THE

COST

OF

KNOWING

ALSO BY BRITTNEY MORRIS

SLAY

'A book that knocks you off your feet while dropping the
kind of knowledge that'll keep you down for the count.
Prepare to BE slain.'
Nic Stone, New York Times bestselling author
of *Dear Martin* and *Odd One Out*

THE
COST
OF
KNOWING

BRITTNEY MORRIS

HODDER CHILDREN'S BOOKS

First published in Great Britain in 2021 by Hodder and Stoughton
First published in the United States in 2021 by Simon Pulse

1 3 5 7 9 10 8 6 4 2

A CIP catalogue record for this book
is available from the British Library.

ISBN 9781 444 951745

Printed and bound in Great Britain by Clays Ltd, Elcograf S.p.A.

The paper and board used in this book
are made from wood from responsible sources.

MIX
Paper from
responsible sources
FSC® C104740

Hodder Children's Books
An imprint of
Hachette Children's Group
Part of Hodder and Stoughton
Carmelite House
50 Victoria Embankment
London EC4Y 0DZ

An Hachette UK Company
www.hachette.co.uk

www.hachettechildrens.co.uk

To all the Black boys
who had to grow up too early

THE CURSE OF KNOWLEDGE: a cognitive bias that occurs when an expert in a particular subject, communicating with a novice, is unable to explain a concept in simple terms that the novice can understand, due to the expert's experience.

A HUSBAND AND WIFE sit at their dining room table one evening, watching a crime report on the news, sipping tea, and lamenting the violent state of the world. They're thankful they live in a neighborhood where crime is rare.

The wife is on the local litter patrol. The husband regularly attends town hall meetings.

The wife is a natural peacekeeper. The husband is a natural protector.

The wife hears a noise outside. The husband gets up to investigate.

1

Scoop's

I PICK UP THE ice cream scoop, and the vision begins.

I see a familiar light-skinned hand with knobby knuckles and dirt under the nails, passing the scoop I'm holding into a new, unfamiliar hand as dark as mine. This new hand is amply lotioned—no ashiness in the crease between the index finger and thumb. The nails are clipped short. A glittering, diamond-encrusted ring indicates this man must have more money in his wallet than I'll make in my entire life. But the most telling detail, the revelation that might affect *my* future, lies in the background. Behind the two hands, sitting on the grass, is the sign that hangs over the front door of this place— the one that says SCOOP'S. In my vision, someone's leaned it carelessly against the white siding, which is coated in a thin layer of green and black grime, the kind that builds up over months of neglect.

Scoop, the owner of this place, is going to sell the business.

I blink, directing all my focus into darkness, the abstract, *nothing*. I breathe. I think the word *stop*, and silently, I command the vision to end. When I open my eyes again, I'm looking down at the scoop in my hand. I'm back to the present day, turning the scoop over in my fingers. Only a second has gone by in the real world, even though I just watched a twenty-second vision. They always last only a moment.

I blink back into reality, still staring down at the scoop in my bare hand, and I briefly consider telling Scoop. But what would it change? What good would it do?

When you *own the shop,* you *can make the rules,* he'd say.

He's never listened to my ideas before—not when I suggested we invest in a shelving unit so we can finally organize the supply boxes obstructing the hallway, not when I suggested we buy blackout curtains for the front lobby so the afternoon sunlight doesn't turn this place into an oven, since we're a damn *ice cream* shop and we can't operate at ninety-five degrees without jacking up our refrigeration costs. Nah, he won't listen to me, and even on the off chance that he does, Scoop doesn't do anything without asking a million questions first. And my only answer to the inevitable question, "How do you know for sure?" will be "I can see the future," an idea so ridiculous that *I* didn't even believe it until I got out of that hospital and it started interfering with my daily life. I can't touch anything with the palm side of my hands without seeing what will happen to it in the next few moments. The longer I touch it, the further into the future I can see. With most things, I can make the vision stop a split second after it begins, so it's more like a photograph flashing in my head, but if I *want* to see further, which is rare these days, I can let it keep going for as long as I'm touching it.

I've picked up this scoop so many times working here. I've seen myself holding it while I'm wearing a tank top and my

4

arm is glistening with sweat. I've seen myself holding it with my long sleeves tucked over my knuckles as the front door swings open and gusts of snow flurries fly in behind a customer who has no business buying ice cream in that kind of weather. Then it changes hands—a white hand is scooping ice cream as customers enter in tank tops. More kids staring from the other side of the counter in bathing suits and sunglasses. Then, gradually, people coming in with their hands red from the cold, fingers curled around hot coffee cups, ordering through the scarves pulled up over their faces. Two summers. Two winters. I'd say Scoop has about two years left before this place goes under. Two. I'll have graduated and gone off to college by then. And even if this place closed tomorrow, there'd *still* be no point in trying to warn him.

I've tried to alter the future too many times to think it'll work anymore.

I remember a vision I had during a camping trip three years ago—a vision I'll never forget. Me, Aunt Mackie, my little brother Isaiah, my best friend Shaun, and his little sister, who's now my girlfriend—Talia—spent a weekend at Starved Rock State Park out in Oglesby. Aunt Mackie was grilling hot dogs, and she asked me to put the bag of buns on the picnic table. I picked them up and caught a vision of Isaiah slipping on the bag, falling, and breaking his arm. So, despite the risk of flies and flying charcoal pieces landing on them, I took all the buns out of the bag, left them open on a plate, and tossed the bag in the garbage.

Crisis averted, I thought.

But then Aunt Mackie asked Isaiah to run the trash to

the dumpster. The crumpled-up little bun bag rolled out at some point while he walked, and on his way back, his foot found the slippery plastic.

Another time, while walking past a construction site, I tried to prevent a beam from falling and bursting a fire hydrant, which I'd touched, by yelling up at the foreman to *watch out!* If he hadn't been distracted, he might have caught it.

No matter what I do, it doesn't help. The mess happens anyway, and I just end up embarrassed, often because it looks like I *caused* whatever I'd been trying to prevent. So I've stopped trying. Better, and less humiliating, to just lie low and let fate happen.

That's the real reason I don't tell Scoop what I saw. Whatever I say, whatever I do to stop it, this place is doomed.

"Alex!" snaps that commanding voice from the kitchen door. I jump, dropping the scoop into the dirty sink water, sending an explosion of suds in all directions, soaking the front of my apron and dousing my face.

God, ew, a little got in my mouth.

"Sorry, didn't mean to scare you," he apologizes. Before I can say I'm okay, he's moved on. "Ross is going on break soon, so I need you up front."

I drag my dry forearm across my face, pull off my other glove, and remove my glasses. The vision flashes. One of me wiping my lenses off on a shirt I'm not wearing. One I don't even own yet. I've touched my own glasses so many times that I must be at a few months into the future with visions of them. I make the vision end, and I do exactly what I just saw myself do—wipe them off. It's become routine for me.

6

Touch item. See vision of exactly what I'm about to do with the item. Do exactly what I saw myself do in the vision.

"Daydreaming again?" asks Scoop. His voice is quieter and kinder this time.

Sure. Daydreaming. That's the closest thing to it that he'll understand, so I nod. I grab the hand towel hanging above the sink and wipe my hands before removing my soaked dish-washing apron. I hang it up by the sink to dry and sigh as the full weight of Scoop's words sinks in, heavy like an anvil on my chest. *I need you up front.*

I *hate* working up front. Not because I don't like talking to customers—I'm actually pretty good at that part, and the customers are usually nice. They're mostly young parents with kids under ten, who are in and out in a few minutes. And the kids are almost always well behaved and happy while they're here because, hey, they're getting ice cream. Nah, I hate working up front because it means touching a million items with my bare hands.

It's an anxiety minefield out there.

Visions fly through my head with everything I touch, like one of those old-school slide-projector things—every tap of the register screen, every dollar I count, every spoon I pick up, every hand I brush while giving out samples, every cup, every cone, every scoop. I can't focus on all of that *and* do my job. I can't constantly be thinking of what's *going* to happen and stay focused on what *is* happening. It's too much.

"Can I go back to dishes after?" I ask. Dishes. My safe place, where I can wear my dishwashing gloves and live vision-free for a while.

7

A droplet of dishwater that was caught in my coily hair races down my forehead, and I wipe it away and sigh, anticipating the answer.

"Sorry, champ," he says, although with his accent, it sounds more like "shamp." He leans against the doorjamb with his arms folded across his black apron and explains, "After Ross takes his break, I've got Ashlynn going home. I need you up there till you're off at six. Okay?"

It's going to *have* to be okay.

I can already feel my heart rate picking up speed, that racing adrenaline that makes me jittery like I've had six cups of coffee and a Red Bull. On really bad days, my mouth gets dry and I start sweating. Sometimes it happens for no reason. Sometimes it happens if I'm anxious about something that would make most people anxious, like an exam, or speaking up in class. Sometimes it happens because I'm with Talia. Today, it's happening because I have to do my job. Just the *thought* of going out there to the front counter freaks me out. It's pathetic. I've been working here for four years. I shouldn't be this afraid anymore. What kind of man am I? *Come on, Alex.* I steel myself, pinching the skin on the back of my hand, which is supposed to help with anxiety.

It doesn't.

I used to be able to wear cheap latex gloves up front. We used to *have* to wear them while scooping, as mandated by the health department. I'd put them on, cancel a quick vision of them, and go the rest of the day blissfully unaware of my—I don't even know what to call this—disorder? Affliction? Curse? I used to wear them home, stealing extra pairs when I could, desperate to keep my brain quiet for as long as possible. But after a few weeks of wearing the latex ones, their protection started to wear off. The visions started coming back about ten minutes after I put them on, and the discomfort of sweaty palms, and the strange looks I'd get in public, began to outweigh the respite they gave me. Eventually, I gave up on them. Now, all that works are those heavy-duty reinforced polyurethane dishwashing gloves that I'm leaving behind in the kitchen right now.

I take a deep breath and follow Scoop through the tiny hallway, which is crammed to the ceiling with unlabeled boxes of flavor powders, industrial cleaning products, ice cream toppings, napkins, and spoons.

This whole place is a fire hazard, a fall hazard, and an accessibility nightmare. Scoop sometimes sends me back here to put bottles and boxes away where they *actually* go, so we can have access to the handwashing sink on the wall behind the mountain, just before scheduled inspections. And it's always *me*, because I can squeeze my five-foot-seven, 140-pound ass into places some of the others can't. I shouldn't have to watch vision after vision of supplies I don't need, just to find some damn napkins. Not when I'm getting paid the same eleven dollars an hour as everyone else.

But I can't dwell on that or I'll get even more jittery and irritable. The quickest way to get through this day, like every day, is to take a deep breath, keep my head down, keep to myself, and keep my hands closed and close to me. I fold them against my shirt and slip between the boxes and the wall. Damn, I swear it gets narrower and narrower every time I walk through here. I keep my eyes on the back of Scoop's head and follow him out to the front counter, where the sunlight has already started cooking the employees. It smells faintly of sugar and dairy products.

The novelty of smelling ice cream all day wore off by the end of my first week. Now I barely smell anything. But I've heard that's normal. Aunt Mackie used to work in a movie theater, and she said eventually she stopped smelling popcorn when she walked in. After a while, it just began to smell faintly of butter substitute and hard work.

There's only one customer out here—a bearded man in his early thirties in shorts, a striped T-shirt, and expensive sunglasses. He's pulling a sample spoon out of his mouth and taking forever to decide on a flavor.

Ashlynn, who stands what feels like a foot taller than me and who always wears a too-tight brown ponytail that's creeping her hairline farther back than any twenty-year-old should have, glances over her shoulder at me with that jaded smirk of hers. Ross, the malnourished Dracula-looking guy whose eyes always look like he hasn't slept in years but somehow always ends up right at the front at the scooping counter, is feverishly tapping his foot, hands on hips, watching the man with the sunglasses, his eyes quietly urging the man to make a decision.

Scoop decides to bail him out.

"All right, Ross," he says, motioning toward the hallway with two fingers. "You're on break. Ashlynn, you're scooping till Ross gets back."

Shit. That puts me at the register.

Calm down, Alex, I tell myself. *Just three more hours and you can go home and nap this stress away.*

Ross can't get his apron off fast enough. He turns from his

10

post behind the counter, yanks his pink apron over his head, and has a cigarette and lighter out before he even reaches the hallway. Ashlynn nods and moves dutifully to the counter where Ross was standing. The customer, who's now watching Ross leave in the middle of the transaction, seems unfazed and points to a tub of green ice cream in the corner. Ashlynn never speaks unless she absolutely has to, so I'm sure she's relieved to be able to scoop ice cream and hand out samples with minimal conversation except "Welcome to Scoop's," "Which flavor?," "Cup or cone?," "What size?," and "Have a great day." That means I, on the other hand, am stuck at the register, touching everything—clicking buttons, counting cash, swiping cards, getting preordered ice cream cakes out of the freezer, distributing receipts, and handing out coupons and allergy info sheets. *And* I have to explain all the time that "yes, sir or ma'am, some of our flavors *do* have artificial colors and sweeteners, but they're all FDA-approved." It's the same answers day after day.

Our only gluten-free flavor is strawberry.

No, strawberry isn't vegan. Coffee and vanilla are our only vegan flavors.

Yes, the coffee is caffeinated.

Vanilla isn't GMO-free, but the sweet cream is.

No, the sweet cream isn't vegan. Only coffee and vanilla.

Shoot me.

I slip on a bubblegum-pink apron and pull my cobalt-blue visor down low on my forehead, canceling the visions for each, right after I see myself hanging both of them up at the end of my shift. I sigh and adjust the visor so it rests comfortably.

My hair is cut short—a fade on the sides and slightly longer coils on top. I was relieved I didn't have to carry an Afro pick and pocket-size styling gel anymore when we switched from baseball caps to visors last year, another expense that Scoop decided would be more effective at keeping us employees cool than blackout curtains. Apparently you lose 20 percent of your body heat through your head or something? I don't know.

In the corner of my eye, I see Ashlynn turn to leave down the hallway.

"We're out of spoons," she grumbles. "I'm going to find more in the back."

As soon as I'm left alone out here, the front door swings open, and I take a long, deep breath and log into the register, clicking my name and typing in my four-digit PIN.

I punch 1. Vision of me pressing the 0 on the register. *Stop.* I punch 0. Vision of me pressing the 0 again. *Stop.* I punch 0 again. Vision of me pressing the 4 on the register. *Stop.* I punch 4. Vision of the register's welcome screen. *Stop.*

"Hi, welcome to Scoop's," I say to whoever just walked in, as the register lights up with my name.

Welcome, Alex Rufus.

Shit, it's hot in here. It's three in the afternoon, and the sun is blinding through the west window, beating down on the whole area right behind the register where I am. Sweat is already beading on my forehead, but I put on my most convincing smile and look up at the customer. A woman about my height with short reddish-brown hair and bright green eyes walks over, looking like she stepped right out of a J.Crew catalog. The redheaded little girl holding her hand looks like she's about seven, but she's

12

sucking her thumb with the enthusiasm of a jittery toddler. When they reach the counter, she buries her face in her mom's stomach and puts all her focus into her thumb.

"Hi," I say, trying to ignore the slippery suction noises coming from the little girl's mouth. I'm sure this woman and her daughter are both cool, but I need them to get the hell out of here with those mouth sounds.

"What can I get you?" I ask. The woman is staring past my head at the board behind me as if it's changed in the last five years. Literally the only thing that's ever changed is our prices. She must be brand-new here.

"Canna get a child's size cone for Mabel, and a single scoop fer me?"

Her accent is either Irish or Scottish—I can't really tell. She's reaching into her brown leather purse, fishing around for something to pay with, but I'm missing information.

"Which flavors, ma'am?" I ask.

"Oh!" she exclaims. "What's the pistachio flavor like?"

It tastes like pistachio, I wish I could say.

"It's nutty and a little less sweet than the others," I have to say.

God, it's so hot in here. I have to remove my glasses and wipe the sweat out of my eyes now, but it doesn't help much because my arms are already dewy. I end the vision of me putting the glasses back on my face. I use her indecisiveness to step away from the register, where the sun is beaming through the window, and stand behind the ice cream counter instead. I rest my hands on the cold metal shelf behind the glass for some relief, until the room fades to black and I see an image of this place drenched in darkness except for moonlight. I see the

13

window, and the summer moon is outside in the sky, shining down on this place. It's peaceful after hours, and cool, and I long for that kind of quiet right now.

But I can't savor this moment forever. I concentrate and command my brain to end the vision. The sunlight zooms at me like I'm flying toward a light at the end of a long tunnel, and suddenly I'm back in the shop, behind the counter, and the J.Crew woman is staring at me expectantly, as if she just asked me a question.

"I—I'm sorry," I say, without missing a beat. "Could you repeat that?"

"Oh, I asked if you go to school nearby. You sound so well-spoken."

Well-spoken? I'm talking about ice cream flavors here, not quoting MLK. But I know what she means. People tell me all the time that I'm "well-spoken," as opposed to however they were expecting me to sound.

"Thanks," I say.

She smiles at me and asks, "Canna try the caramel peanut butter pretzel?"

I pick up a plastic sample spoon and see a vision of it being thrown into the dirty spoon bin in just a few moments, and when I cancel the vision and the real world comes zooming back, I'm staring down at the ice cream flavors. I scoop out a tiny bit of the caramel peanut butter pretzel, not really caring that there's not a single piece of pretzel in the sample, and hold it out to her. She takes the spoon without touching my hand, thank goodness. Every vision I can prevent is an act of precious self-preservation.

"Oh, that's delicious!" she marvels. My head is spinning. My temples are throbbing. I'm dizzy.

I miss the days when my gloves used to work.

I finally get through scooping a scoop of caramel peanut butter pretzel into a cup, and a scoop of cookies and cream into a cone for Mabel, and get all three of us back to the register so they can pay and leave and take Mabel's thumb-sucking sounds with them. The mom hands me a twenty-dollar bill. Dammit. I have to count back two fives that I see are about to get stuffed into her purse, and two ones that are about to be dropped into the tip jar.

"Thanks." She smiles at me. "Mabel, say thank you to the nice young man."

Mabel looks up at me through her straight red bangs and blinks a few times in gratitude. I'll take it.

"My name's Ena," the woman says with another grin. "Mabel and I are new to Chicago. I own a consignment shop down the street. Maybe you've heard of it. It's called Mabelena's?"

I don't care. I *can't* care. I don't have the *energy* to care. My eyes are throbbing. The pressure in my sinuses is crushing. Ena and Mabel are kind, and I should probably be glad that they came in instead of some entitled asshole who's a hair trigger away from asking to speak to a manager. I suddenly feel guilty for hating this interaction so much. I should be grateful.

"I've heard of it," I finally say.

An explosive crash behind me rattles my ears, and I flinch. I look to my right to see Ashlynn standing behind the counter, looking over her shoulder at me with huge eyes. The empty plastic napkin dispenser lies in pieces on the floor next to her.

"Sorry," she says, her voice monotone and unwavering as she kneels and picks up each plastic shard and heads back down the hallway to retrieve the broom and dustpan, leaving

15

me alone in here with Ena and Mabel again.

I turn back to Ena, whose eyes are still bright and trained on me.

"You have excellent customer service skills. In this industry, that'll get you far," she says, glancing around the room before reaching into her purse.

I may live in Naperville now, west of Chicago, but I was born and raised in East Garfield Park, where people don't reach into their bag at the register after paying unless they're about to rob the cashier. I flinch and step back reflexively, and Ena looks up at me with a hint of confusion on her face. She pulls a single business card from her purse and holds it out to me.

"I just wanted to give you this," she says. "Come over to Mabelena's and apply if you ever get tired of working for"—she leans in close and lowers her voice to a whisper—"Scoop. Met him in here a couple times myself. If you ask me, *you* should be the one running this place."

This woman has clearly been here before, scoping the place out. Maybe she's the mysterious buyer that Scoop will eventually sell to? But the person I saw in my vision grabbing the scoop was Black. Whatever. I'll be outta here before any of that happens. I have to keep reminding myself not to care what happens to this place. The pope could buy it and it wouldn't change a thing about my life.

I take the card with trembling hands and a polite "Thanks," and Ena turns and guides Mabel to the front door. I force the vision of me throwing the card in the garbage can under the register to end. When I zoom back into reality and find myself staring down at the card in my hand, I toss the card in the trash.

I'm alone at the front counter, so I do what I always do when I have a moment to myself—allow my brain to torture itself with "what-abouts" and "what-ifs." Did I throw away that card because I saw the vision first? Or did my vision happen because I would've thrown the card away anyway, even if I was normal? If it's the former, are these visions altering my life timeline? Could I have had a different future without them? What happens if I pick the business card out of the trash and don't throw it away again? I guess it wouldn't do anything because the vision was that I would throw it in the trash, and that happened already, whether I pick it out of the trash or not. But what if, just to see what happens . . .

I lean down and pick the card out of the trash and force the ensuing vision to end—the vision of my hand sliding it into my pocket. I'm back to reality, and I glance around the room as if I'm about to test some unwritten rule of the universe by trying this. I lean down, hold the card over the trash, and begin to spread my fingers to let it go, and just as it's about to fall from my hand, Scoop's voice explodes through the hallway.

"Hey, what was that noise, huh? Did something break?"

I hear Ashlynn's dry voice from down the hall.

"Broke a dispenser. Sorry."

"Another one?" asks Scoop, stepping into the front room and marching up to the ice cream counter. He looks over to the other side, where the full napkin dispenser sits intact. "That's the second one this month! Those are thirty bucks apiece, Ashlynn. Be careful, please!"

He's clearly frustrated, but his voice breaks at that last "please," and something tightens in my chest. When I first met Scoop, his

17

smile was bigger, his eyes were brighter, and he weighed about thirty pounds more than he does today. His glasses didn't used to have scotch tape around the bridge between the lenses, and he didn't used to have dark circles under his eyes. I remember sitting across from him four years ago, at the round blue table that's still right here in the lobby. I was eleven. My résumé was a joke—I mowed Mrs. Zaccari's lawn for a few months and vacuumed around the house for Aunt Mackie whenever we'd visit—but my mother insisted I have a résumé, even if I was asking a childhood friend of hers for a job tidying up his ice cream shop's break room once a week. So there I sat at that little blue table, heart pounding, as Scoop—then I called him Mr. de la Cruz—pretended to scrutinize every word of my list of qualifications before shaking my hand to make my employment as official as under-the-table work can be.

That day seems like forever ago. That was a year before I lost my parents. A year before I woke up in that hospital bed seeing my very first visions, of what would become of my hospital blankets and the IV drip bag. A year before I started frantically googling what the hell these visions were, why I was getting them, where they came from, and how to get rid of them. Google can be hella scary. I found whole forums full of people with "visions" who said their premonitions were from God or Satan or their "higher self." None of them wanted to get rid of theirs.

They just wanted to charge people for their services.

So I googled. I searched. I read. I prayed. And, after months, nothing.

No solutions.

No answers.

No peace.

I catch myself staring out into the lobby at that little blue table until Scoop's voice throws my train of thought off its tracks.

"Hey!" he snaps, startling me. I clutch the card a little tighter in my hand.

"What's that?" he asks me, nodding to my hand with his chin. I look at the card, and then at the trash can, where I'm supposed to leave the card. If I leave it there, I'll have proven my vision wrong. I look back up at Scoop, and when his eyes narrow slightly and he takes a step toward me, I realize I can't leave it in the trash. He'll pull it out, read it, figure out I've been offered another job, and hire my replacement before I can quit.

I end up slipping the business card into my cargo shorts pocket and whipping up a lie.

"A therapist just walked in. We got to talking, and my parents came up."

Scoop's eyebrows soften and his shoulders fall a little. His dark eyes blink a few times, searching mine.

"Sh-she," I stutter for maximum believability, "she gave me her business card . . . in case I need it."

Scoop folds his arms across his chest, takes a deep breath, and stares at the ground as if he's trying to find words. You could get Scoop talking for hours about literally anything, but when I bring up my parents, my mom especially, his childhood friend, he locks up. Freezes. Can't get the words out, or doesn't want to. Sometimes I wonder if he remembers her at all.

If he ever thinks of her. Maybe when this store goes under, he'll pretend it never existed too. I turn my attention back to the register, pick up a nearby rag, get through the vision of me dragging it across the counter, and then drag it across the counter. I shut my eyes and pray to whatever name the greatest force in the universe goes by that I can make it through this shift without having to touch anything else, and that miraculously, no customers will come in for the next two and a half hours.

And then the front door opens again.

"Hi, welcome to Scoop's," I say, focusing all my attention on making my voice sound less exhausted than I feel. I drop the rag and look up at the front door. A girl slightly shorter than me steps into the shop in all black—ripped jeans pulled up to waist height, a crop top that leaves about half an inch of midriff right in the front when she turns to close the door behind her, and combat boots. She grins up at me with a knowing smile framed by bubblegum-pink lips. All of her hair is tucked up into her hat, but I'd recognize those big brown eyes anywhere. Relief washes over me like rain across the wildfire of stress I've been battling all morning.

"Hey, Tal." I smile, genuinely, for the very first time today.

You ever just be standing somewhere—like at a bus stop or something—and someone gets the giggles, and everyone around them starts smiling, and then you start smiling, and maybe even suppressing laughs, just because they are? That's how it works with Talia—her laugh, her smile, the way she flips her hair. The whole room feels brighter, and for a split second, I forget how miserable I am.

20

"Hey, babe!" She beams, clasping her hands in front of her and rocking side to side. She glances up at Scoop.

"¡Hola, señor de la Cruz!" she exclaims, a bit too loudly for the space of this lobby.

"¿Cómo estás, Talia?" he says with sparkling eyes. "¿Cómo está tu mamá?"

"¡Bien!" She smiles.

Talia's always been like this—always smiling and bursting with energy. But she's bouncier than usual today, even for her. Her whole face, the color of a perfectly toasted marshmallow, is pinker than usual. Maybe it's from the summer heat. But her eyes are twinkling, like she has something important to tell me.

"You good?" I ask her.

What we used to ask each other after my parents died. After her dad left. After we lost Shaun. Whenever we *really* need to check in with each other. *You good?* is code for *Tell me everything*.

"Nah-ah-ah." She frowns, holding up her index finger and pretending to pout as she looks away. I roll my eyes and sigh. Oh, right. Spanish.

"¿Estoy bien?"

"Yo no sé," she says, rolling her eyes. "¿Estás bien?"

I blink.

Talia's been trying so hard to teach me Spanish, throwing phrases at me constantly, leaving sticky notes all over Aunt Mackie's stuff whenever she comes over to study with me after school, pointing to random objects when we're out in public and quizzing me on whether I know the Spanish word for it. I can't keep up. Nothing sticks. I appreciate it, though. I've

21

always wanted to learn a second language, and since Talia speaks Spanish fluently, it might as well be that one. It's a great addition to my résumé. Mom would be proud. I hope.

"Hey," she says, "are you listening?"

"What?" I ask. Shit, I was lost in thought again. "Oh, sorry. I mean . . . ¿qué?"

Talia takes in a deep breath and opens and closes her hands, which she does whenever she's decided to just move on and not make the situation an incident. She's on to the next sentence before I can correct my error and ask *¿Estás bien?* instead. She's talking to Scoop again.

"¿Te importa si hablo con Alex por un momento?"

"Sure," he says in English, nodding at me before switching back to Spanish. "En realidad, Alex, Ashlynn me ha estado pidiendo más horas últimamente, así que si quieres irte a casa ahora y dejarla tomarse las últimas horas de tu turno, siéntete libre."

All I got out of that was Ashlynn's name and the word for "hours."

"What?" I ask. But Talia's halfway through an eruption of squeals and jumping up and down. She reaches over the counter, grabs my hand, and guides me around to the front of the store. Her hand feels hot—blistering, like I'm touching red coils on a stove—and a vision overtakes me that's more powerful than all the others I've been through today. My chest feels like it's being squeezed in a vise. Talia is standing in front of me, looking up at me with those captivating eyes of hers. Her dark curls just barely touch her shoulders. Her black sundress flutters slightly. It's night outside, and I can feel a gentle breeze against my skin,

22

with the moon high above us. This whole place is bathed in moonlight. No, harsh yellow light. *Lots* of harsh yellow lights, actually. I think they're cars, passing by slowly, crawling down the street. We're on the sidewalk, staring each other down. It's cool enough outside to raise goose bumps on my arms, but my heart is pounding with fear and shame and regret. I look at Talia's eyes. They're traced with the blackest liner I've ever seen her use. Big black circles and huge lashes. Dark lipstick. Dark everything. And, the scariest part, Talia is looking at me like she wants to kill me. Like I've done something unforgivable. Like it's over. I don't recognize her. She's *never* looked at me like this. Even as I watch her in this vision, glaring at me like she's trying to drill straight through my head with her eyes, I know she's actually standing in Scoop's ice cream shop right now, holding my hand, but I don't know if she'll hold my hand like this tomorrow. I don't know if she'll look at me the same way next week. I don't know if we'll be together next month. I don't know if I'll have her number in a year. But *this* moment, standing with her on the side of the road, with her looking at me like she doesn't know me, with searing hatred in her eyes—I don't want to know when that moment is coming.

I don't want to know what happens after that.

When I return to the ice cream shop, I'm gasping and pulling my hand from hers.

"Hey, you good?" she asks, looking over her shoulder at me in confusion where her smile used to be.

I'm not good. There's a lump in my throat that I can't swallow. My armpits are soaked with sweat, and my right eye is burning from a sweat droplet that's fallen into it. It's getting

23

harder and harder to find the differences between my visions and my anxiety attacks.

I think this time it's both.

I breathe and try to think. I've never seen her look at me like that—like I did something horrible, like I really hurt her. Like she never wants to see me again.

Are we going to . . . break up soon?

I don't want to think about it. We've been fine. We're fine! . . . Right?

I blink, trying to steady my breathing so she doesn't get nervous and think something's up. I look at her to see if it's working.

It's not.

She reaches for both my hands, and I flinch away before she can touch me.

Her eyebrows sink down, and the look of disappointment in her eyes breaks me.

"Tal, uh," I say, scrambling for control of my words, "I've, uh, been feeling kinda sick. I don't think I should be holding your hand."

What kind of man has to make up excuses *not* to touch his own girlfriend?

And . . . how long can I *go* without touching her?

I've never had to before. I've always just cancelled the vision before it took over.

I don't know exactly when that night is coming, but at least I know I've got some time. As far as I know, she doesn't own a black sundress—I've never seen her in one anyway, and at some point her hair is supposed to go blue. I've seen it. She's going to dye it electric blue soon, and then brown again. That should give me a while until we're somehow standing on the side of a road jammed with traffic, right? But what happens if I see what happens after that? What happens if I find out that's the night we break up? What happens now that I'm too scared to even touch her, and she thinks I'm mad at her or something and my fear *causes* her to break up with me?

"Oh, uh . . . okay, then," she says.

Talia tries not to let it bother her by smiling at me, but her eyes betray her. My heart is still pounding and my head is spinning. I'm relieved when she keeps talking.

"Scoop said Ashlynn wants to take your hours," she says cheerfully, leaning in so close to me I can smell her shampoo and whispering, "Which means *we* can head back to your place early. Come on. Let's grab some ice cream and get the heck outta here. We're burnin' daylight."

"Okay," I concede with a sigh, still reeling from that vision. How am I supposed to keep from touching Talia without her figuring out something's wrong? "Just let me get some cash out the ATM for bus money first."

"No need. I drove your car here so you wouldn't have to take the bus."

I smile, but inside, my heart sinks. The bus is so much cheaper than gas, and it requires me watching zero visions of my steering wheel and gear shift, so lately I've been leaving my car—my little 2001 Geo Metro—at Aunt Mackie's house. I don't know when I'll be comfortable enough with it to call it *my house*. Maybe when my parents come back from the dead and start living there too.

"Thanks, Talia," I say instead.

2

The Photo

BY THE TIME TALIA orders her double scoop cone of half s'mores, half rainbow sherbet, which sounds absolutely disgusting together but has always been her favorite, and I order my plain old chocolate scoop in a cone, and we squeeze into my blue Geo, it's begun to rain, despite the heat. Talia makes a fantastic copilot. She flips on the radio, blasting static into the car for a brief moment before switching it to Bluetooth and cranking "Feel Good Inc." This car may be a piece of crap as old as me, but the sound system is bumping. I can feel the rhythm in my chest as we fly down Clark Street.

I glance over at her as she licks some of her s'mores into her sherbet. I like her hat like this. It sits right at her hairline, with all her hair tucked up into it so I can see her whole face. It sharpens her jawline. Then I remember that she asked Scoop if she could talk to me about something.

"Hey," I say. "Did you say you had something to tell me?"

"Oh yeah!" she exclaims. She bounces with excitement in her seat and nestles her ice cream cone in the cupholder, then reaches up and dramatically rips off the hat. Waves of electric-blue hair fall over her face, and she shakes her head and beams at me proudly.

"*Whaaat?*" I grin, sounding pleasantly surprised, even though I'm actually terrified.

The blue hair.

It's happening.

One step closer to her breaking up with me.

"You like it?" she asks, raising her left shoulder to her chin, lowering her eyes and pouting her bubblegum-pink lips slightly.

Damn, do I like it.

I nod and swallow the lump in my throat. If I can't even hold her hand without seeing her breaking up with me, how can I even *think* we could ever have sex?

"Ready for a lick?" she asks, jarring me from my thoughts. I turn my head and stick out my tongue, she holds the cone up to my face, and I lick, savoring the cold, creamy sweetness. Talia and I used to visit Scoop's all the time when we were little, when Shaun was with us. I'm sure my face betrays that I'm thinking about him, because I can feel Talia's eyes linger on me before she faces forward again and licks her own cone in silence. I glance over at the rainbow and white and brown all swirled into a monstrous tower.

"I swear I'll never get used to looking at that," I say with a grin. The rain picks up, pelting the windshield mercilessly, and I take a long, deep breath and glance at Talia. She doesn't reply, her eyes transfixed on the road, her mind somewhere else.

"Hey," I begin, trying to distract her from the rain. I look down at her hand. I wish I could take hold of it, look her in the

27

eyes, and tell her that it's okay to grieve every time it rains, even if it's been three years. But I'm better at offering distractions.

"Did you check on Isaiah while you were at the house earlier?"

She smirks at me, and her eyes brighten.

"You know I did. He's been playing music in his room all day, though. He used to be fun to play with, once upon a time. When we were kids."

"We're *still* kids," I remind her as we stop at a red light. The words don't sound convincing when I say them. I don't know what I feel like, but I don't feel sixteen. It's hard to feel like anything in the present when I'm staring into the future every thirty seconds. The light turns green and I put my hands on the wheel again, triggering a vision of my car sitting at the top of a junk pile the size of my house at the dump, years from now because I've touched the wheel so much, and seen *so* many visions of it.

This car, my little Geo that I love so much, will end up flooded with water one day. A few weeks ago, on one of the hottest days of the year, I stopped for gas on the way to Talia's house. We had everything planned out for a perfect summer day. We were going to put on our bathing suits and head to the Garfield Park Community Center for a swim. Talia had stocked her freezer with Popsicles for us to enjoy on the walk over. I was leaning against my car at the gas station, excited, happy for a moment. I was about to see my favorite girl. But when I put the pump away, sat down in the driver's seat, and grabbed the steering wheel at four and eight, I saw a vision I'll never forget. Two hands, white, seeming to belong to a man in his twenties or thirties, wearing a wedding band, took the place of my black hands on the wheel. A torrent of water barreled down on the windshield and sprayed glass into the car, releasing the flood into the cabin.

I panicked.

I thought about stopping the vision.

But curiosity, I guess, is a helluva drug. It's like standing in front of a train as it barrels across a broken bridge. Yeah, it's horrific, but is any normal person going to look away? Nah. So I watched on. A notebook flew past my face, and my left hand went to the driver's-side door, but it wouldn't open. I couldn't see anything with the surge of water battering my face. When I opened my eyes, I still saw nothing. Just inky blackness. Those hands with the wedding band were slumped over the wheel in the dark, unmoving, probably cold.

And then, red.

Then I commanded the vision to stop. I couldn't take any more. I was back in my Geo—my dry, functioning, safe little car parked at pump two on the corner of Harrison Street and Independence Boulevard. It was sunny outside, and sweat was beading on my forehead. My chest was pounding. I wanted to go back to thirty seconds before, when I was looking forward to Popsicles and swimming, and seeing Talia in a swimsuit. But I couldn't. I was stuck in that moment, sitting in my car alone, staring in a daze through my windshield at two carefree girls about my age in jean shorts with swinging brown ponytails. They were laughing and climbing into a Jeep in front of me, while I was absorbing the fact that whoever gets my Geo next is going to drown exactly where I was sitting. Exactly where I *am* sitting. How could I go have a day at the pool with Talia with that on my mind? I went home.

That was the day I learned to avoid seeing anything I didn't have to.

It was going to happen whether I knew about it or not, and I might as well protect myself from the knowledge.

"Hey," says Talia. I look over at her and realize she's holding my chocolate cone inches from my face. It looks like it's about to drip. I dutifully lick the outside, and she rotates a little too fast, and a huge glob falls and lands on my shoulder.

"Ah!" she exclaims, handing me my cone and reaching for the glove box, where I always keep extra napkins. "Lo siento."

"Uh . . . ," I begin. "Is that 'Let me get that'?"

She sighs.

"No. 'Lo siento' is 'I'm sorry.' You could at least make flash cards for yourself or something. *Act* like this is still something you want to do."

"It is," I say.

I'm trying. Spanish is hard. Or at least for me, without the time or energy. I guess she's had to tell me what "lo siento" means more than she should have.

"I'm sorry," I say. "Uh . . . lo siento."

She carefully wipes the chocolate from my shoulder without a word as "Feel Good Inc." fades into silence. There's a gap between it and the next song, and in that moment, I absorb the sound of the rain pelting the car. Talia does too. I know this when I hear what she says next.

"I'm bringing Shaun flowers tonight." I can feel the weight in her voice. I keep my hands on the wheel and my eyes on the road, and I realize I've been tensing my jaw. I take a deep breath and wait for her to keep talking.

"I was wondering if you want to come with me."

Shaun. Her brother. My brother from another mother.

"I . . . ," I begin, wanting so badly to be able to say yes. I choose to be honest instead.

"I can't, Tal," I say. I struggle to find the words. What do I say? How do I tell her that I can't hear Shaun's name without feeling like I'm going to fall apart? "I'm so tired," I continue. Always a good excuse. "I'm *so* grateful for you coming to get me from work, and I'm glad to be off early." But I'm scared. "But I'm tired."

It's not too far-fetched. I've been working all day, so it's believable that I'd be too tired to do anything more than heat up something for dinner and go to bed. My stomach twists into a knot of apprehension. The number of things I have to touch just to make dinner, even something microwaveable, is going to be mentally exhausting. I wonder what tonight might look like if I were . . . "normal." Aunt Mackie is probably home, unless she's showing someone a house, but she wouldn't ask questions if Talia and I stole away into the theater room in the basement together for a few hours. And we wouldn't have to worry about Isaiah, since he's been going to his room for the evening earlier and earlier these days.

Talia and I would have the house to ourselves.

"I get it," says Talia, crunching into her waffle cone and licking the dwindling brown-and-rainbow ice cream tower. I lift my own cone and savor another lick of creamy chocolate. We ride in silence for the rest of the trip, which Talia doesn't do unless she's retreated into her thoughts, which she doesn't do

31

unless she's hurting.

I sigh and decide that if I can't distract her from the rain, I can at least leave her to endure it in peace. But it kills me to just leave us to the sound.

I can feel her pain.

I'm remembering him too.

I try not to let the hard knot in my stomach turn itself into nausea, which has been known to happen with me, usually when I'm hungry. The merciless rain has receded to a drizzle by the time I drive through the black iron gates of Santiam Estates, the gated community Aunt Mackie has lived in since before I can remember.

Each house in this neighborhood costs over a million dollars. All of them are at least two stories tall, with a basement, forced air, and a well-maintained lawn, as is mandated by the Santiam Housing Association. I should know. Aunt Mackie is a real estate agent. Kind of a famous one around Chicago proper. Her face is on buses, park benches, and taxis. She knows the rules of the homeowners association better than anyone else in the community, and has had a hand in shaping so many of them over the years.

As she says, "Whoever makes the rules controls the narrative."

We drive past Talia's favorite house. It's a humble one compared to its neighbors, gray with a bright yellow door. I see why she likes it. It's the only house with any color. Bright pink hydrangeas line the front of the house, all the way up to the front door.

"We'll have a house like that one day," she said dreamily, six months ago when we announced to Aunt Mackie and Talia's mother that we were officially together. I haven't held her hand long enough to find out if we will.

And now, I don't know if I ever can.

We pass a cream-colored house with black shutters. The sprinklers are spewing water across the front lawn, even though it's just finished raining. Mr. and Mrs. Sanderson must not be home yet. Isaiah and I have been mowing their lawn and trimming down their dogwood bushes every summer since we moved in with Aunt Mackie four years ago. Mrs. Zaccari's house next door to the Sandersons' is looking a little overgrown too. I consider asking Isaiah if he wants to walk over here with me tomorrow to make an extra twenty bucks, but I doubt he'll say yes. We have nothing to talk about anymore. Nothing in common except one thing—that aching empty space where our parents used to be, and that topic will probably always be off-limits for him.

We finally reach Aunt Mackie's house—the brown one halfway down the block. The *sunset-auburn-colored* house halfway down the block, Aunt Mackie insists. Looks like plain old reddish-brown to me.

"Dammit," hisses Talia as I pull into the wraparound drive-way and park my car around the side of the garage so the neighbors can't see it.

A two-decade-old Geo isn't exactly the curb appeal I'm looking for, Aunt Mackie said to me when I first drove it home from the used car lot.

"What's up?" I ask.

Talia pops the last of her ice cream cone into her mouth and holds what remains of my chocolate cone out to me.

"Your aunt's already home."

I eat the last bite of my cone and she swings open the door and jumps out. She shuts it a little harder than I think she meant to. I suddenly realize why she wanted us to come home early, why she was so happy to show me her new hair, why she was looking at me like that when she took off her hat.

I sigh in relief and get out of the car. For the first time in my life, I'm grateful that Aunt Mackie is home early. Better to have her home than risk being left alone in the theater room with Talia and see the disappointment in her eyes when I have to bail out before she reaches for me. Goddamn it, I hate this. If I can't touch her for fear of seeing the future, how am I supposed to convince myself that our future includes a big gray house with a yellow door and hydrangeas, and us *not* touching each other forever? By simple logic, we *have* to end at some point. I just want to go through life blissfully unaware of when that'll happen.

I pull my keys out of the ignition and lock my car door. I shoo away the vision of me locking my keys in the back seat of my car in a few years and follow Talia through the jet-black front door into the foyer. The unmistakable smell of pizza bites and baked sweet potatoes overtakes my sinuses. This smell combination means two things: Isaiah has eaten dinner, which is always pizza bites, and Aunt Mackie has been home for at least twenty minutes to meal prep—one of the few times she cooks each week.

"Alex?"

"It's us, Aunt Mackie," says Talia, slinging her black

messenger bag off over her head and running her hands through her new electric-blue hair. She sets the bag down by the copper console table, with a mirror the size of a standard sofa above it, and steps farther into the house until the carpet begins. Then she steps out of her black combat boots and makes her way into the living room and around the corner.

"Oh my gah—" comes Aunt Mackie's hushed voice. Talia's giggling starts immediately.

"What did you do?" asks Aunt Mackie.

I kick off my Vans and take a shortcut to the dining room through the kitchen, around the island, and through the walk-in pantry with boxes and cans neatly arranged to the ceiling.

"I wanted something a little different," says Talia, just as I reach the dining room. Aunt Mackie is sitting at the other end of the dining table, which has papers strewn all over it. She looks up at me over her glasses with her mouth agape in shock.

"Do you see what your girlfriend did to her hair?" she asks me. I don't know why she expects me to be outraged. If she knew any of the music I listen to, saw any of the artists, she could've anticipated my response. I hold up the devil horns with my right hand and shut my eyes for maximum effect.

"I think it's pretty metal."

Talia raises one hand to the ceiling, twirls around in a circle, and curtsies.

"Hella metal," she says.

Aunt Mackie slips her glasses down her nose and reaches up to touch her edges. She's got a new hairstyle herself—her normally shoulder-length wash-and-go is now twisted up into

Marleys, tied into a giant bun right at the crown of her head—neat and professional. She's looking over her glasses at Talia's blue hair, which seems to glow in this dining room otherwise filled with beige, brown, white, and black.

"I just hope you dye it back before the start of the school year. What'll happen if colleges ask you to send in pictures of you doing extracurricular activities throughout high school, with your applications?"

"Pretty sure plenty of college students have blue hair," says Talia.

"But not during the admissions process."

"Well, then my pic will be even more accurate. They should know exactly what they're getting themselves into if they admit Talia Gomez—nose ring, blue hair, eighteen-inch back tattoo and all."

It takes a solid five seconds of staring before Aunt Mackie processes that last part.

"Did you say eighteen-inch back tattoo?" she asks.

Talia nods, and I try not to smile as she drags out the joke.

"Yeah, I got it when I went to Mexico with my cousin last summer. It's a picture of you with the word 'gullible' underneath."

That's my girl.

Even Aunt Mackie has to smile in defeat at that one. She taps the table a few times.

"All right, all right, I'm glad you think it's funny to watch my blood pressure go through the roof," she chuckles. "But I'm serious. Colleges can deny students based on absolutely anything. I'd hate for you or Alex, or Isaiah, to get skipped over

36

because of something so silly. You kids are my babies, y'know? I hate to say it, but sometimes you have to play by rules you don't agree with, just to make it in life."

"Yes, Aunt Mackie," says Talia with an eye roll.

Aunt Mackie nods in reply, rising from her chair and rubbing her temples as if she's been straining her eyes all day. "I have to leave in a few minutes to pick up a petition from Mrs. Zaccari about this concert at the Wall this weekend—"

"Ooh, ooh!" cries Talia. "Rex and the Thimbles? Icey London?"

"Who?" asks Aunt Mackie.

"Plush Frog?" presses Talia.

"I don't—"

"Who's playing this weekend?" asks Talia.

I have to smile. If a concert is happening anywhere near us in the next three months, Talia usually knows about it. Rex and the Thimbles and Plush Frog are both playing at the Wall this weekend, which is only a mile away from here, but I can think of only one artist playing that would warrant a petition from Mrs. Zaccari.

"Shiv Skeptic," I say.

Talia's eyes double in size and her mouth drops open.

"Shiv Skeptic is going to be within two hundred miles of here, and you didn't tell me?!"

I shrug.

"I assumed you knew about it already," I explain, but that wasn't the only reason. General admission tickets are 150 bucks. Talia's mom hasn't been able to afford bread and milk comfortably since Shaun died. His funeral expenses blew away the little she had saved up as a single parent, and her disability checks don't cover much else. Why would I tell Talia about a Shiv Skeptic concert if there's no way in hell she's going to be able to go? What's the point in me telling her, except to disappoint her?

"Have you two eaten yet?" asks Aunt Mackie, conveniently changing the subject. "Isaiah's already raided the last of the pizza bites, but you can order something—"

"No I didn't," mumbles a voice from somewhere in the living room.

Talia looks at me as if we're about to enter a war zone. Then she turns to face the big gray sectional facing away from us into the living room. The sixty-four-inch flat-screen TV on the other side of the room is displaying a soccer match on mute, but I know Isaiah well enough to know he's not really watching.

"Hey, Isaiah," offers Talia.

No response from the other side of the couch.

I look to Aunt Mackie to press him to say hello when people walk into the room, like my parents used to. But she just shakes her head and turns her attention back to the papers on the table. Not that I really care if we say hello or not, but it was something our parents wanted. More and more of who they were seems to get forgotten every day. She could at least *pretend* they existed. I step past her, past Talia, and peer over the couch, carefully, without touching it. Isaiah, reclining with his bare feet resting on the cup-holder section—gross—is holding his phone only inches away from his eyes, tapping the screen to bounce a bright yellow ball up and down to create sound waves against the ceiling and floor of the room

38

it's in. I've played this game before. It's a music game called BeatBall, in which you have to tap a ball to stay on rhythm with the EDM song playing. Some, like me, get bored of it within minutes. Others, like Isaiah, play it all summer, buy the fifty-dollar expansion pack that lets you add your own songs to the game, and publish custom levels to the app store.

I could ask him if he wants to mow the Zaccaris' lawn tomorrow morning, like we used to do together, but he probably wouldn't answer me. But I can't blame him. Since the accident, he doesn't really talk unless he has to.

Sometimes, when I'm at work, I wish I had that luxury.

"Well, I'm hungry," says Talia. She throws up her hands and steps back into the kitchen. "Anyone else want pizza?"

"They have a new number now, Talia. It's on the fridge," says Aunt Mackie without looking up from her papers, which I notice, now that I'm standing right behind her, are actually photos. The burgundy photo album lies closed on the table. I hate photos. Not the ones on my phone. Actual physical photographs. I picked up a stack of them once for a school project last year, and the rapid-fire visions I got were a full-blown assault on my psyche. I couldn't focus on anything. Stressful as hell. And dizzying.

"I don't see anything on the fridge," calls Talia, a little too loudly, from around the corner. This house is so big, you get an echo if you stand in certain spots.

Aunt Mackie sucks her teeth in realization, calls back, "Oh, right, I put the flyers in the top drawer. Hold on," and stands up from the table a little too fast. Her left elbow catches the corner of the photo album, sending it flying off the table to the floor.

Only a few loose photos scatter away from the album, which is lying facedown on the carpet. I watch one fly under the sofa. Aunt Mackie sinks to her knees and begins picking them all up and carefully sliding them back into the album, all except the one that slipped under the sofa. But before I can inform her that she missed one, she's standing back up and jogging into the kitchen to help Talia.

"It's in this one," I hear from the kitchen. Their voices dwindle into nothing, and I weigh my options. I could just wait until Aunt Mackie is back in the room to point out that the photo is under the couch, but then I'd have to sit here and remember to let her know. But then she might wonder why I didn't just pick up the photo myself. I'll tolerate one more vision just to keep her from asking questions.

I kneel and reach my hand under the sofa, palm up, so I don't let it touch the floor.

My fingers find the photo and take hold of the edge, and the vision begins. It's strange to see what the photo looks like in my vision when the actual photo is under the sofa where I can't see it.

Mom. Dad. Isaiah. Me.

Dad's holding the camera at an angle that captures all four of us. His smile is crooked, like it always was, and one of his front teeth is grayer than the others. He's wearing his favorite black hat with the Chicago Bulls logo front and center, and his dark eyes, full of warmth, are staring up at me. I sometimes forget what he looks like, but now, looking at this photo, I remember everything. I remember him leaning down to kiss my forehead after I went to bed angry once, right before the accident.

I pretended to be asleep, but he kissed me anyway. Maybe he knew I was awake and wanted to tell me he loved me, and maybe I pretended to be asleep because I didn't want to hear it.

Mom is wearing a matching Bulls hat, holding her backpack strap with one hand and glancing over her shoulder at the camera, as if the camera caught her off guard—Dad loved taking pictures that were posed for him but impromptu for the rest of us. Her eyebrows are perfectly arched. She looks so young she could be mistaken for a college student—bright smile, bright eyes, ready for the world. I guess that's what she hoped I'd look like in college, whenever I got there. Looking at her now, I can almost remember what she smelled like. It was a sweet smell, unmistakable. I noticed it once getting off the bus downtown as a lady in her forties walked past me to get on. By the time I realized what it reminded me of and turned around to look at her, the doors had closed and the bus was taking off down the street.

Maybe it was a perfume she used to wear? A soap she used to use? I don't remember now. I hope I meet that woman on the bus again. If I could just get the name of whatever that scent is, I'd buy a bottle or a bar of whatever it is, I wouldn't care how expensive—one for me, and one for Isaiah. He wouldn't even have to thank me. I would just know that he understood, and he would know I did too.

I look at the two of us in the background of the photo. Mom has her arm around me, pulling me close, and I'm smiling like I probably never will again. There's a light in my eyes that's gone now. I barely recognize myself when I look in the mirror in the morning. I look tired. All the time. But here, in this photo, my mouth hangs open mid-laugh with braces, and I look like I'm excited about what's going to happen next. We're about to walk through the gates at United Center to watch the Bulls play the Spurs. It's my first live game ever, and Isaiah's, too. I look at his face. I look at his smile, at his sparkling eyes. There's something in the curve of his mouth that indicates this photo caught him by surprise just like Mom. But he looks happy. He looks curious. He looks hopeful.

That was when he used to talk to me. We used to play ball outside in the summer and *Smash Bros.* inside when it rained, and I used to obliterate whatever strategy he'd have cobbled together in *Catan*. We had game night every Saturday, and Scoop's was our favorite after-school hangout spot before Mom and Dad came home from work.

Everything was so different back then.

As always, the vision lasts for only a moment in real life, so I prepare to cancel the vision and wait for Aunt Mackie to come back into the room. But just before it fades into darkness, I notice something. I hesitate. I expect to see myself slip the photo into the album, or put it on the dining table next to the others, or hand it to Aunt Mackie.

But I don't.

The photo sinks down to my waist, and I stuff it into my jeans pocket.

Why would I do that?

I have no intention of continuing to relive this memory. Mom. Dad. Isaiah. Me. The Spurs game. A week before it happened. It's easier to just forget we had a life before we lost them. It's easier to forget. Forget everything.

But . . . apparently, I won't.

I'm back in the living room, staring down at the photo in my hands.

Think, Alex.

Why would I put this thing in my pocket?

If there's no way I would decide to put it in my pocket with what I know now, I must discover something in the next few moments that will make me *want* to put the photo in my pocket. Something significant. And if I can't tell why, from the past or the present, there's only one other source of information I haven't checked.

I set the photo on the dining room table and, with trembling hands, pick it back up again, triggering another vision.

I watch the photo shifting around inside my pocket, pitch black. Shortly after, I pull it out again, this time with my ceiling behind it. I'm lying in bed looking at it, torturing myself, dwelling on memories, so it must be night. Then darkness takes over again as I slip the photo into the pocket of my jacket, wadded up on my nightstand.

It feels like I stand in the dining room for hours, watching this vision, but I know the whole thing is taking a split second. When I take the photo out again after watching the darkness for forever, I see the photo in my hands again, with grass behind it, and when I look up past it, I see gravestones. Hundreds of them. In a lush green field with morning sunlight peeking through the trees, and colorful flowers dotting the hills where the grave plots are. The photo goes into my jacket pocket this time. Darkness again, with occasional flickers of

43

sunlight through the mesh waterproof layer, in different colors. Looks like a rave in my pocket, wherever I am. Darkness again.

Graveyard again.

This time, my eyes travel. At first I'm looking at the photo with more gravestones behind it, dotting the hillsides, scattered among the trees. But then I look down, at the gaping rectangular hole in the ground, and my vision goes red.

Red.

Red, like I'm looking through one lens in a pair of 3D glasses. Red, like I saw in my vision of Shaun before he died. I freeze, staring down at the rectangular hole. My shiny black shoes, peeking out from under my black slacks, are covered in dew from the grass, standing only inches away from the edge. I watch myself reach my hand forward and let the wind carry the photo from my fingers. It falls, like a leaf, landing squarely in the middle of a floral arrangement on top of a small white casket at the bottom of the hole in the ground. Before I can will the vision to stop, I see the inscription on the side. I see the name before I can backpedal out of this nightmare.

ISAIAH RUFUS, DEARLY BELOVED.

3

The Graveyard

MOM AND DAD USED to tell us, when we were still young enough to believe people can understand anything about the universe, that people are always chasing after impossible things. We want what we can't have. We ask questions we don't fully understand, looking for answers we wouldn't be able to handle. People pay accountants and psychologists to give them power over the here and now, and they pay life coaches, fitness trainers, doctors, and tarot readers so they can control more of the future.

But none of them really want to be *sure* of what will happen.

You can't convince me that anyone really wants to know when they'll die, or when they'll get married, or when they'll have kids, or how many. The not-knowing is what makes life meaningful, the surprise of my girlfriend picking me up at work with blue hair, the suspense of wondering if she'll turn to me and kiss me, or if we'll get into a massive fight and she'll break up with me like in my vision, whenever that night comes. Spending summer days on the sofa across the room from Isaiah, the two of us on our phones, not acknowledging each other except to ask if the other wants a snack, happily unaware of the hours we have left to get to know each other. My visions took all of that away.

I sigh and roll from my side to my back to stare at my ceiling.

The moment I saw him, the last living piece of my immediate family, lying inside a box at the bottom of a hole in the ground, he was already dead.

I know that I can't stop it, but I shut my eyes and begin ripping through the facts I have in my head regardless. Everyone dies. Isaiah's going to, just like me, but is it really in only a few days?

Less than a week left?

Lying in bed looking at the photo, which is happening now.

The morning in the graveyard. At least, I *think* it was morning.

The evening I'm going to spend sitting in my chair looking at the photo again.

Darkness.

The evening—what I assume is evening—lights flickering through my jacket pocket.

More darkness. The morning in the graveyard.

I shake my head.

There's no way this is happening. Isaiah's a healthy—excluding all the cereal and pizza bites—twelve-year-old kid. He can't just . . . no. It's not happening. Maybe I'm stuck in one of those time-loop things I've heard about. Maybe I'm *still* stuck in a vision of me lying in bed, staring at my ceiling. Maybe I'm dreaming.

I shake my head and pinch the back of my hand. No vision, since touching my *own* body doesn't count.

The pinch doesn't help.

I reach down and grab my comforter and shoo away a vision of me, fast asleep in bed, probably years from now.

Nope. This is reality.

Maybe Isaiah fakes his own death?

Then I shake my head and scoff at my own thoughts. How the hell would he pull that off? He'd have to be some boy genius, and Isaiah is *no* genius. He'd have to dig or hire someone to dig a rectangular hole, get a casket off eBay, *and* convince me the whole thing wasn't staged. There's no freakin' way.

And that red in my vision. The whole world looking like I was watching through blood. My heart races out of control again. I don't want to believe it, but that red can mean death and nothing else.

But what if . . .

I'm out of ideas, but desperate for another.

What if *anything* but this?

My heart is thundering. Then another thought crosses my mind. Maybe it's a different Isaiah Rufus. I dive for my phone, banishing a vision of me unlocking it, and unlock it. I take to Google.

"Rufus last name how common," I search. I click the first result and read, and my stomach twists into a knot. Apparently, the last name Rufus hasn't been in circulation in the US since . . . 1988? That can't be right. Isaiah and I are here. Our parents were here. Did we not even show up on the radar? I scroll and see that even in 1988, our last name only belonged to .005 percent of the US population.

We're likely the only two Rufuses left, and even more likely the only two Rufuses in Chicago, Illinois, USA, which means the Isaiah Rufus who's going to be at the bottom of that hole in the ground in that graveyard in less than a week is probably my brother.

Panic crawls into my stomach like a colony of ants, and I try to breathe as the futility of this whole situation sets in. What do I know? What can I piece together? In a little while, I'm going to pull the photo out of my pocket again, in a graveyard. Why the hell would I be in a graveyard? *Which* graveyard?

Why am I doing this to myself? It doesn't matter what I know, or what I do. Isaiah is going to die. *So why am I still anxious, like I can do something?*

Why do I still have adrenaline coursing through me like there's some way to fight this?

I open my eyes, stare at the ceiling, and follow all the steps that are supposed to calm me down and help me sleep:

> Take a deep breath.
> Hold my breath and count to ten.
> Count to a hundred.
> Lie in corpse pose.
> Get up and get a glass of water.
> Open the window and get some fresh air.
> Stare at the ceiling.
> Lie with my ass against the wall and my legs up, so my body makes an L shape.

None of this works.

The window is open, the blood that was in my feet is now in my legs, there's water in my stomach and air in my lungs, and I'm still wide awake. Even as I stare at my ceiling, which is a solid white sheet of nothing, my brain charges full speed ahead through the hypotheticals, the *what if I just . . .* , the same fear

48

that swallowed me after I foresaw Shaun's end.

It happened the summer after I'd lost my parents.

We were both thirteen.

I didn't really know how to handle my visions yet or understand the damage they could do to me, until that day we stood in Shaun's backyard, kicking a soccer ball around, just the two of us. It was an otherwise normal day. Sunny. Summer. Shaun offered to teach me how to make the Shiv hand symbol, and for some reason—must've been a moment when I wasn't thinking—I agreed. There's a certain way you can bend your fingers to spell *S-H-I-V*, and Shaun was determined to teach it to me by the time I left his house. But I couldn't get it. My ring finger wouldn't bend into a sharp V for anything, so Shaun put down the ball, rolled up his sleeves, and took both my hands in his, guiding my fingers into the correct positions. I was sucked into a vortex of colors. Brilliant flickers of what was once the sunshine and Shaun's tan skin and dark eyes, and the green grass in the backyard and the clear blue sky, faded into a dull gray-green hue. I was suddenly in the back seat of a car with soft fabric seats and mud stains on the back of the front passenger seat. The rain was so violent, the droplets dancing against the windows made a consistent collective *hissssss* instead of infrequent pitter-pattering. Twin headlights emerged from the darkness before I could realize what they were, zooming straight at me, and the *sound* . . .

The sound was like something out of an action movie, the ones where everyone important miraculously dodges every bullet, evades every crash, and survives every explosion. But we weren't in a movie.

And then, the red.

Once Shaun let go of my hand, we were back in his backyard, with the soccer ball on the grass between us and my hands in the perfect position, spelling out the word *S-H-I-V*. He was smiling at me. His eyes were searching mine, like he could see through me, like he knew I'd seen something. Or maybe I just thought he was looking at me like that. Maybe I wanted so badly to tell him what I'd seen, I mistook the approval in his eyes for curiosity.

I shut my eyes against the memory and cover my face with my hands. What else could I have done? I was scared. I didn't know exactly when the crash would happen, except that it would be raining hard outside. All I knew was that I didn't want to be anywhere near that car when it did. I ran all the way home without another word to Shaun that day, the whole two miles. Talia still lives in that house with her mom, on the south side of East Garfield Park, and I can't even go over there without remembering what I did.

I *hid*. I ignored Shaun's texts. I left him wondering what he'd done or said to lose his best friend in the last few days of his life, and a couple of days later, when I woke up from my nap to the sound of rain tapping against my window, I sobbed into my pillow, *knowing* it was happening.

I never saw Shaun again.

Never even saw his face.

His casket was closed at the funeral.

I can't even go with Talia to take him flowers. I'm afraid looking at his headstone, knowing I could've stayed with him so he wouldn't be alone, would break me completely.

I think of Aunt Mackie and how I'll have to look her in the

eyes across the dinner table every night until I graduate and go off to college, knowing I knew about Isaiah before it happened, whatever "it" ends up being. Whatever happens in the next few days, I'll have to live with the decisions I make leading up to it. I'll have to make it count. I may not be able to keep Isaiah with me for much longer, but I can make sure that in the last few days of his life, he knows he's not alone.

I don't have to make the same mistake twice.

I *can't*.

I force my body to peel itself from my bed, even while it's still dark outside. I can see the sky from my window, deep and dark and dotted with sparkling stars. The faint warm purple of sunrise is slowly creeping into view, and my phone clock reads 5:45 a.m. I should be tired, but right now my body is buzzing. I can't sleep. I can't eat. I have to get up.

I don't even know where to begin with this. Isaiah is the only person I know who legitimately hates everything. He doesn't watch movies. He doesn't hang with friends. He doesn't even leave the house unless he has to, like, for school, or a doctor's appointment. He just sits in his room eating Lucky Charms and pizza bites, playing BeatBall and listening to music.

Occasionally, a box from Amazon will arrive at the door addressed to Isaiah, and either Aunt Mackie or I will knock, pass it to him through his bedroom door, and leave him to open it in the solitude of his hobbit hole. They're usually just new clothes, with the occasional phone case or headphones thrown in. I know because sometimes I watch the visions of him unboxing things as I carry the boxes to his room.

Just because I'm cursed doesn't mean I can't get *some* fun

out of it.

But . . . *how* do I make the next few days meaningful for him? What would that even look like, besides offering to sit with him in his room, eating Lucky Charms and pizza bites, and playing BeatBall and listening to music? If that's all he likes, what can I give him to make it special?

How do you bring joy to someone who just wants to be left alone?

I swing my legs off the bed and my feet find the carpet. In the dark, I find my T-shirt draped over the back of my desk chair—the Gorillaz one that's going to end up at Goodwill in a few years. I'll take that as a gentle nudge from the universe that I'm headed in the right direction.

I slip the shirt on and step gingerly over the piles of clothes scattered all over my floor. Aunt Mackie claims there's a smell of body spray and fried food in here, but maybe, like the smell of ice cream at Scoop's, or the popcorn at her movie theater, it's just begun to smell faintly of sandalwood incense and anxiety to me.

I ease my door open. It stopped creaking when Aunt Mackie had it replaced last week. I miss my old door. That's where I kept my band sticker hall of fame. I'd been collecting them for years, a sticker for all my favorite artists—the Gorillaz, the Fray, the Weepies, Kendrick, Logic, Panic! at the Disco, Nicki Minaj, Lizzo, Lady Leshurr, and the king himself, Shiv Skeptic. So many people I respect, whose art has gotten me through so much. So many people who I've always wanted to see live, but imagine me, an already anxious, cursed kid, dealing with all those people. No way in hell am I about to walk into such a huge place with so many people, and so many surfaces to touch, and so many things out of my control. But with my door, I could dream. I had *all* the greats until Aunt Mackie decided the doors in the house needed an update, and I came home to a brand-new, boring white door that still smells like fresh paint. All my stickers, all my memories, gone.

But the house's market value is now higher, so it's fine.

I roll my eyes. Aunt Mackie's job is important. I get it. I like food. I like having clothes. I like having a bed to sleep in. But she could've let me keep the old door under my bed or something.

Talia's sticker hall of fame is on her ceiling above her bed. I should've put mine somewhere smart like that, somewhere that could withstand all my aunt's "home updates." That way, I could stare up at good memories while I try to fall asleep. My blank ceiling is an empty canvas that prompts my mind to wander.

I wonder if Isaiah has anything like that in his room.

I haven't been in there in a million years.

I make my way down the hallway, hardly able to see anything except the light from the moon shining down through the skylight in the ceiling. I step through the shower of moonlight and disappear into the darkness on the other side with my arms outstretched, feeling for the door at the end of the hallway.

My fingertips meet brushed nickel, and I end the vision of me turning the knob. I glance over my shoulder to make sure I'm alone. What am I doing? Isaiah's probably asleep at this hour. Even *he* has to crash at some point. But better to check just in case. Hours are precious now, and if he's awake, we're wasting them. I take a long breath in and obey my vision, turning the knob, easing the door open. I'm immediately hit with the odor of must, and the ineffective scent of body spray. It smells like my PE bag in here. God, I forgot. He has to be *reminded* to shower these days.

I'm surprised to see the blue glow of his computer lighting up the otherwise pitch-black room. He's sitting, hunched over at his desk, staring intently at the screen. His big white head-phones, the size of grapefruit halves, peek out from under his oversize sweatshirt hood. He's swimming in it, but it was Dad's favorite. The black one with the Bulls logo on the chest.

A pang of guilt hits me. I didn't even know he still had that, let alone wore it.

His eyes are wide, only inches away from the screen. I whisper into the room.

"Isaiah."

But his headphones are too loud. He doesn't flinch. He doesn't even notice me until I step into the room and ease the door closed behind me. The glow of the screen dances on his face.

"Isaiah?"

Still no response.

I step gingerly closer. I know what it's like to be staring at a screen too closely and then someone steps out of the darkness behind it and scares the living shit out of you. I don't want that to happen to Isaiah, but it does.

His eyes dart to me and grow huge, and he reels back in his chair.

"Dude!" he exclaims, one hand over his chest and one hand scrambling to find the mouse and shut down whatever was playing. He stands up and flicks on the desk lamp next to him, filling the room with a brilliant yellow glow. My eyes haven't adjusted, and I quickly squeeze them shut.

"What are you doing in here?" he demands, stepping out from behind the desk.

I squint my eyes open and realize he's not wearing pants—only checkered boxers and white socks. His leg hair is almost as thick as mine now, and even in this poor light, I can see that his knees are ashy as hell. He's standing with his feet wide and fists balled, like he's prepared to literally fight me out of here. I raise my hands humbly.

"I'm sorry," I begin. Always a good place to start. It's hard to be mad at someone who's apologizing to you. Hard for me anyway.

"Get out," he says, his eyes narrowing. He takes a step toward me, and I move backward.

"Bruh, calm down. I just came to talk."

"How about 'bruh, *no*'? Get out."

I weigh my options. I could insist he calm down, or I could leave and try talking to him later, if there *is* a "later." Or I can bargain with him.

"Let me finish what I have to say, and I'll buy you all the Lucky Charms you want."

"Aunt Mackie already buys all the Lucky Charms I want."

Fair enough.

"Get *out*," he hisses. "*Now.* Or I'll tell Aunt Mackie you woke me up."

I don't like fighting. It makes me all clammy and shaky and uncomfortable. But I'll bring out the big guns if he makes this difficult.

"Sit down and listen, or I'll tell Aunt Mackie what you're watching in here."

Panic spreads across his face. He sinks down into his desk chair and folds his arms. His jaw is clenched and he's staring at the wall, refusing to look at me. He and I both know that Aunt Mackie will start cutting some cords if she thinks he's abusing his internet privileges, and I don't want that for him. I'm sure the internet is all he has, being in here all day.

"Look," I say, kicking a few clothes out of the way to clear a space on the floor. I sit down cross-legged and stare at him, hoping he'll look at me. "I didn't want to have to threaten you into talking to me. I just came in here to ask what's up."

He looks at me now, eyes flashing.

"What's *up*?" he asks. "You want to know . . . what's *up*?"

I nod.

I don't think all the Lucky Charms in the world could make this conversation less awkward.

"Yeah," I say with a shrug. "We haven't talked much since . . . well, really since we moved here. I feel like I don't really know you anymore."

He rolls his eyes and shrugs.

"You don't."

I nod, a lump forming in my throat. He has every right to be angry. After the accident, I shut down, and then when we lost Shaun, I shut everything and everyone out. Including him. Now I have to recover before it's too late.

"I know," I sigh, scrambling for the right words to say. "Do you, uh . . . do you remember when we used to play basketball

56

with Shaun in the driveway?"

His frown deepens and his crossed arms tighten around himself. I continue.

"We used to be . . . I don't know . . . we used to hang out. It's just that, after we moved here, and after Shaun . . . you know . . . we didn't have much in common, so—"

"We *don't*."

"Well," I say with open hands, "now I'm trying to fix that."

"You couldn't text me that? Like, way later today? You had to bust down my door at six in the morning to ask 'what's up?'"

It does sound ridiculous when he says it like that.

"Okay, fine. You want me to cut to the point?" I ask. "I came in here to ask what you want to do today. Anything you want. Literally anything, and I'll make it happen. I know I haven't been there for you. I haven't been a big brother to you. Like, at all—"

I realize, now that I say it aloud, that I really *haven't* been a big brother. I haven't taught him anything. I haven't even talked to him, not for real. Not like this. My cheeks are burning and I take a deep breath. I *really* don't want to cry right now.

Man up, Alex. Man up.

"I want to make things right," I say. "Just tell me what you want to do."

Isaiah glances over his shoulder at his computer. Then he leans forward with his elbows on his knees and opens his hands.

"You know what I wanna do today?" he asks. "I wanna finish what I was watching, then go to bed, wake up this afternoon, eat some pizza bites, and then rewatch what I was watching. And I want to do *all* of that . . . *alone*."

It's taking all my self-control not to say something I'll regret right now. I shut my eyes and focus on my breathing. I picture Shaun's face, smiling at me as we stand face-to-face in his back yard. He would've known what to do, what to say. He used to stand between Isaiah and me when we'd get into it, especially on the court. Isaiah didn't like that I kept dunking on him, and I didn't like that he kept whining about it instead of pushing himself to jump higher or learn to bob and weave around me. I wasn't *that* much taller than him, after all. Shaun would've offered to swap teams with me so Isaiah and I could play along-side each other instead. He would've suggested we switch it up and do a free throw contest or something. Anything to ease conflict.

Anything to keep us all happy.

I guess Shaun really *was* the glue holding us together after our parents died. We only hung out when it was the three of us. With Isaiah and me at home, we lived in separate worlds.

Ay, man, Shaun would say if he were standing in this room right now. *Why don't we go for a walk or something to cool off? Or ice cream. That'll cool us off too. Oh, actually, it's too early. How about we go look up a recipe and learn to* make *some?*

He was always so much more adventurous than I was. So unafraid.

I play a sound that's been burned into my memory, the sound of his voice, his laughter. I think of what I'd give to be able to go back to that day I left him standing in his backyard. I think of what I'd say to him if he were here. If he could hear me.

"Can I drive you anywhere?" I press.

"If you could stop driving me up the *wall*, that'd be sick. Are we done here? Can you go away now?"

"I'm not leaving until we have this day planned out."

"I'd give Aunt Mackie my entire browser history before I'd spend a whole day with you."

"You don't mean that."

There's no way he can mean that.

"I don't say things I don't mean," he spits, "like 'I wanna make things right.'"

"You don't think I want to make things right?"

"I don't even think you know what that *means*."

He's right. I don't.

"Mind *telling* me what that means?" I ask. Then I realize I'm getting defensive, and I revert to my original plan. "There has to be somewhere you want to go. If you could drive anywhere in the world right now, where would it be?"

He's silent for what seems like forever, staring at the floor with his hands clasped. So much time passes that I think he'll let the question go unanswered. Then he breaks the silence.

"You don't care."

That stings. I hear him saying this to me, but it just sounds like Shaun.

"You never care about anything," he says, pushing himself up out of the chair and walking to the window with folded arms. He leans against the wall and stares at the sill, since the blinds are closed. "Just Talia and your job, and panicking about everything."

My cheeks are on fire. I know he's right, but it still hurts to hear it. I *do* care, but . . . I guess he would never know that. I never talk to him. I never reach out to him. I never hang out with him or help him with homework or even play ball with him. Not even in the summer, when I have plenty of free time. I watch him closely, shoulders hunched up around his ears, so much rage boiling up inside such a small person. How does he live like that? I mean, I'm pissed too. These are insults he's throwing at me. But something soft and cool is seeping into the cracks between the blocks of rage stacked into a wall between us.

Pity?

He continues, "Whatever nightmare you had last night to make you realize you should *start* caring, leave me out of it."

"I didn't have a dream," I say quickly, spotting the escape route.

I would promise never to listen to another Gorillaz song again in my entire life, if I could make that vision a bad dream.

"Whatever," he grumbles. "I'm done talking."

I stick to my guns.

"You were thinking about somewhere to go for a long time there," I press. "You have to have thought of *somewhere*. The pier? Millennium Park? Scoop's? Want to start with ice cream and talk?"

"About what?"

I shrug. "Whatever's bothering you."

"*You're* bothering me," he snaps, "and ice cream won't fix my problems."

What problems? Missing Mom and Dad? I'm not trying to "fix" that. His anger issues? I wouldn't touch those with a thirty-foot pole.

"What will?" I ask, giving him the benefit of the doubt.

He's quiet for a long moment before shaking his head.

"You'd never take me there," he says.

"Try me. I promise. I'll drive you wherever you want."

It can't be anything *too* wild, right? He's twelve. Chuck E. Cheese's? The aquarium? The zoo?

"Twenty-fifth and Jefferson," he says.

"What's there?"

He looks up at me and says, "Elginwood Park Cemetery."

Why in the name of Biggie Smalls would he want to go to the cemetery where Mom and Dad are buried? My chest pounds as I remember my vision. Just six events will happen before I lose him forever:

The morning in the graveyard.

The evening I'm going to spend sitting in my chair looking at the photo.

Darkness.

The lights flickering through my jacket pocket.

More darkness. And then . . . I'm back in the graveyard alone, looking down at his casket, never to hear his voice again.

"I knew you wouldn't take me," I hear him mumble. "You're probably too scared." Apparently I've taken too long to answer.

"No, no," I say, frustrated at my voice cracking while I take a deep breath and say determinedly, "Let's go. Mind telling me why we're going there, though? You really don't want to get ice cream or something instead? You really want to talk in a graveyard?"

Somewhere that *doesn't* progress the vision any faster than it has to? If we go to the graveyard this morning, that leaves four events.

"I never said I wanted to talk," he says.

"That doesn't sound like a no."

"Fine, I'll go. But no questions," he says, grabbing a pair of

61

pants off the top of a pile of clothes on the floor and stepping into them. He grabs his black Vans sneakers from the foot of his unmade bed and steps past me. "Let's go."

Once I get back to my room and get through visions of my jeans, my socks, my shoes, my jacket, my wallet, and my keys, Isaiah and I tiptoe through the front door and get into my car, looking out at the winding streets of Santiam Estates.

The sun is peeking over the city skyline, dulled by morning fog and pollution, like a glow stick at a Wiz Khalifa concert. Isaiah is slumped against the window with his hood over his head, staring out at the driveway. It's surreal having him in the passenger seat. I'm so used to seeing Talia next to me. I realize I don't remember the last time he rode in my car. Must have been at least a year. He was so much smaller back then, his legs fit just fine without adjusting the seat. Now he's had to slide the seat back six inches just to keep his knees off the dash.

I realize he's not wearing his seat belt.

"Hey," I say. "Seat belt, please."

He glances over his shoulder at me and sucks his teeth.

"Now," I insist.

My vision wasn't specific. I have no idea when or how it'll happen. In my vision, I didn't see him in the graveyard with me that first time, I didn't see him while I was lying in bed staring up at the photo, and I didn't see him the whole time the photo was tucked away in darkness in my pocket. I didn't see him until I took it out at the funeral and looked down. I don't know when my last moment with him will be. We could crash in the next five minutes. And even though I know I'm powerless to prevent it, Isaiah's seat belt gives me the illusion of control.

62

My chest tightens as an idea hits me. I could . . . what if I just . . . touched his hand? Or arm or something? If I want to know exactly when it'll happen, I could just . . .

My hands are clammy around the wheel, and my heart starts pounding. I remember to breathe, trying to ward this off before it turns into a full-blown anxiety attack. *Breathe, Alex. Isaiah's here. He's fine. You don't have to do anything you don't want to do.*

It would be the smartest option. If I could just get over my fear . . .

Do I really want to know?

Would it change anything?

I've taken too long to think it over.

Isaiah rolls his eyes and reaches for his seat belt, clicking it into place and resuming his mopey slump against the window. I sigh and focus on a spot on the driveway pavement. The hum of the engine isn't enough to cut this silence. I feel my shoulders getting tense, and I become desperate to fill the air with something, even if it's awkward conversation. My mind wanders to our destination.

"So, of all the things you could choose to do today, you want to visit Mom and Dad?" I say, probably a little too flippantly, conveniently leaving out the implied *or Shaun?* I try to soften it with, "I just want to know if I should be mentally preparing for—"

"Yeah."

I have to ask.

"Why?"

His voice is softer this time, and I swear I can hear an unsteadiness in it.

"I just do."

I'm not going to force him to keep talking. I turn to the other thing I often use to fill silence, so I don't let my mind wander to whatever embarrassing thing I said the day before to someone who has probably already forgotten about it, or any other social interactions in my past that I've utterly butchered.

Music.

When I'm lying on my bed with my eyes closed and headphones on, just listening, nothing can touch me.

As I pull out of the driveway, I flip on the radio, and it finds my phone, automatically starting my playlist off with "Black Dragon" by the great Shiv himself. This song goes so hard. The lyrics always stir something deep within me that I've never been able to identify. When those first four bass booms come pounding out of my sound system, I feel like I could park this car, hop out, and sprint ten miles. If I were alone in here, I'd be rapping and dancing to those opening lines. I glance at Isaiah and decide, screw it, life is too short.

I'm going to do it anyway.

> *"Bangin', ballin', bobbin', bouncin', bumpin'*
> *Black Dragon.*
> *Got them bottles poppin', yeah we hoppin' in*
> *the station wagon.*
> *Bitch, yo' Lam ain't paid off, made of money?*
> *More like made o' debt. Bet.*
> *Call me when yo credit score is set like*
> *Aquanet."*

I glance at Isaiah, who's looking at me like I've lost it, and I launch into the next verse. This is my car. I'll rap if I want to.

> *"Let my crew find out you slingin', bringin'*
> *Crissy to my shows, bruh.*
> *Shit turn you a zombie, leave yo body for the*
> *crows, bruh."*

At "crows, bruh," I hear my voice double. Isaiah raps with me through the next lines, and that lift in my chest from earlier, that feeling like I could run ten miles, multiplies by fifty.

> *"Niggas think they'll catch me slippin', sippin'*
> *on this juice, mayne.*
> *Cobra got my keys cuz had enough to get me*
> *loose, mayne."*

"You listen to Shiv?" asks Isaiah. His eyes are wide, and his hands are on his knees. He's leaning forward in his seat and looking at me, totally perplexed.

"The king?" I ask. "Of course."

"Since when?"

What a question. Since his first EP, *The Rush*, which he dropped six years ago. Most people haven't even heard of it. I glance at Isaiah, turn down the radio, and decide to test him.

"*Goin' down to the corner store armed with my hatchet, machete, grenade, and my gun,*" I rap. Isaiah, without hesitation, jumps into the next part with me.

"*Just to have company, someone to talk to, but I make it look like I play this for fun.*"

Holy shit! He knows "The Rush"!

65

"How did I not know this about you?" I ask. He gets suddenly quiet, and I feel the weight of what he said earlier, when I said I feel like I don't know him.

You don't.

I haven't been around enough *to* know him.

We've had the same favorite artist for—what, months? Years even?

"I'm sorry," I say, glancing down at his hands, which are still resting on his knees. I wish I could offer him some kind of solace in resting my hand on his. But the vision I'd get from that might dissolve whatever sanity I have left. I decide that, no, I don't want to know what happens to him in the next few moments, or hours, or days.

"For what?" he asks.

I shrug and sigh. "For not getting to know you."

"You still have time, you know," he says, so softly I almost don't hear him. That catches me off guard, and for a second I wonder if he knows. I look over at him, but he keeps his eyes staring straight ahead until he notices me.

"What? I don't graduate for another six years." He shrugs gloomily. "I'm not going anywhere."

It sends a pang of hurt through my chest, the fact that he's counting down the years he has until he gets to leave—where to, I don't know. I bite back the next question at first, wondering if I want to start that conversation. But we're heading to the graveyard.

~~Lying in bed.~~

~~Graveyard.~~

Sitting in my chair.

66

Darkness.

Flickering lights.

More darkness. Graveyard.

We're about to head to the first event that happens before *it* happens, and I decide that if we're on some Final Destination shit, I'm not going to waste the little time we have.

"Where are you going when you graduate?" I ask.

There's silence, and then he shrugs. He rests his head in his hand, with his arm propped against the door, dead eyes ahead.

"I don't know. But wherever it is, I'll be writing rhymes."

"*You?*"

He frowns at me.

"I didn't mean that like I'm laughing at you," I say. "I'm just surprised!"

"You think I've been spending all that time making BeatBall beats and *not* writing lyrics to go with any of them?"

Fair point.

Silence drags on for so long that I start to get jittery. I don't know what to say, so I turn to the road and crank the music again just as the chorus drops, wanting to return to thirty seconds ago, before I posed the question, when we were singing together as if we didn't have a care in the world. Wasn't that what I was supposed to be trying to do? Making his life easier?

"Say it wit me, ooh, there go my crew that's Black Dra—"

The music vanishes, and I look down to see Isaiah's hand on the dial.

"Shh," he urges, pointing past my face out the driver's-side window. "That's the Zaccaris' house."

I look out the window at the white house with the white rosebushes and slightly overgrown front lawn that I'd be offering to mow any other day. But with Isaiah's time dwindling, there's no way I'd waste a minute over there. Not today.

"Right," I say.

The Zaccaris have always been nice to Isaiah and me, ever since we moved in. They have a son who's never home, but they don't talk about him much. I heard his name's Eli. I've never met him in person before, and Aunt Mackie says she hopes I never do. I haven't told her that he sent me a friend request on Facebook. She told me once, "Eli is always strung out on something, running from somebody for some kinda charges." Apparently, he's only a few years older than me.

I glance at Isaiah and thank God he never got involved in shit like that. As mouthy as he is to me, he's never been in trouble with the law, and he knows how to sound professional when he leaves the house. He can rap "Black Dragon" as well as I can, but once we knock on the Zaccaris' door, it's "Good morning, Mrs. Zaccari. How are you today?"

As I drive past the house at a responsible speed, the wooden gate at the side of the house swings open, and in one fell swoop, Isaiah yanks off his hood and clicks the radio off completely. Mrs. Zaccari steps through the gate in her shiny pink silk pajamas, with a matching silk robe over the top. Her shoulders are hunched, and her arms are folded as if it's too cold for her to be out here. Her hair, which I imagine was once all blond and is now mostly a warm gray blond, is tied into a loose braid at the nape of her neck, so loose actually that bunches have fallen down into her face, indicating she probably slept

68

with her hair like that. She immediately spots us, and her face melts into a smile. She waves, and we wave back, and she steps forward as if she wants to talk to us.

"You think she has cookies for us?" asks Isaiah. Mrs. Zaccari's white chocolate macadamia nut cookies are the best. She chops up the nuts really small so you're not even mad when you find out the bite you took was more nuts than white chocolate. But it's wishful thinking to imagine she has any freshly baked right now.

"At six in the morning?" I laugh. I slow down to a complete stop and roll down the driver's-side window.

"Morning, boys!" she calls, stepping gingerly across her front lawn and down the slope to the sidewalk in her black Nike flip-flops. "Up early?"

I nod and glance at Isaiah, who's looking at me. I'm sure he's thinking the same thing I am: I don't really leave the house except to go to work, Isaiah is practically nocturnal, and the Rufus boys are *never* out together. Especially not at no six in the morning.

"Thinking about starting a paper route," Isaiah hollers out the window. Smart. That's something we can easily explain to Aunt Mackie if she happens to notice my car is gone this morning. People in this neighborhood talk too much to keep secrets. "Thought we'd try out waking up this early to see if we like it."

"Oh, that's so responsible of you!" She beams. "I *love* that."

"Thanks," replies Isaiah convincingly.

I'm not gonna lie—I'm impressed at his quick thinking. He whipped up that lie faster than I could think of one. Maybe I've underestimated how much street smarts he's learned without me already. I forget sometimes that he grew up in East

69

Garfield Park too.

Mrs. Zaccari looks around, up and down the street, before stepping forward and continuing in a lowered voice, like she's telling a secret, "Y'know, if you do decide to do a paper route, you could get some exercise and take Eli's old bike. We were about to sell it in a garage sale next Saturday, but if either of you can use it, it's yours!"

Isaiah and I look at each other. He's probably, like me, realizing how much money the Zaccaris must have to just be handing out bikes like that. Back in East Garfield Park, you couldn't leave a bike chained up in the backyard without somebody jacking it. He looks past me again, out the window to Mrs. Zaccari, and I answer for both of us.

"Thank you! We'll let you know!"

She nods.

"And be safe out there. And don't stay out too late tonight, okay? You know with that concert tomorrow night, we're supposed to get all kinds of people around here."

I'm used to it by now—the code-switching, the two-facedness, the pretending to empathize with white people's concerns about Shiv Skeptic concertgoers, while in another reality in which I mowed Mrs. Zaccari's lawn several more times and could afford it, and I wasn't so scared stiff of huge crowds, I might *be* one. And, in another reality in which Isaiah gets to grow up, he might have made it big as a rapper himself.

My chest tightens.

"Aunt Mackie told us," I say. Mrs. Zaccari even went as far as to start a petition about the concert, when, as far as I know, the Wall is a public venue. It's fair game for any artist popular

70

enough to fill seats. Shiv fits the bill.

"Even right here, in Santiam Estates," she says. Her eyes are wide and her mouth is pursed with disgust. "People around here shouldn't be allowed to rent out their house to just *anybody* with a concert like this going on so close, especially in a gated community. It's just dangerous. I don't want you boys getting hurt, okay? Tell your aunt to sign my petition as soon as possible."

"Yes, Mrs. Zaccari," we say, almost in unison.

Her stern expression melts into a smile before she continues.

"And come over later for cookies. Double the white chocolate chips this time."

Isaiah and I exchange glances, and something sinks in my chest. Is eating cookies at the Zaccaris' house really going to impact Isaiah's time left? Is it really going to help him so much that we shouldn't do *anything* else instead? I guess we have time to decide that. Maybe.

We wave our goodbyes, and Mrs. Zaccari gets her mail while Isaiah and I sail down the road.

The radio stays off.

4

The Cemetery

ELGINWOOD PARK CEMETERY IS only a mile away from Aunt Mackie's house. I've walked past it late at night when Aunt Mackie is out of town at a conference and I can't sleep, and Talia's not awake to text me.

I park my little blue Geo in the mostly empty parking lot. The only other car here is a single white hearse. I intentionally park as far away from it as possible, because I don't want to look at it. I shut off the engine and take in the silence as the engine clicks a few times while it cools down. A few birds chirp sweetly nearby, welcoming us to this place of the dead. I take a deep breath and open the door. Isaiah hasn't moved since the engine shut off. He's just staring straight ahead at the sea of gravestones and plaques dotting the field, just like I'd be doing if I hadn't trained myself long ago to avoid unnecessary silence.

I rest my elbow on the door and run my fingers over my curls, twirling one around my finger nervously. My heart is racing as I stare out the windshield. I'd rather be *anywhere* but here. But if it's what Isaiah wants, if it gets him out of his room and talking to me, then here we go. Mom and Dad and all. Shaun and all.

"Ready?" I ask.

He nods, and I take that as confirmation that he'll follow me once I climb out of the car.

The morning air is crisp, and the birds are even louder out here. I've always enjoyed that sound, but today it just makes it hard to focus. I shove my hands in my pockets and cancel the vision of me walking across the grass in these jeans. I hear Isaiah's door slam shut.

"Did you lock it?" I ask, glancing over my shoulder at him.

He nods and steps over the curb onto the dewy grass.

"Hey, watch out," I say. "You might slip."

If he falls and breaks his neck right here in this graveyard, I swear to God I'll never forgive myself. He's still looking around, looking especially small now, his shoulders hunched, hands in his pockets. He looks like he's about to walk through Shelob's lair. Eventually, he nods and falls into step beside me, hands still in pockets. I wish he'd hold them out for balance as we walk through this slippery grass, but I decide the argument isn't worth it. He's quiet. He's calm. He's scared of something. So instead, I walk, ready to catch him if he slips. I'm wondering why he wanted to come here to visit our parents when he could have been anywhere else, and why he looks so terrified.

"Hey, you okay?" I ask. "You look a little . . . nervous. What's up?" I can feel the dew soaking through my cloth Vans, and I suddenly wish I'd worn my leather ones like Isaiah's black pair he has on. I breathe in the morning air, listening for Isaiah's reply, which takes forever.

"A lot," he says.

Moments go by, and I realize it's going to take some gentle

nudging to get more out of him.

"Like what?" I ask.

He lets out the biggest sigh I've ever heard him make.

"Like, weird questions that nobody else thinks about."

Now I'm curious, because I too think of weird questions nobody else thinks about, like why are the letters of the alphabet in the order that they are? Who decided that vowels should be scattered throughout instead of neatly organized at the beginning? What would happen if Batman were bitten by a vampire? Why do we have to wash bath towels if we only use them to dry clean hands and bodies?

"Questions that nobody thinks about. Like what?" I ask.

He glances up at me and folds his arms tight around himself before answering.

"Do you ever feel like the world is screaming at you?"

Screaming at me? I hadn't thought about my visions like that before, but that's a great way to describe them. It's like having someone behind you all day and all night, yelling facts about the future into your ears.

"Yeah," I say, "I do."

He nods. "Me too."

Him too? For a split second I think he could be talking about having his own visions. Maybe he sees the future too. But then I remember how casually he uses his hands, opening the freezer door with them instead of the back of his fingers like I do, picking the note up off the fridge instead of leaning down to read it. He doesn't seem to care what he touches. The hope of solidarity was nice while it lasted.

We meander in silence across the grass.

"Do you know where we're going?" I ask. I certainly don't.

"Yeah," he says. "I walk here all the time. Mostly at night, after you and Aunt Mackie are asleep."

Again, *why* would a twelve-year-old kid want to go to a graveyard, much less at night, by himself? As if he can read my mind, he answers.

"It's easier to think when nobody else is out here."

I feel that.

"Please don't tell her," he says, his voice on the verge of pleading.

I don't even need to ask who he's talking about. If Aunt Mackie ever found out her nephew was out walking around in a graveyard in the dead of night, she'd snap completely. Not gonna lie, I'm a little alarmed myself. I know how dangerous it is for *anyone* to do that, and if you're Black and out walking, at night, in the wrong neighborhood, the danger doubles.

But I'm not here to judge him, or try to be Dad. I'm here to just *be* here.

"I won't, dude."

We walk a few more yards, stepping between gravestones and over flat grave markers, and suddenly Isaiah stops and stares at the ground, hands deep in his sweatshirt pockets, and he looks up at me. I turn around and take my place next to him.

"Here they are," he says.

I look down at their plaques, nestled side by side in the grass, and read them both quietly to myself.

Levi Rufus
Born February 9, 1977

75

Died November 8, 2016
Katie Rufus
Born June 19, 1976
Died November 8, 2016

It's weird reading these. This is the first time I've seen them, because I haven't been back here since the funeral four years ago, and these markers were installed later. It seems like forever ago. I was twelve. Isaiah's age. I remember not talking much after they passed, mostly because everything just felt weird. Mom wasn't around to drive us to school or pick us up, and Dad didn't go to work in the morning or come home in the evening. It was just me and Isaiah at Aunt Mackie's house again, except we kept getting reminded that our parents were never coming to pick us up. Both people who I used to talk to, the two people I saw the most, were just gone. It happened so fast, I didn't really know what to talk about, with anybody. Add my visions to the mix, and I turned into a complete shut-in. Besides school, I didn't go anywhere, didn't talk to hardly anybody except Shaun and Talia, who came over all the time afterward to keep Isaiah and me company and take our mind off the fact that we were orphans. Isaiah and I reciprocated the company after Shaun and Talia's father left for a business trip months later and never came home.

But after the accident, Isaiah and I stopped talking. We went to therapy, as ordered by the courts, and we moved in with Aunt Mackie, also eventually ordered by the courts, although we were already living there. I guess in avoiding the elephant in the room, we both shut ourselves off from everyone, including each other. Maybe I was afraid to lose him, too?

Well, the universe is cruel. Now I'm *really* about to lose him, and I've been pushing him away instead of using the time we have.

Isaiah sinks to the ground and sits crisscross in the dewy grass. I almost launch into something like, *You're not getting back into my car with your ass soaking wet*, but I realize this may be the last time I have the privilege of riding in the car with him, and I let it go. Not to mention that he's much less likely to slip on the grass if he's sitting instead of standing.

I even decide that if the passenger side is going to be wet, the driver's side might as well be too, and I lower myself to the grass, careful not to touch it with my hands, and sit beside him.

Isaiah looks shocked.

"You know this grass is wet?" he asks.

"Yeah, I know."

Silence.

"Your car seats are going to be wet."

"I know," I say again.

"And you're okay with that?"

I nod.

"I . . . I thought you'd be mad . . . at me."

Before today, I would've been mad. I would've been furious. That's how you get moldy seats and mildew smell and fungus and shit. But not today. Not me. Not anymore.

More silence passes until I break it.

"What do you do when you come out here?" I ask.

He's staring at Mom's plaque, which is white with loose blades of grass over it. I'm relieved when he reaches forward to brush

77

them off, but I'm surprised when he rests his fingers over her first name—Katie—and closes his eyes, leaving the grass blades right where they are. He bows his head and sits perfectly still, the only movement the slight expansion of his back as he breathes.

He looks like he's praying. Maybe he is.

Then he speaks.

"I listen."

I get it. He loves the silence as much as I do.

I pull my knees up to my chest, close my eyes, and sigh. My breath comes out in a cloud, like Shiv Skeptic does with smoke on stage. I still can't believe my own brother knows *The Rush*, and I didn't know until today.

"Listen to what?" I ask.

He's quiet for a while, until I look at him.

"Nothing," he says, but his sigh reveals there might be more he's not saying.

"What does nothing sound like?" I ask.

Come on, Isaiah, give me more than just one word at a time.

Out of nowhere, he changes the subject. "Do you think the dead would talk to us if they could?"

I feel something tickle the underside of my left pinkie finger, and before I can look at it, I'm snatched into a vision. A ladybug flies past my face, and I cancel the vision and look down at the little red creature crawling down my baby finger toward my nail.

"I don't know," I answer absentmindedly, as the ladybug lifts its wing shells, which I've always thought look like a space-ship, and zips off into the air to join whatever other insects are waking up in this place. "I would guess they might? I mean, I would. If I were dead."

"Me too," he says.

"You would?" I ask, surprised. Isaiah doesn't talk much as it is, so I'm surprised to hear him say he'd want to talk in the afterlife. "Why?"

He shrugs. "I'd give advice to people who outlive me. I'd tell people what I know."

"Do you think you'd know anything in the afterlife that you don't know now?"

"I think Mom and Dad do."

Mom and Dad.

I look down at their plaques. I read the fine print at the very bottom of each.

Beloved sister, daughter, wife, and mother,
who loved as fiercely as she lived.

Cherished brother, son, husband, and father,
with the heart and soul of an angel.

Such short captions to sum them up. Two whole lives, most of which happened before I was even born, and so few words. I remember the day I was finally old enough to sit in the front seat of the car. I felt grown up, back when growing up sounded fun. Even though it was just the passenger seat, I felt like I was being given a privilege and a responsibility that I took way too seriously. My seat belt was on as soon as I sat down, and my hands stayed folded in my lap the whole time. The windows were bigger than the ones in the back, there was way more leg-room, and I could look in the visor mirror and see Isaiah back

79

there, pouting, jealous.

"Why can't I sit up front?" he seethed, arms folded, brows knit together in an angry knot.

Mom just smiled. "Because you're not a big boy yet, Isaiah. Just wait a few years."

It's been a few years, Mom, I think. *Neither of us are "big boys" yet.* Not big enough not to need our parents.

My mind wanders.

I wonder what they'll say about me after I'm gone.

Alex Rufus. Son, brother, hopefully husband one day. Afraid of everything.

"You ever wonder what they'd tell us if they were here?" he asks. "What they'd say if they could see us now?"

I don't want to think about it. I take a deep breath and pinch the skin on the back of my hand to calm me down, but it doesn't get rid of the lump in my throat. Everything in me wants to change the subject. Not all men are comfortable being "in their feelings" like Drake. We're wasting time out here! I'm supposed to be helping Isaiah, not sitting in the middle of a graveyard with him, talking about shit we can't change. But if this really is going to be his day, I guess I need to give him space. I did ask him to talk to me, after all.

I've taken too long to answer. He continues.

"I think Dad would wonder why I'm not taller," he says.

I have to chuckle at that.

Dad was always reminding us about the height that runs in our family, and how we could both go pro if we kept up our practice. I had a mean bob and weave that would leave Isaiah on the ground while I went straight for the hoop.

"You've got time," I say without thinking, and then when the realization hits me all over again, I clear my throat and continue with, "I think Mom would be happy with our grades. Heard you got straight As this semester."

He looks up at me.

"I have to keep them up, or Aunt Mackie will yell at me. She and Mom are like . . . clones or something."

"They both want the best for us," I say. "But Mom was . . . softer."

"She would let me sit in her lap, and she'd rub my head and ask what's so wrong that I'm bringing home grades like this," says Isaiah. His voice trails off into nothing, like he's stopped mid-thought. "I miss her, Alex."

"I miss her too," I croak.

"Do you . . . ever wish you could talk to them?"

Maybe this is how he grieves.

Ever since the day we lost them, I've been running from everything death-related I possibly can. That's how I grieve. I *don't* grieve. I run. And now, here I am, sitting next to the last piece of my parents left on earth, who I'm about to lose, and all he wants to do is hold their memory in front of my face. He wants me to face it.

He wants to face their death *with* me.

Breathe, Alex. Let me just calm down and answer the damn question.

No running now.

"Yeah," I concede. "Yeah, I do sometimes."

"Do you think there are people who *can* talk to the dead?" he asks.

81

"I don't know," I say, and then I realize I've said *I don't know* twice in five minutes. I have to give him something more than that. "I mean, I *hope* there are?"

So I can talk to Isaiah.

"But then," I continue, "I feel like I'd also hope that dead people are actually at peace, like, not having to think about what's happening in the world. If they can still talk to living people, wouldn't that mean they actually care about what's happening on earth? And if they care, wouldn't that mean it stresses them out when bad things happen to the living? The ones they love, anyway?"

I'm probably overthinking things again.

"They mostly talk about the past," he says.

The silence that ensues happens mostly because it takes me a solid ten seconds to realize that he said *they talk* instead of *they* would *talk*. I look over at him. His eyes are open now, staring straight down at Mom's grave, where his fingers are still resting. They're trembling even as he presses them against the stone, and his forehead looks especially shiny, and I realize he's broken out into a cold sweat.

"Isaiah?" I ask.

He sniffs, and I realize he's crying.

"You said the world screams at you, too?" he asks.

I don't know what to say. Is this kid really telling me he can talk to the dead? Would it be so impossible? I can see the future, after all. Maybe he does have powers?

I nod.

"Yeah, it does," I say.

"How?"

82

Oh, how.

"I feel like I can't stop thinking about what's going to happen. I just . . . worry," I explain. "I can't stop worrying."

"Worrying?" Isaiah says, wide-eyed. There's realization in his face, like he's put something together in his head, like everything's clicking for him. "What do you worry about?"

Talia hating me. Scoop's going under. Aunt Mackie's new door. Mrs. Zaccari's lawn.

"Everything," I say. "All the time. That's what anxiety is, Isaiah. It never stops."

It never sleeps, and consequently, neither do I.

I would give *anything* to be rid of the visions. Once, two years ago, I was sent home from school after having my first panic attack, to be expected after years of vision-induced anxiety, right in the middle of the lunch line, out of nowhere. Aunt Mackie was at work, and Isaiah was still at school. I texted him and told him he'd need to take the bus alone that day. I stood by myself in Aunt Mackie's kitchen, staring at the knife block for a solid twenty minutes, working up the nerve to rid myself of this torture once and for all. I picked up the smallest paring knife I could find, about three inches long, as if the smaller the knife, the less intense the pain would be. I tested the tip against my left thumb, pressing harder and harder against the pink of it, the underside where my print was. I wondered if I was ready to let go of having fingerprints, not to mention the rest of my palm. How I'd explain this stunt to Aunt Mackie. I could cut a small bit every day and swap out Band-Aids and maybe no one would notice.

"Everything?" he asks. "You can't . . . relax? Like, at all?"

I remember jumping at the searing pain, drawing blood. A cut as long as the width of a dime spanned my thumb, red slowly filling the crack. I took a deep breath and steadied my head. I knew there was no way I could bring myself to raise the knife against my thumb again. Not with blood already all over my thumb. So I put the knife down on the counter, took the skin between my other thumb and index finger, and pulled.

"Nothing," I say, my eyes transfixed on somewhere in the distance across the grass as I relive the rest of the memory. "I've tried everything. I've meditated. I've prayed. I've—"

I remember thinking it would rip like a Band-Aid and be over in a second, but I yelped and slipped my thumb into my mouth, wincing against the pain, knowing it would be a long journey. By the time I worked all the way up to my thumbnail, my forehead was coated in layers of sweat that had dried over the course of hours, and bloody paper towels were piled high on the counter. I thought the taste of copper would never leave my mouth. But I looked down at my thumb, half in horror, half-hopeful, and I reached out my arm, found a clean corner of a paper towel on top of the pile, and pressed my thumb against it, making sure to touch only the bloody exposed part. It stung, but not nearly as much as the disappointment that came with the vision of the paper towel.

After all that pain, it hadn't worked. The skinless spot on my thumb still brought visions, so there was no use even trying to cut away the rest.

I went to bed that night, hopeless. Helpless.

I would give *anything*.

"Trust me, Isaiah," I say, my voice breaking, "I've tried *everything*."

I look up at him.

He's gone silent, his fingers still trembling against Mom's plaque. The company of his grief is like a radiating heat lamp next to me in the middle of this cold morning. I'm suddenly so glad we came out here. Somehow, he needed to get this out. I want to help. I want to know what he's thinking.

"What does the world scream at you?"

He looks up now, at me, his eyes red and brimming with tears. "Different things."

"Like what?"

He's quiet for a moment.

"What might've happened," he finally says.

"If?"

"Just, *if*."

I'm getting nowhere with him. He's plucking at blades of grass and pressing his thumb into them, flattening spots into a darker shade of green.

"What might've happened if *what*, Isaiah?"

He shakes his head. "You're not going to believe me."

I want to laugh. If he knew about my visions, he'd know that whatever he's about to say can't be nearly as unbelievable as *I can see the future*. But I don't want to push him. The whole point of today was to do whatever he wants—*needs*—to do.

"You don't have to tell me if you don't—"

"Yes, I do, Alex."

Again, he said my name. I guess that's his way of saying he's serious.

"Okay," he breathes. "So, you said you worry about everything. Would you worry more or less if you spent all day thinking about what could have happened differently?"

What *could* have happened?

"What could have happened differently if . . . ?" I ask.

"If," he says again with a shrug.

Goddamn it.

"If *what*, Isaiah?"

"If a million different things, Alex!" he says, slapping the back of one hand against the palm of his other between each of his next words. "Come on, bro, keep up."

"I'm trying!" I have to laugh. He's smiling now, still staring straight ahead at the millions of other gravestones around us. I continue, "Clearly, you're just too smart for me. Break down what you're trying to say."

"I'm saying exactly what I'm trying to say," he insists, his face suddenly growing solemn again. "If you could see what you could've done to save Mom and Dad, would you want to know?"

I freeze. What the hell kinda question . . . ?

"No, I wouldn't."

I have enough to worry about, being constantly reminded of the future while I'm trying to live my life. I don't need to live in the shadow of the past, too.

"Me either," says Isaiah. "And I wish I didn't."

"You . . . do?"

"Yeah, I do. I get these"—he hesitates and glances at me before continuing—"I get these . . . visions," he says. My heart stops. "I, uh . . . ," he continues, "I see myself that day in the

86

back seat. And I just . . . I think about all the things I could've done to keep it from happening. And I think about what Dad would say about my height if he knew all I eat now is pizza bites and Lucky Charms, and what Mom would say if she could've seen me at my fifth-grade graduation . . . *if*."

The realization hits me.

If.

If it hadn't happened.

Damn. Isaiah gets visions just like mine, only . . . backward. He relives what happened every day, suffering inside his own head. It's like the accident froze him in time and won't let him move forward. I guess it's not much different from what it did to me, pressed a wall up against my back that's always pushing my mind into seeing what'll happen tomorrow. Isaiah's shoulders are shaking. He's rocking back and forth in the grass, and he sniffs again. He looks so small right now, like he's sinking into the earth, retreating into himself. Imploding. Like there's too much inside of him for him to handle.

"Why didn't you just tell me after the accident?"

"I mean, it sounds pretty wild, doesn't it?"

I swallow and suppress this sick feeling in my stomach. It's like watching him drown. I have to physically fold my arms and focus to keep from blurting out that he doesn't have to do this to himself, that he has to fight off these thoughts or they'll pull him under. Even though it never helps when people say that to me about my anxiety, I feel the burning need to say *something*. To *do something*.

"Isaiah—"

"It's . . . kinda like your worrying, only it's what's already

87

happened." He's staring at the gravestones, but his eyes are empty. His mind is somewhere else.

"I can see my soccer game," he says. "I can see me taking that picture with my coach after—I don't even remember his name. That picture wasn't even worth it. Nothing was worth it. I took forever getting my equipment in the car, and I was mad about something, so I wouldn't wear my seat belt. Mom took extra time forcing me to put it on. I could've skipped *any* of that shit. I did a million things that day that put us in the wrong place at the wrong time."

"You . . . relive that day?" I ask.

"Over, and over, and over. Do you have any idea what that's like?"

Yeah.

Yeah, I really do.

My fingers inside my jacket pocket find the corner of the photograph, and a vision flashes to life in my head. I cancel it before I can see anything else, since I *cannot* bear to watch more of Isaiah's funeral, and suddenly I'm back in the graveyard. I sigh and take the photo out of my pocket and stare down at it, with the grass and the gravestones behind it. Then I slip it back where it belongs. Darkness. I absolutely do.

Knowing sucks.

Isaiah looks at me again, his top lip trembling as two tears roll down his cheeks.

"*Do* you know?" he asks.

I glance down at his hand, resting on his knee, and I want to take it in mine. I want to squeeze his fingers and pull him into a hug and let him know he's not alone. I want him to know I understand. All this time, I've been enduring these visions

88

in silence. Suffering alone. But I had company this whole time, just down the hall from my room. Isaiah's had company. Isaiah's been reliving the accident since the day it happened, somehow. He can see what happened just like I can see what will happen. I can't imagine which is worse—getting premonitions of things you can't change, or getting flashbacks of how you or someone else fucked up the past.

"Is that what the world screams at you?" I ask.

He nods.

"It screams what happened?" I ask.

He nods again. "All the time."

"Anywhere?"

He nods. "Whenever I leave my room."

"So then . . . why did you want to come out here?" I say, hoping he'll stop this. Why does he torture himself like this, coming to a place with so many bad memories? My heart is pounding so hard, and my hands have curled themselves into fists. I can't even process what's happening right now. All I want to do is make Isaiah happy, but it's hard enough making a regular kid happy. It feels impossible to do it in spite of *this* kind of . . . of . . . *whatever* this is. He starts talking again, softer this time. Slower.

"You really wanna know why I wanted to come out here?" he asks, wiping his hand across his cheek. I glance over. His fingers come away wet. "I *miss* them, Alex. I come out here to see them. I . . . don't know why. I guess maybe I'm afraid if I don't, they'll get forgotten? Left behind? What if I forget what they look like?" he says, nodding down to our parents' graves.

"You won't forget," I say, nodding down at him decidedly. "*We* won't forget. Okay? I won't let you. Remember that time Dad

89

shaved his mustache off and you cried?" His next sob comes out a bit brighter and rolls into a laugh as he wipes his eyes.

"He looked so weird," he says. "I never knew his upper lip was so big."

I nod. "See? And how Mom always used the same tortoise-shell hair clip? Every single day?"

He looks up at me. "I have that in my drawer. I . . . I asked Aunt Mackie if I could have it."

My heart swells at that. Part of me wants to ask to see that hair clip, so I can remember too. And then I decide that if we're truly in our last days together, what have I got to lose?

"Could I see it when we get home? Assuming I'm allowed back in your room?"

He's silent for a long moment and then says, "Sure. But be careful. It's in a plastic bag because it still smells like her hair oil. Sometimes I open it and pretend she's still here."

I remember the woman on the bus, the one wearing mom's perfume.

My pulse is racing as the full weight of it sinks in—Isaiah is suffering so much, and I haven't been there for him. What kind of brother would I be if I didn't try to stop this? I have to do something. Forget making Isaiah's last days happy. What good is that if he has to deal with visions like this? I have to find a way to stop them.

We have to find a way to stop them.

"Have you tried to get rid of them?" I ask.

He nods. "I thought about telling the therapist. The one we had to see after the accident? But you know how she was."

"Felt like she was reading from a book the whole time, right?"

"Like I was the fiftieth kid she'd talked to that day."

"Box checked, right?"

"Right."

His smile falls a little and he sighs.

"Once I snuck into the medicine cabinet and took one of Aunt Mackie's sleeping pills," he says.

Damn.

"Really?" I ask.

He nods and sighs.

"Don't tell, okay? I didn't like it. It made me really tired the whole next day. I never did it again. Swear you won't tell her?"

"Of course not, Isaiah," I say. "I promise."

"Thanks." He smiles, his eyes glistening. "I really have tried everything, though. I tried praying. I'm not sure God is up there. Or if he even cares. He must not, since I'm still seeing things."

"That's not what Aunt Mackie says," I say.

"Well, it's what I say," says Isaiah, his voice shattering into a million squeaky little pieces as he drags his arm across his eyes. "He doesn't care. I know it. If he did, I wouldn't be like this. But I get it. It is what it is. So I just avoid 'em."

"The visions? How?"

Isaiah looks up at me and smirks.

"Why do you think I stay in my room all day?"

Holy shit, he doesn't stay in his room all day because he hates me or Aunt Mackie or the world. He stays in there because he's scared. And I've been down the hall the whole time, clutching my pride like it's my last lifeline. That shit stops today.

"It just seems like no matter what I do—"

"It doesn't stop," we say together.

91

I look at him, and he looks up at me, and my cheeks burn hot with tears.

There's silence where my words should be, and I realize there's only one thing I can say to make this better, to make him realize he doesn't have to suffer through this alone.

"The world really does scream at me, Isaiah," I say. I take a deep breath and say what it's taken me four years to say out loud. "I can see the future."

It sounds weird hearing it. He looks up at me for a long time, and I sigh and eventually look at him.

"Wait, you *what*?!" he practically screams. I shush him and look around. Even though there's no one else nearby, it feels wrong to be screaming among so many dead people. Irreverent or something.

"You *what*?!" he whispers again.

"I said what I said," I say.

"You're not kidding?" he asks.

"On *God*."

"Wait . . . how long?"

"Since the accident," I answer.

"Yeah, that's when it started for me too. But how far into the future can you see?"

"It happens when I touch things with my hands. Anything. The longer I touch something, the further into the future I can see."

"So," he says, "when you eat something, can you, like, see what your poop will look like later?"

"What the hell is wrong with you?" I laugh, shoving him with my elbow. He giggles, and I wish I could record that sound and play it over and over and keep it in my phone forever. "It's more like, if I'm holding whatever I'm eating, I can see myself chewing it."

"Or if you're like, scooping ice cream, you can see the person eating it."

"Nah. I can see myself scooping it, though. I can only see what I touch with my hands, so just the scoop. It's complicated."

"Sounds awesome, though," he says, gasping as he realizes something. "Oh my God, you could touch a scratch-off and see if it's a winner!"

He still doesn't get it. I would just be able to see whether I'm going to scratch it off, and the numbers that are under it. But if I see myself scratch it, even if it's a losing ticket, it means I *will* eventually scratch it anyway. It's not like I can just decide to put it back and have the universe just accept the difference.

"That's not how it works," I say. But his mind is off in another dimension with bad ideas.

"Oh my God, you could hold Talia's hand and see if you guys are going to get married!"

Okay, maybe he kinda gets it.

"Yeah," I say.

"That's not a curse, dude, it's a superpower!"

Yeah. Sure. Superpower. Seeing things you can't prevent and don't have to care about yet. Dandy. But seeing into the past also sounds miserable. To have to live with that every day, forced to dwell on the grim past all the time, I can't imagine how demoralizing that would be.

"At the same time, though," I say, half to myself, "being able to touch something and see its history instantaneously, when it's not significant, sounds pretty cool. But . . . you didn't see the

93

history of the gravestone. You saw . . . Mom. So you touched the gravestone, but you saw . . ."

"I don't have to touch anything. I just have to be near someone who's thinking about their past regrets—"

He stops mid-sentence, and I finish it for him.

"Or yours."

He nods solemnly. "Or mine. It's so weird. Sometimes I can just *feel* what's around me on another level."

"Like Spider-Man?"

He smirks at that.

"Yeah, I guess. The closer, the louder. Sometimes it's like a buzzing feeling, like when you hold a balloon to your arm and all your hair stands up. Sometimes it's voices, like a play where all the characters are narrating what's going on. Everything. The trees, the grass, the ladybug that flew off your hand, the girl walking on the other side of this place. She's across the field over there, visiting her husband who died in the army. That's why I can see them. She's wishing she never let him go back again. She's with her daughter, Mabel."

Mabel. I follow his eyes, but I don't see anything.

"She's like a hundred feet away. You probably can't see her. Your boss is here too somewhere."

"What?"

At the thought of talking to either Scoop or the consignment shop owner—what was her name?—Ena, a knot forms in my stomach. Isaiah and I will have to finish this conversation at home, before the start of my shift. I press my hands against my knees, cancel the vision of me standing up in these jeans, and push myself to my feet, careful not to let my hands touch the grass on the way up.

"Come on," I say. "I think we'll both feel better if we go home and have some breakfast." I consider texting Talia and inviting her over before my shift starts at one. But then a realization hits me. What the hell am I doing even *thinking* about going to work today? If these are really the last few moments I'll get to see Isaiah, to talk to him, why wouldn't I call in sick? My hands are suddenly clammy, and I remember sitting at our kitchen table across from Dad. I held up my first "paycheck," $37.86 cash in an envelope with the balance written on the front. It was more money than my twelve-year-old self knew what to do with. Dad leaned forward over his coffee and smiled proudly at me. He took my small hand in his big, strong one and said, "You know what this means, Alex? This is a big step in becoming a man. You're a leader. A supporter. An example to Isaiah and other Black men who will follow you. You're a future provider for a future family." Isaiah, who was sitting next to me, looked up at Dad and said around a mouthful of cereal, "What does that have to do with being a man?" and Dad replied, "Son, a man's not a man without his paycheck."

Is that why I feel guilty now? Is that why calling in sick feels so wrong? Against everything I've ever been taught, as we walk to the car, I pull my phone out of my pocket and cancel the vision of me texting Scoop.

Me: Hi Scoop. Sorry but I can't make it into work today. Feeling pretty sick.

Scoop texts me back almost immediately.

Scoop: ok do u have someone to cover you?

95

"Are you going to invite Talia over?" asks Isaiah.

"Should I?" I ask.

I don't know why I asked that out loud. I'm really asking myself. If I have only a little bit of time with Isaiah, do I really want to spend any time at all talking to anyone else? I finish my conversation with Scoop with:

Me: No, sorry. Really not feeling well. Going back to bed . . .

I hate doing this. I hate skipping out on a shift at the last minute. It makes me physically ill to think that Scoop might think I'm unreliable—that anyone, actually, would think I'm unreliable. Or that I don't care about my job.

A man's not a man without his paycheck.

But today, I'm choosing different. What kind of man chooses his job over his family? Isn't that a cliché by now? You see it all the time in hetero sitcoms. Husband comes home later and later, spends less and less time with his wife and kids. Wife complains that he's not paying her enough attention, or that he doesn't care about his family. He wonders how she can complain when he's working so hard. An affair is usually the last straw, and then a messy divorce, blah blah blah. It's the classic American romance.

And, as a man, that's not what I want.

Is that where my dad's advice would've had me?

I'm surprised at the burst of anger that swells in me. I know my dad was looking out for me. Didn't want me to end up broke. Didn't want me to end up selling drugs. Didn't want me to end up in prison, or abandoning my kids, or gambling my life away. I get it. But did he ever stop to ask what he *did* want for me? Have *I* ever stopped to think what I want for me? I take a deep breath and dwell on the idea that in thirty years, maybe when I look back on today, I'm going to be glad I climbed back into my car and drove back to the house with Isaiah instead of going to work for another forty bucks. And I'm going to hope I did so quick enough that Scoop didn't see me.

Just as we drive past the Zaccaris' house, Isaiah looks up at me and asks, "So . . . do we ever get rid of this?"

"Get rid of what?" I ask, my mind off in the middle of nowhere.

"This . . . curse?"

A lump forms in my throat. He used the same word I do. Curse. That's exactly what it feels like. I decide right then, that if nothing else happens before Isaiah dies, if I get nothing else right, if I can't make up for years of not being there for him, I *have* to help him get rid of these visions. No kid should have to live with that.

My hands tighten around the wheel and I take another deep breath.

"I don't know," I say. "But I'm game to try if you are."

For the first time since we stopped rapping "Black Dragon" together, he smiles with hope in his eyes.

5

The Dress

WE MAKE IT BACK to Aunt Mackie's house with Isaiah still alive.

But the relief lasts for only a moment. With every minute that goes by, we're inching closer and closer to the end.

This morning in the graveyard, which . . . has already happened.

The evening I'm going to spend sitting in a chair.

Tomorrow, where the photo will stay somewhere dark, probably in my pocket.

Lights flickering through my jacket pocket.

More darkness for who knows how long.

The morning in the graveyard.

I shake my head.

I guess that's the case for all of us, but knowing that it's going to happen to my brother so soon makes me keenly aware of every little thing in this house that could be dangerous. A loose cord holding up the chandelier in the foyer could finally snap and the whole thing could come down and crush him. He could start making his lunch—probably pizza bites—and faulty wiring in the kitchen could blow up the oven. Or he could choke on one of them. Or his heart could give out at age twelve from all that cholesterol.

I step out of my shoes and put them on the rack. We enter the living room, but not before he kicks his own shoes across the foyer, and I worry that maybe the water from his shoes will make him slip when he runs into the kitchen for some pizza bites. I lean into the kitchen to grab some paper towels and wipe up the droplets, which are all over the floor. My hands are clammy. My chest aches, and I practice my deep breathing. I watch Isaiah disappear around the corner into the kitchen without even noticing what I'm doing, and I swallow the lump in my throat.

When I saw Shaun's end—watched the accident in that red haze—I didn't know what to do. All I could think about was avoiding being in the car when the fateful moment happened. I thought for the longest time it might have been because I was a coward, or maybe because I was only thirteen—not much older than Isaiah is now—and scared of being in a car accident. But now, I think it's because I didn't want to believe it. Maybe I thought if I could just avoid Shaun, I could keep running from reality. Like I did after we lost our parents. Like I've done even more ever since losing Shaun—hiding in my room, in my car, at school, and at work, and trying to forget about everything else. About this . . . curse. I ran, hoping to forget. And maybe, if I was lucky, I wouldn't have to *watch* him die. I follow Isaiah into the kitchen and absorb the weight of the fact that if I stay by his side like this, I'm going to have to be there when it— whatever *it* is—happens.

New determination rises in me like a flood. We *have* to figure out how to get rid of this thing. And we're running out of time. I glance at Isaiah and think to invite him into my room so we can figure out a game plan here.

"Isaiah, why don't we—"

"Hey, you guys are home!" interrupts a familiar voice from the dining room.

Talia steps into the kitchen in a black sundress with a V-neck that cuts low enough for me to see . . . a lot. My face turns hot. Normally, I might be distracted, but the only thing on my mind is that vision of us, the one in which she's wearing a black sundress and glaring up at me with hatred like I've never seen, somewhere with lots of white and yellow lights behind her, and my heart sinks.

She's just bought that dress. Time goes on.

I turn to finish what I was about to ask Isaiah, but he's across the kitchen, unfolding a step stool and swinging open the high cabinet above the fridge to reveal about ten boxes of Lucky Charms stacked to the ceiling.

"There's a note on the fridge," he says, stooping to pull a sticky note off the door. "Says 'Going to Mrs. Zaccari's for a meeting. I'll be home around five. Pizza bites in freezer. Or order something. Love you, Aunt Mackie.'"

"Yup, saw that. She won't be home for hours," says Talia, smiling at me and flipping her electric-blue hair over her shoulder. "By the way, do you like my dress?" she asks, spinning around for me.

"Yeah, is that new?" I ask, trying to sound as warm as possible, even though that dress is the last thing I want to see. It means that night of our huge blowup is getting closer.

"¿Te gusta?" she asks. "Mamá lo compró para mí en la

100

tienda de segunda mano."

I can piece several words together.

Mama.

Bought.

For me.

Store.

Secondhand.

She's speaking in simple sentences for me, and I try to piece together a response.

"Sí," I say. "Te gusta malo."

"¿Mucho?" she asks with a grin, reaching behind her and picking up half a sandwich I didn't notice before. "¿Me gusta mucho?"

"Yes," I say. "Sí, me gusta mucho."

I realize now that I initially said "you like bad" instead of "I like it a lot." Sometimes it feels like I'm never going to get the hang of this language. Too many words sound too similar, and I can't roll my *R*s properly. She takes the sandwich in both hands and sinks her teeth in. But I don't see any peanut butter, or jelly, and I realize it smells like bananas in here.

"What's in that?" I ask.

"¿Qué es esto?" she asks for me. "Plátanos y mayonesa."

Plátanos must be bananas.

"¿Qué es mayonesa?" I ask, and then I realize, when I hear it escape my mouth, that it's mayonnaise.

"¿Qué mierda?" I ask. "Banana and mayo?"

Talia's eating habits have always been a little . . . out there. She's used to piecing together whatever is in her mother's cabinets at home. Struggle meals, she calls them. Bologna and mustard sandwiches. Hot dog wrapped in a slice of white bread. Potato chips and ketchup, PB&J with Cheetos, and her classic s'mores-and-sherbet ice cream combo. But banana and mayo is enough to make me gag.

"What?" she asks with a shrug. "It's not as gross as it sounds. Plus, Aunt Mackie wasn't home, and I didn't feel like eating pizza again. Try it! It's super gooey." She rips off a piece and holds it out to me, and I hear Isaiah's voice behind me yell, "I wanna try it!"

I immediately want to say no. I think Aunt Mackie stores her mayo at room temperature in the cabinet. I've never really thought or cared about getting salmonella before today, but what if Isaiah eats this monstrosity and dies? Can you die from salmonella? I look down at the piece in disgust. I can see the banana slices mingled with the creamy white mayonnaise, and I shake my head and turn to leave so I don't have to smell that eggy-banana-y smell anymore.

Isaiah goes down quick.

The step stool flips and knocks over a stack of papers on the counter, and a thud shakes the floor. Panic sinks in, and Talia and I hurry to the other side of the island.

This might be it.

It might have just happened, while I was talking to Talia about a sandwich that Isaiah was climbing down a ladder too fast to try. But Isaiah, still lying on his back with one leg under the upturned step stool, and one arm above his head, is laying his head against the floor with his mouth wide open in a laugh.

"You okay, dude?" asks Talia, reaching down and grabbing his arm to help him up.

"I'm fine," smiles Isaiah, clearly laughing at his own clumsiness as if there's no way his neck could be broken or he could have a concussion.

"No, wait!" I exclaim, kneeling and swatting her hand out of the way. Panic is still racing through me. "Have you never seen any of those ER shows? *Never* move a person who's just fallen. He could have a broken neck or a spine injury or something. Isaiah, how do you feel? Are you okay?"

"I'm fine," he says again, rolling to his side.

"Don't move," I urge him. "You might be hurt," I add, remembering every last thing I've ever read online about brain injuries. "Do you see any flashing lights or dark spots? Do you feel nauseous or tired?"

What do I do? If I touch him, I'll trigger a vision of what will happen to him in the next few minutes, and I don't know if I can go through that right now. I don't want to know what will happen. But he's sitting up anyway, ignoring my concerns, and pushing himself to his feet.

"I said I'm fine," he insists. "I'm okay, really."

"You *have* to be more careful," I say, a bit harsher than I mean to. "Watch your step, okay?"

"Okay, okay, fine. Jesus. What's your problem?" he says with an eye roll, dusting off his shirt. I decide not to take any chances. I reach up and open the freezer door, pulling out two boxes of pizza bites for him and canceling visions for each.

"Here," I say. Then I remember what I thought earlier about the oven. "Actually, you know what? Go sit on the couch. I'll make them for you."

Anything to get food in Isaiah, so he and I can go somewhere we can talk.

Isaiah and Talia exchange glances, and I keep my hands and eyes busy with opening the cardboard boxes, canceling the vision of me pouring out the pizza bites, grabbing a baking tray from the drawer under the oven, canceling the vision of me setting it down on the stove, preheating it to 425 degrees Fahrenheit, and canceling the vision of me letting go of the oven knob. I feel a low growl erupt through my stomach, and I'm suddenly glad I grabbed two boxes of them. I'm starving.

I hear Isaiah's footsteps retreat into the living room behind me, but I can still feel Talia's eyes on the back of my neck. I glance over my shoulder at her, only for a second.

"You okay?" I ask.

She moves toward me and says, "I was going to ask you the same thing."

Then I feel her arms slide around my waist, and her chin press against the middle of my back. I feel her chest expand, and her soft breath on the back of my arm as she sighs. She smells good. I can't put my finger on what it is. She doesn't wear perfume, and her lip balm is strawberry scented, but there's a scent of something else about her, a scent I know well. It's sweet to me, and unique to her.

She smells like *her*.

"It was raining too hard last night, so I went to visit Shaun this morning instead," she says.

That hungry rumble in my stomach from earlier twists into a knot of something else.

"Oh," is all I can come up with to say. What else is there *to* say?

But then she goes and complicates the conversation.

"I saw you and Isaiah across the lawn. At your parents' grave. Are you *sure* you're okay?"

I sigh, soaking in the warmth of her arms around me. I want so badly to turn around, pull her close against me, run my fingers through her blue hair, and hold her. I want to comfort her. I look down at my hands, at my fingers, which I know will set off a vision if I'm not careful, and I rest the back of my right hand against her forearm. The only solace I can give her without setting off a vision I can't handle.

"I'm sure," I say, but my voice breaks. I clear my throat and say it again, although I don't believe it myself. "Yes, I'm sure I'm okay. Did you go see Shaun by yourself?"

I feel her nod behind me.

"I didn't really have a choice, did I? Mom was off at a job interview, and you never go with me."

That stings. I'm quiet.

"I just sat and talked to him," she continues. "Gave him updates."

"Updates on what?" My hands go to work laying out the frozen pizza bites over the tray as the oven beeps, alerting me that it's preheated. Talia slips her arms from around me and steps away, knowing I can't open the oven with her holding me like that.

"Everything," she says, folding her arms and leaning her hip against the counter on the other side of the oven. "Mom. School. You."

"Me?" I ask. A pang of guilt rings out through my chest and down my arms. God, I hope whatever afterlife Shaun is in, he doesn't remember me. He's earned the right to forget

105

all about me.

Talia grins and lets out a chuckle. "Yeah. I told him how much you *love* working at Scoop's."

I roll my eyes and smile.

"Jokes," I say playfully. "You got jokes. A'ight."

"And how well you and Isaiah get along."

More jokes.

"*And,*" she continues, pushing herself off the counter and closing the gap between us. Her chin is down, and her eyes are migrating from my eyes to my chest to my eyes. "How it took you three months to kiss me." I look into her deep brown eyes smiling up at me, surrounded by long, thick eyelashes. Without thinking, my eyes move down to her pink lips with the clear gloss on top, and finally, down to her breasts. I can see straight down her black V-neck dress now. I can see her blue lace bra with pink polka dots and a little pink bow in the center, and I don't know what to do.

I'm frozen like this. I can't look away. My heart is pounding, and I realize I'm making a fist with each hand, and I'm leaning away from her. It's like staring down the barrel of a gun, knowing what could come next if I don't do something quick to stop this.

That word "sex" bounces around in my mind, and there's suddenly a lump in my throat that I can't swallow. I open and close my hands at my sides and imagine looping my fingers underneath the thin straps of her black dress, reaching behind her and sliding the zipper down, unhooking her bra.

If I let things get out of hand and we started giving in to things—namely each other—my mind would be somewhere else.

And if the palms of my hands touch her, I'll be locked into a vision that might break me, one that will show me what happens *after* our fight.

I might see where we end.

Since that day I woke up in the hospital with my first vision, and the doctors told Aunt Mackie, who told me and Isaiah, that we'd never see our parents again, I tried to navigate my power as best as I could. The following summer at the pool, Talia froze up at the top of the high dive, and some asshole shoved her off because she was taking too long to jump. When she came up, gasping for air, something went off in me like a grenade—a switch flipped, and I was in that pool before I could think. When I grabbed her arm and pulled her to the pool's edge, I expected a vision of us, but I didn't expect a vision of us *kissing*. I was so shocked, I gasped. Water surged into my throat. I couldn't focus on stopping the vision while I was so focused on saving Talia and staying afloat and not drowning.

Maybe I was too afraid?

Come on, stop! I remember crying out in my head. The vision ended, and I kicked my feet blindly and determined that if I swam in a straight line, I'd find a wall eventually. But there was water in my eyes, and I could feel myself getting tired. Talia was latched onto me like her life depended on it, and I'm sure she thought it did. More water surged into my mouth, and I began to prioritize coughing over swimming. A huge, strong hand clamped around mine, and Talia and I went sailing through the water until my hand found tile.

Both of us floated there, hugging the wall, while we coughed out all the chlorinated water and caught our breath. I heard somewhere in the background a man's voice asking, "You kids okay?" but I could barely think. I barely managed to nod at whoever it was behind me who had pulled us to the edge. She was getting words out between coughs like "Thanks" and "saved me," but I was hardly listening, frozen in shock.

What kind of vision was that?

And then she looked over at me, with her dark hair soaking wet, stuck to her forehead and cheeks, and her huge brown eyes, and her face slightly flushed red amid the panic of almost drowning. Call me delusional, call me unrealistic, call me a hopeless romantic, but I realized that day that I love that girl.

It just clicked. It all suddenly made sense.

And I'm a logical person. I realize how illogical the whole thing sounds. But if there's anything this curse has taught me, it's that there are some things humans will never be able to explain. Why can't insta-love be one of them?

I blink myself back into Aunt Mackie's kitchen and force myself to look up at her eyes, and she's grinning like we're in the middle of a chess game, and she's just won. She blinks a couple of times, and her lips part. She's on her tiptoes with her hands on my elbows, pulling me against her into a kiss. Something in me breaks. A warmth melts into my brain, and I can feel my pulse in my neck.

I take a deep breath and take in that sweet scent that only she has.

Come on, Alex, I think. *Forget it, man.*

I think of how soft her skin would feel under my hands.

Her lips are soft and plump against mine, and I rest my

hands on the counter behind me as her hands wander to my waist. To my belt. Her fingers stop when they reach the buckle, and she ends the kiss, her face lingering only an inch from mine. She's smiling up at me and biting her bottom lip.

"I think Isaiah can make his own pizza bites," she says, her voice soft and breathy.

I nod.

What the hell are you doing, Alex? hollers my brain in protest.

"Yeah," I say, although I don't recognize the strain in my own voice.

What the hell *am* I doing?

"I mean, no!" I say suddenly, as if I've been snapped from a stupor. I slide out from between Talia and the counter and brush the crumbs from my hands into the sink.

"Sorry, uh," I say. "Tal, I'm really sorry, but I can't. I just . . . can't. Okay? Not now. I'm not—"

What am I not?

Not brave?

Not strong?

Not ready?

That's it! I'm not ready. I'm not ready to tell her. I'm not ready for her to know about my power. No, that's not true. I don't care if she knows I can predict the future—it'd be an easy enough thing to prove to her, and I know I can trust her with that knowledge. She's always believed me. She's always taken me at face value. She never questions my fear of the police, or the public, especially convenience stores, or my fear of being pulled over. I can trust her, but I'm not ready for her to know what I *didn't* do with my power.

I'm not ready to look her in the eyes and tell her I knew about Shaun.

I'm not ready for her to know I let her brother die alone, thinking he'd done something to lose his best friend in the world.

I look up at her and shake my head apologetically.

"I'm just . . . sorry."

Talia's eyebrows are knit together in a determined stare, and tears glisten in her eyes.

God, I can't look at her. I fold my arms against me and look down at my feet. That creeping, thorny vine of guilt is making its way through my solar plexus, up through my chest, and into my throat until it chokes me. I can't look up at her. I'm a coward.

"Why can't you just say what you mean, Alex?"

What *do* I mean?

"Why can't you tell me what you're feeling?" she says.

I just stand there, staring down, wordless, directionless. I don't know.

"Tengo que ir a casa," I hear her say. She turns suddenly and disappears around the corner and down the hallway. I tap my foot, not taking my eyes from my toes, and I hear the rustling of her picking up her backpack, the *tap-tap* of her sliding her feet into her shoes, the sound of the front door opening and slamming shut.

And she's gone.

6

The Bedroom

BY THE TIME I get through the visions of the baking tray, the oven door, the oven light button, the oven door again, a pizza bite, and finally, the knob to turn the oven off, Isaiah is asleep on the living room sofa.

Here I am with a tray of a hundred pizza bites, and no appetite.

I set the tray down on the sofa, pick up my phone, cancel the vision of me unlocking it, and unlock it.

No texts.

I breathe a huge sigh and lean my head back against the sofa. Man, I've fucked up. Who knows what Talia thinks of me? Probably that I'm a coward. Probably that I'm self-conscious about my body or something and *that's* why I'm not ready when, admittedly, I am. I'm *so* ready. I dream about her sometimes. Picture her naked. I've seen her in a swimsuit so many times that I have enough material for my imagination to fill in the rest.

I glance across the room at Isaiah and consider leaving him here while I go to my room to masturbate. I need to relax. My head hurts. My chest hurts. I'm tired.

But then I realize that Isaiah still isn't safe, even in sleep. What if he has a nightmare and rolls off the sofa and snaps his neck? I look at the pizza bites. What if he wakes up while I'm away and eats one and chokes? Maybe I should wake him up? We only have a couple of days at most to figure out where this curse came from and get rid of it, and here he is, sleeping it all away! But I glance at him again. His face is completely relaxed, his mouth slightly open as his chest rises and falls. And I sigh.

How can I wake him up when he looks so . . . at peace? He's probably dreaming about . . . I don't know . . . Lucky Charms and pizza bites. Or BeatBall. Or maybe he's hanging out with Mom and Dad. Maybe he's finally happy.

I should let him sleep. But I should stay in here, at least until he wakes up, just to make sure he doesn't stop breathing or something. Besides, sleeping off a headache is sometimes as effective as fapping it away. I slide the pizza bites to the other side of the sofa, curl up in my corner, rest my head on the arm-rest, and shut my eyes.

I dream of Talia in that black dress, smiling at me in the moon-light, pulling me up a hill. The night air is cool against my skin, and she looks over her shoulder at me and mouths the words "Kiss me." And then the sky flashes white. Thunder explodes, chasing the lightning, and rain hisses down in sheets, soaking both of us. Her hair is black against her forehead, cheeks, neck, and shoulders, and her face is contorted into a grimace. And suddenly we're standing in a glowing yellow haze, with head-lights creeping alongside us. She turns to face me.

"Why?!" she shrieks in the darkness. "Why didn't you tell me?!"

She falls to her knees, clawing at the sidewalk, boring all the way through the concrete, her fingers bloody, her fingernails gone. She reaches wet earth and hurls globs of grass and soil at me. I hold up my hands for her to stop, and I try to speak, but my throat is blocked with something. She keeps digging at the earth, throwing chunk after chunk, and when I look back, there's a perfectly rectangular hole in front of her.

"I'm sorry," I mouth to her. She stops mid-throw, each fist full of mud and grass and blood, and looks down into the hole. Curious, I follow her gaze, stepping forward until I can see the casket at the bottom. I read my name.

Alex Rufus, dearly beloved.

What the hell?!

I fall backward, my body slamming into the ground, clutching at my chest, looking down at my caramel-colored hands. I turn them over and over again. And then Talia says his name.

"Shaun."

I look up at her, confusion and fear ripping through me like a hurricane. The rain is running into my eyes, and I can barely see her silhouette as she continues, "Why didn't you tell me?"

I end up being the one who tumbles off the side of the couch, my foot catching the corner of the pizza bite tray and sending it flying across the floor, crumbs and all.

Fuck.

I lay on the carpet, staring at the ceiling, heart pounding. I smell sweet potatoes. I hear Isaiah's laugh. Oh thank God, he's okay. And that's when I notice, the tray that used to be covered in pizza bites, the one that now sits overturned on the floor, was *all* crumbs.

Did . . . did Isaiah eat them all?

"Whoa, dude," he giggles, picking up the tray from the floor. I see his impish face over me, all smiles. I haven't seen him smile like that in years, and relief flows through me like medicine.

"Isaiah," I begin, clearing my throat, which is still raspy from sleep. "What time is it?"

"Dinnertime. Aunt Mackie's home. Mrs. Zaccari's here."

Mrs. Zaccari's *here*?

I look up and around at the living room and hear the faint sound of talking coming from the kitchen. Suddenly a shrill explosion of two women's laughter cuts the otherwise almost silence, and I jump.

"Told you," says Isaiah. He kneels and scoops the crumbs from the carpet into his hands. "You didn't predict that she'd come over?"

"Shh," I say. "Isaiah, that's between you and me, okay? You better not tell *anyone*."

"Okay, fine," he says. "Don't tell anyone about mine, either."

I nod. "Of course. I won't."

I would never.

Aunt Mackie's voice rings out from the kitchen.

"Boys, what was that sound?"

"Nothing!" hollers Isaiah.

He and I both know we're not supposed to bring food into the living room. The tray is back on the sofa, and most of the crumbs are in Isaiah's hands, being dusted off onto the tray.

"Thanks, man," I say, and then I think of something. "Did you eat *all* those pizza bites?"

He picks up the tray, looks at me, and shrugs.

114

"You judgin'?" he asks.

I smile. That's the title of another single from *The Rush*.

"Nah," I say.

"Good," he says, hurrying across the living room to the kitchen. "'Cause I'm still hungry."

I shake my head with a smile. And then I remember our mission.

"Hey," I say, reaching out to touch his shoulder, and then recoiling when I remember my power. I clear my throat as he turns to face me. "Uh . . . after dinner, I *really* think we should go figure out how to get rid of this"—I gesture between me and him—"this *thing* we've got."

He giggles.

"It's not a disease, you know," he says.

"Sure feels like it sometimes."

"Definitely still feels like a curse."

"About that word . . . 'curse,'" I whisper as he starts walking again. "Come on, it's not *all* bad, is it? You get to see all the stuff in our history played out like a movie."

"And you get to see the future like a movie," he says. "I'll bet neither is all bad. But it's not all great, either."

"A little of both?" I ask.

After a moment of staring at the floor, he looks up at me and nods determinedly.

When I follow Isaiah into the kitchen, Aunt Mackie and Mrs. Zaccari are sitting at the island bar, each with a glass of white wine almost as big as half a bottle. Aunt Mackie gives me a brief smile before directing her attention to Isaiah.

"Did you have that tray in your room?" she asks as Isaiah

slips it into the deep sink with a *clang!*

"Yup," he says casually. His voice is lighter and brighter than it usually is around Aunt Mackie. Then I put it together. He's trying to sound cheery because we have a guest over. A guest who might just pay him to mow her lawn soon.

"Hi, Mrs. Zaccari," he chirps, smiling big.

Mrs. Zaccari looks much more awake now that she's out of her satin robe and into pressed white pants and a blue-and-white-striped top like she's on vacation. She's washed and blow-dried her hair so that it falls in gold and silver waves over one shoulder.

"Hi, Isaiah," she says, beaming, her smile pearly white and her eyes warm. "Hi, Alex. Looks like you boys were tired. When I got here, you were fast asleep on the couch."

"Yeah," says Isaiah. "Sleeping and eating are what I'm best at. And mowing lawns."

Oh God, the pandering. I roll my eyes and cringe internally, but Mrs. Zaccari just chuckles and takes a swig of wine. Aunt Mackie is pursing her lips at Isaiah with that *boy, if you don't stop* look of hers. She knows his game. I'm sure Mrs. Zaccari knows it too, but she's playing along great. I smile at both of them. Mrs. Zaccari speaks next.

"I think I saw chicken salad in the fridge. Right, MacKayla?"

Aunt Mackie nods and sips from her wineglass.

"There's chicken salad, roasted sweet potatoes, and mandarin oranges. They're already packed in individual lunch containers, but help yourself."

A bit of the light leaves Isaiah's eyes at the news of chicken salad, roasted sweet potatoes, and mandarin oranges.

I already know what he's thinking: None of that is fried. None of that is especially high in sugar. None of that is tasty.

"Ah, on second thought, I'm okay," he says.

"If you're hiding Lucky Charms in your room, I *will* find them," says Aunt Mackie.

Normally, I'd be making my *oh shiiiit* face snidely at Isaiah, relishing him finally getting caught for hoarding all those sticky, marshmallowy boxes of cereal in his room. But I look at him now, with his hands in his pockets, staring at Aunt Mackie with a stone face even though he knows several boxes are back in his room, and I think to myself, *Let him have them.*

He's only got a little time left. Let him have them. Let him have every last little thing that makes him happy.

"Bring them here," says Aunt Mackie. Her words are blending together a bit, and she's probably a little extra agitated now that she's had wine. I've tried it before. It's bitter and miserable and I'd be agitated if I had half a bottle of it in me, too.

Isaiah's shoulders slump forward and he lifts his face in a grimace.

"Aunt Mackie, come *on*," he says.

"Nah-ah-ah," says Aunt Mackie, pointing down the hall. "Go. I'll have no contraband in my house."

Isaiah turns and slumps out of the room, disappearing down the hallway, and my anxiety shoots through the roof now that he's out of sight. What if he trips on the rug in the hallway and goes flying into a doorjamb? What if there's a loose wire somewhere in his room and one of the dozens of half-empty disposable water bottles decides to spring a leak too close to the wire? What if—

"Sweet kid," says Mrs. Zaccari, nudging Aunt Mackie playfully and taking another sip of wine. "You must be so proud. They're both so smart."

Mrs. Zaccari smiles up at me, wrinkling her nose a bit as she does.

Aunt Mackie's smirk melts into a smile and an eye roll.

I watch Mrs. Zaccari's smile fall slightly.

"Actually"—she clears her throat—"*they're* part of the reason I want to get this petition moving before tomorrow night."

Aunt Mackie lets out a huge sigh and reaches for the wine bottle, even though there's a whole two inches of wine left in her glass. The wine glug, glug, glugs into her glass as Mrs. Zaccari leans forward on the counter and prepares to keep talking.

I glance at the door and hope Isaiah didn't fall and hit his head on the desk or choke on a piece of gum I didn't know he was chewing or—

I take my first step in making a break for it before Mrs. Zaccari stops me cold.

"Alex, could you stay for a sec? I really want your opinion on this."

Shit.

"I want to make sure all our kids are safe," she continues. "There's so much crap out there in the world, MacKayla, outside Santiam. They're having this event in our backyard tomorrow night. That doesn't scare you at all?"

She says "they're" as if she's not referring to the worshippers of the king himself. The fire-breathing wizard of rap. The Black Dragon.

She looks up at me as if she can hear my thoughts.

"Alex, back me up here on this, please. You're a sensible kid with internet access. Don't you feel the *least* bit uneasy about them having a Shiv Skeptic concert a mile away?"

No. Not even a little.

Mrs. Zaccari has no idea of the concert footage I've seen—the pills I've seen passed from pocket to pocket, the elixirs hidden inside water bottles and flasks and even squeaky toys—yes, I saw someone do that once, with a rubber ducky the size of my fist. The woman whose front lawn I mow every other week has no idea who I am or what I dream about, and I guess in the name of professionalism, she probably never should.

"Uneasy?" I ask coyly. *That's it, Alex,* I think, *play coy.*

"Uneasy," repeats Mrs. Zaccari. Aunt Mackie is already halfway through downing her wine refill. "Maybe even a little *scared*?"

I know what she's doing. She's trying to bait me into ganging up on Aunt Mackie about this. She wants me to help pressure my aunt into signing the petition and pushing it forward so she can get this concert canceled.

"I try not to be afraid of anything, Mrs. Zaccari," I say, being as diplomatic as possible. "But I understand your concerns about having it so close."

Aunt Mackie picks up on my apprehension and lowers her glass to the counter, looking from me to Mrs. Zaccari.

"I think you may be overreacting a bit, Karen," she says, leaning forward on one elbow. "Shiv Skeptic is one of the biggest artists in the world right now. You don't think they'll have ample security and metal detectors there? You don't think they'll be checking tickets and IDs at the door?"

"I'm not worried about security at the *event*, MacKayla," says Mrs. Zaccari with a tone that says my aunt grossly misunderstood her point. "I'm worried about security *after* the event, when all those drunk, high, strung-out people come back to the homes they might have rented for the weekend, many of which could be right here in Santiam Estates. I just think the homeowners association could use a vetting process for out-of-towners, especially when events like this come around."

I really want to ask her what she means by *events like this*, but Aunt Mackie is speaking again.

"What kind of vetting process, Karen?" she asks with a sigh. Mrs. Zaccari might not know my aunt well enough to realize how tired she is of this conversation.

Mrs. Zaccari swirls her wine and glances up at me before answering.

"Background checks would be a great start," she says.

"So we'd bar anyone with a record from renting a house here?"

"Does keeping convicted felons out of our homes sound unreasonable to you?"

I hear Isaiah's footsteps racing back down the hall to us, and he leaps into the kitchen with a four-foot slide across the wood floor in his socks. It happens so fast. He reaches out to catch himself before sliding into the corner of the island. His feet fly out from under him, and he lands flat on the hardwood with an "Oogh!" that sounds like it's been forced from somewhere deep within his gut.

Shit! It's happened. This is it. I knew I should've followed him down the hall!

"Isaiah, oh my God!" cries Aunt Mackie. She's off the barstool and around the side of the island so fast she almost knocks her wineglass over. Mrs. Zaccari stands and races around the other side of the island past me, almost knocking into me. They both kneel over my little brother, whose hands are resting on his stomach. He coughs, coughs again, and then, to my surprise, he laughs, again.

And he doesn't stop.

His face is looking up at the ceiling, mouth open, eyes shut tight as he cackles and clutches his stomach.

"Isaiah John, what the hell?" snaps Aunt Mackie. She's made the leap from flustered bystander to exasperated guardian in less than a second, but all I feel is relief. Clearly Mrs. Zaccari feels the same, because she reaches out and tickles more laughs out of him.

"You have to be more careful, goofball!" she laughs.

"This isn't funny," says Aunt Mackie, rising back to her feet and resting her hand on her forehead. "Don't run in the house again. And where are those Lucky Charms you were supposed to come back with?"

I realize just how light-headed all this is making me. The vision of Isaiah. The *knowing* it's happening, only for it not to. That's how my visions work. Much like my anxiety. I grab the back of the only unoccupied barstool, cancel the vision of me sitting down in it, and sit down in it just as Isaiah's laughter dwindles enough for him to speak.

"I recycled them," he says with a grin.

"I don't believe you," says Aunt Mackie.

"It's true!" he insists, rolling onto his side and pushing himself to his feet. "Look in the recycle bin. There's four empty boxes in there."

"You had *four* boxes of Lucky Charms in your room, Isaiah?" asks Mrs. Zaccari.

"They're good!" explains Isaiah.

Mrs. Zaccari laughs. "I *know* they're good. My husband eats them every once in a while, but *four boxes*? How long did it take you to get through those?"

"I haven't been keeping track," says Isaiah, his grin suddenly sheepish.

Mrs. Zaccari and Aunt Mackie look at each other, Mrs. Zaccari with that scrunched-nose smile of hers, and Aunt Mackie with another eye roll. Suddenly it hits me. Hard. I realize that in just a few days, those smiles will be gone. Isaiah will be gone. Aunt Mackie and Mrs. Zaccari will never hear his laugh again. And here I am just watching in silence. My brain knows telling them would just make it worse, but I wonder if I did, and they miraculously believed me, if they'd do anything differently. If they'd let him eat as much sugar as he wants. If they'd let him listen to whatever music makes him happy.

If they'd help me figure out how to get rid of this.

We *have* to get rid of this.

I have to get rid of this.

For him.

"Well, I guess we'd better let you two get back to your conversation," I say, shuffling toward Isaiah. "Wouldn't want us kids to get in your way. Come on, Isaiah, let's go—"

"Now, hold on, Alex, your opinion matters here. Both of your opinions, actually."

Mrs. Zaccari studies Isaiah for a moment, and as she picks

up her wineglass and sinks back down onto her seat, she says, "Isaiah, maybe you can help me out with something here. Did you know that Shiv Skeptic is going to be in town tomorrow night for a concert?"

Isaiah glances at me, and I hope he can sense my telepathic big brother advice: *This is a loaded question. Answer carefully.*

"Um," he says, shifting his weight a bit. "Yeah, I heard."

"How do you feel about that?" she asks.

Isaiah looks at me again, and Mrs. Zaccari follows his gaze as if she doesn't understand why her questions are concerning. His eyes are panicked, and I decide to step in.

"I don't even think Isaiah knows who Shiv Skeptic *is*. Do you, Isaiah?"

He looks to Mrs. Zaccari, then to me, then back to Mrs. Zaccari, then back to me.

"I—I've heard of him. . . ."

I give him a look that I hope says, with claps between each word, *Bruh, keep up.* His eyebrows go flat and his eyes ask me what the hell I'm trying to do. Aunt Mackie jumps in and saves us both.

"Why the fascination with the Shiv Skeptic concert specifically, though, Karen? They have concerts at the Wall all the time."

"I mean, you have to admit a Shiv Skeptic concert has a much different clientele than, say, a Nyein Chen concert."

"Who's that?" asks Isaiah.

"Concert violinist," says Aunt Mackie.

"An *award-winning, classically trained* concert violinist," interjects Mrs. Zaccari. "And she's so young. Can you believe she's only twenty?"

I've heard Nyein Chen's music. She does things with a violin that I thought could only be done with a synth, modifying her violin to take on different tones so they sound like different instruments. In a video I saw of her performing live, she clipped several hair clips to her violin in different spots and played, changing the tone each time she added a new one. But comparing Nyein Chen to Shiv Skeptic is a bit unfair.

"You saying people can't get drunk or high at a Nyein Chen concert?" asks Aunt Mackie.

"I'm saying the types of people to attend a Nyein Chen concert would be less likely to get drunk and high than people who attend a Shiv Skeptic concert."

That phrase, *types of people*, makes every hair on the back of my neck stand up.

Isaiah breaks character.

"It sounds like you're saying *bad* people listen to Shiv and *good* people listen to the violin lady," he says, folding his arms and narrowing his eyes. *Come on, Isaiah, you're throwing our money away.* But at the same time, what he's saying is bold. It's honest. It's . . . exactly what I'm too afraid to say. I stare at him, hoping he'll look in my direction, but his eyes are trained on Mrs. Zaccari.

"Well, his lyrics alone are cause for concern, Isaiah," Mrs. Zaccari explains, her voice brightening as she breaks it down gently for the child in the room.

"Lyrics like what?" asks Isaiah.

Aunt Mackie, who's been unusually quiet, gets up and heads for the pantry, where she keeps the rest of the wine.

Mrs. Zaccari glances at me before letting out a helpless laugh.

"Well, I'm not going to quote them. But he references crystal meth quite a bit."

"Yeah." Isaiah nods. "He raps about people who bring it to his concerts. He's asking them not to."

Leave yo' body for the crows, bruh.

"There's also quite a lot of sexual content," she says. "Sex workers, promiscuous women, video girls, things you shouldn't even know about yet, Isaiah—"

"I know those people exist, Mrs. Zaccari," he replies.

And then he just looks at her. The silence is tangible. My heart is pounding. Isaiah's eyes haven't wavered. I've never seen him like this before, but I guess if you question Shiv Skeptic's character, you get Isaiah's horns.

"Well," says Mrs. Zaccari, "that may be. But that doesn't mean any of it belongs in our neighborhood. You boys may not understand what a serious responsibility it is to keep the neighborhood safe, but one day you're going to grow up and be thankful that your aunt and I have worked so hard to provide a safe, happy place for you to live."

"We're thankful," I say. Perfect time for me to defuse this. Mrs. Zaccari might just get her way, but I'm not going to this concert, so I guess I don't have to care if it's canceled or not. "I get why you want this concert canceled, Mrs. Zaccari."

Isaiah is glaring at me like I've betrayed him somehow, and it stings. I make up my mind to talk to him about it later, and then it hits me all over again that with every passing moment, the time frame called "later" dwindles.

We don't have much time. Not much at all.

125

I can feel myself getting angry. Fuck this whole stupid conversation. Isaiah and I have a past to discuss. But before I can jump in and ask Isaiah to follow me to my room so we can talk, Mrs. Zaccari is talking again.

"Oh, I don't necessarily want the concert canceled," she says with a smile. "I'm not here to ruin anyone's fun. They can do whatever drugs they want as long as they keep it out of Santiam. All I'm suggesting is some kind of criteria that should be met before we allow out-of-towners into our homes, starting with background checks. We pay good money to live in this gated community, you know."

Isaiah looks from me to Mrs. Zaccari, and back to me. His jaw is clenched, and he takes a deep breath before turning back to the hallway and waving goodbye.

"I'm going to bed early," he says, with a smile that's probably convincing to everyone in this room but me. "Good night, Mrs. Zaccari. Alex, you coming?"

Thank. *God.*

I follow him this time, dead set on explaining why I leveled out the conversation at the expense of Shiv Skeptic's honor, and dead set on figuring out how to get rid of this curse.

"Good night, Mrs. Zaccari," I say with a smile. "Night, Aunt Mackie."

On my way down the hall to our rooms, my phone buzzes in my pocket. I pull it out and blink away the vision of me unlocking it, and then unlock it. My heart skips at the thought that it might be Talia.

Nah, wishful thinking. It's Scoop.

Scoop: Hey, so, think you'll be better by tomorrow? Ashlynn and

126

Ross both called in sick with the flu.

I stop underneath the skylight in the middle of the hallway and sigh. I'm running out of excuses. I was out sick today already. Would he buy it if I'm out sick tomorrow, too? It takes me at least two minutes to think of a reply, which I'm sure looks even more suspicious, but I'm doing what I can.

Me: Still not feeling well, Scoop. Sorry. I need tomorrow off too.

Those three dots spring to life and I take a deep breath, focus on expanding my lungs into my belly like my school guidance counselor advised, and let it out slowly through my nose. When I look down at my phone, it vibrates.

Scoop: To be honest, Alex, I saw you and Isaiah this morning at Elginwood.

Shit. A lump forms in my throat and I suddenly feel sick. Isaiah was right. Scoop *was* there with us.

Scoop: I understand if you were having a rough day and needed to visit your parents. I wish I could give you as much time as you need. But without someone up front tomorrow, I can't open the store. If I lose a day at the store, I lose lots of money.

Come on, Scoop, I think, *any day but tomorrow.*

I'm so lost. If I go to work tomorrow, my goodbye to Isaiah tomorrow morning might be the last time I see him alive. If I stay home, Scoop's will take a huge financial hit, and who knows what that'll mean for a man who already won't spend a dime on his employees. Work from here on out might suck even more for me if a piece of equipment breaks, or, God forbid, we have to work some hours without pay. Scoop's might go under faster than I expected.

I take a deep breath and settle on the real reason I want to

127

go to work.

Not going feels *wrong*.

I shut my eyes and remember the moment my dad drove me to work when I didn't want to go. I was sitting in the front seat, arms folded, head against the window, fuming, as Dad explained to me that I'd made a commitment. And from that day on, Dad would make me go to work. Hail, sleet, or snow. Hell or high water. Sickness or health. Not going feels like I'm turning my nose up at something Dad hammered home that I should be grateful for.

Not going feels like I'm slapping my father in the face.

Okay, Alex, think. What do you know? What can you reason out?

I realize a few things. First, that no matter what I do, Scoop's is going under at an already predetermined time. Second, no matter what I do, Isaiah is going to leave this earth at an already predetermined time.

That knot in my stomach twists at having to realize that all over again.

I have a finite number of hours left with my brother.

His peace, his well-being, come first.

Me: I'm so sorry, Mr. de la Cruz. I can't. On any other day I would, but I absolutely can't.

That guilt vine is back, creeping up through my middle and into my throat. *Breathe, Alex,* I think. But I don't listen to myself. My heart is racing. *Breathe in. Breathe out.* I crack my neck and open and close my fists, and my phone vibrates again.

Scoop: Listen, Alex. Don't make me play hardball. I know the concert is tomorrow and you probably want to get there early.

128

Could you just help me open the store until 11?

What?

The concert?

Scoop really thinks I'm the type of person to skip work for a concert? I've *never* done something like that. Every single time I've asked for time off, I've given him every detail. I've never lied. I've never missed a day of work unexcused in the four years I've worked for him.

I don't know whether to feel hurt or angry, but these heart palpitations tell me it's probably some combination of both. It suddenly feels a bit warmer in here, and I reach up to touch my forehead, my palm accidentally brushing against my glasses. I grunt in frustration and cancel the vision of me slipping my glasses off God knows how far in the future and feel my forehead, where I find a sheen of sweat. Another heat wave washes over me.

My pulse is still thundering against my ribs. Jesus, what do I say to Scoop? If he thinks I'm skipping work to go to a concert, what kind of person does he think I am? Does he trust me? Has he *ever* trusted me? What the fuck, what the fuck, what the fuck?

I type, then erase, then type, then erase. Then type. And send.

I breathe in, and breathe out, surprised when my own voice escapes as a whistle. Or a wheeze. I don't know what that was.

"Hey." I hear a voice behind me and let out the sharpest gasp. More like a yelp. Whatever you call it, it doesn't sound human. I spot Isaiah's head peeking out from behind the door. Not his door. Mine.

"What are you doing in my room?" I ask, a bite to my voice that even I didn't expect. The moment I say it, his smile disappears and he looks at me like I'm someone he doesn't recognize.

"What?" I ask, wondering why I'm suddenly out of breath.

"Uh," he says, easing his way out into the hallway. He's already changed into gray basketball shorts and taken off his socks. He's back in Dad's sweatshirt. "Are you okay?"

I don't remember the last time he asked if I was okay, and suddenly I feel guilty all over again. How did I somehow screw this up so bad that Isaiah's spending the last of his time worrying about *me*?

"Hey," I say, shutting off my phone and slipping it back into my pocket. My pinky finger slips and I touch the pocket of my jeans, and cancel the vision of me walking into my own room wearing them. *Fuck, visions, stop it just for a second while I try to get my thoughts out.*

"Isaiah," I say, catching my breath. "I'm fine."

He doesn't believe me. I can see it in his face.

"I, uh," I continue, still wondering why he's in my room instead of his own. "What's . . . what's up? Ready to talk? And when did we decide to meet in my room?"

He shrugs.

"Just thought you . . . wouldn't mind? Y'know. Since we're friends and everything now?"

My pulse is still racing, unnaturally fast. But the word "friends" repeats over and over in my head. He's looking up at me with confusion and timidity that I'm not used to seeing in him. It breaks me.

"Come on," I say, squeezing my hands over and over, wishing I could pull Isaiah under my arm and give him one of those extra-spirited big-brotherly hugs. But my power. Holding me back. It's *always* my power. "Let's go."

I usher him back into my room and cancel the vision of the door behind me before shutting it.

"You sure you're okay?" he asks.

"Yeah," I say. It's weird seeing him inside my room. He looks oversize in here, like a chess piece in the middle of a checkerboard. And then I realize, it's probably because he hasn't been in my room since we lived in our old house.

"So," he says, hopping up onto my bed and reclining exaggeratedly with his hands behind his head. "What's my future like?"

"What?"

"You said you can see the future, right?" he asks, holding out his hand to me. "Touch my hand and tell my future! What am I going to be when I grow up? Where will I live? Will I have kids?"

"Isaiah—"

"Am I going to get married? Is she pretty?"

Oh God. What do I say to *any* of this?

"Isaiah," I say, sinking into my desk chair across the room, careful not to touch it because my thoughts already feel like a tower of cards, fragile enough to fall if I add one more.

He looks up at me in confusion, his dark eyes studying me.

"You sure you're okay?"

"Yeah."

"Why are you sweaty?"

I'm sweaty because I can't fucking take this. It feels like my brain is attacking me when things get this bad, when I get this anxious. Do I take on the weight of explaining to Isaiah what an anxiety attack is? Why would I do that when we have so little time left?

"I don't know," I say. "It doesn't feel hot in here to you?"

"Nah," he says. He's silent for a minute, and I latch onto the hope that he's dropped all the questions. But then, "So, can you tell me what happens to me?"

No, I absolutely cannot.

I don't even know if I can make up something convincing. And he's still holding out his hand to me, because like an idiot I told him exactly how my power works, so he knows I have to touch him. But there's no way I'm doing that. I don't want to know what happens to him. I *can't* know what happens to him. And since I can't know *how*, all I can do is keep him from any danger possible. Illogical or not, I'll take steps to avoid whatever kills him. I'll keep him out of my car, I won't let him go into the kitchen, I won't let him leave the house if that's what it takes. And I don't want anything getting in the way of him having a fantastic time. I couldn't live with myself knowing I got in the way of that.

"Listen, man," I say, leaning forward in my chair and focusing on my breathing. "You don't really want to know what's going to happen, do you? I mean, what's the fun in that?"

His eyebrows flatten. "Nah, I want to know so I can plan for it."

"Since when do you plan for anything?"

He shrugs. "Maybe I *would* if I knew what to plan for."

Wow. I didn't expect that from him. He's still staring at me, bright round eyes full of life, studying my face. His chest rises and falls with his breathing, and I can't imagine how anything but a freak accident could be his end. He's so young. So bright.

"I'll make you a deal," he says. "If you tell me my future, I'll tell you how we got our powers."

That gets my attention. If we're going to try to figure out how to get rid of our powers, we'd better start with how we got them in the first place. He crosses his arms and gives me the proudest smirk I've ever seen on him. I have to smile. Little negotiator.

"How about I tell you the future of anything else in the world?"

He thinks for a minute, staring off into space before turning back to me. "Mrs. Zaccari?"

"Why do you want to know *her* future?"

He shrugs. "I want to know if her petition goes through."

"Why?"

"Just 'cause. I don't think it should."

I'm curious now. "Why not?"

He's quiet for a moment, before clapping his hands once and leaning back into a shoulder-shrug dance while rapping, "*Redeemed! My brothers! I been, I been what? I been redeemed!*"

In keeping with our new tradition, I jump into the second line with him.

> "*Recovered! Twelve years, did my time. But man, I'm clean!*
> *Discovered! The most important people on my team! My brothers!*

Recovered, nigga, I have been redeemed!"

"Yeah, boi!" laughs Isaiah before throwing his arms up in a dab.

"Bruh, no," I say, waving my hand. "Get your 2016 dance moves out of my room."

"Whatever," he says, tossing a pillow at me. "I've never even *seen* you dance."

"You never saw me rap Shiv before today either."

"True," he says, sitting up and resting his hands on his knees. "My point is, if Mrs. Zaccari gets her way with that petition, Shiv *himself* wouldn't be allowed to stay in this neighborhood. And I thought maybe he might stay around here and I might see him, without having to go to the concert?"

Sadness melts through my chest, cold and unwelcome. He really loves Shiv, even more than I do. I study him as he stares at the floor, and I suddenly wish so badly that I wasn't cursed and that I could take him to the concert tomorrow. We'd waltz in there like kings. I can picture it now—Isaiah on my shoulders, fist pumping, rapping along to every song with me. It's what *should* be happening tomorrow. We should both be blissfully unaware of the future, and going to concerts like normal kids. This isn't fair.

My phone buzzes again, and I sigh. I blink away the vision of me unlocking my phone and unlock my phone, preparing to face Scoop again.

But this time, it's Talia.

Talia: ¿Soy asquerosa para ti?

Is she *what* to me?

"Uh, Isaiah, hold on one second, okay?"

134

He shrugs, leans back onto my bed, and stares at the ceiling. I take to my translator app to search the word "asquerosa," and the translation confuses me immediately. *Disgusting*, it says. That can't be what she asked me.

Am I disgusting to you?

I type.

Me: Why would you think that?

Talia: That's not a no.

I roll my eyes.

Me: No. You're beautiful.

She's more than beautiful. She's a dream.

Me: I've never seen eyes like yours. And your hair.

What do I even say about her hair? It's so loud and bright. It's perfect. It's her. She's typing again, and my heart begins to race again, unnaturally fast. *Come on, Alex, not another panic attack. Not now.* She's typing again.

Talia: Are you doing this because I'm size 14?

Oh no. Oh no, no, I get it now.

Me: No. I promise that's not it. It's not you. You're perfect.

Talia: I want to be close to you. I want you to come over.

Fuck.

Me: Me too. I'm just not ready, okay?

Talia: Are you scared?

Yeah. I am. But not scared of what she thinks.

Me: No.

Talia: Why won't you just tell me what's wrong?

I try to blink away the nervousness. It doesn't work. My phone vibrates again, and this time, Scoop's name pops up on my screen.

Scoop: Alex? Don't leave me hanging here.

Jesus Christ, my head is spinning. I can't handle all these messages. Isaiah starts talking again.

"Did you ever notice Dad had a scar under his chin?"

I try to gather my thoughts.

"No," I say. "What scar?"

"You wouldn't see it unless you were looking for it. He got it in a skiing accident when he and Mom were dating."

"I . . . didn't even know Dad skied."

"Neither did Mom until he did his first run." He smiles. "He flew down the mountain trying to show off and hit a patch of ice. Busted his chin open."

"*Our* dad?"

Me: I'm sorry I'm complicated.

Talia: I'm sorry I like you so much it scares you.

I sigh. My phone buzzes again.

Scoop: Alex?

I look up at Isaiah, who's silent again, staring up at the ceiling, lost in his own thoughts. His words from earlier echo in my head. *Do you ever feel like the world is screaming at you?* His eyes are fluttering back and forth, and I wonder what he's thinking, what the world is screaming at him. And then it hits me. The only time I've seen him happy—genuinely joyful—is when he's quoting Shiv. It's the only time I've seen him where the world *isn't* screaming at him. It's him playing BeatBall. It's him always wearing his headphones. Music. That's what silences the screaming. And that's when it hits me.

Maybe that's it! Maybe the answer to this curse is doing

something that brings us joy even if it means facing what scares us most? I . . . *guess* that could be a concert? With all those crowds . . .

Just thinking about it ties a knot in my stomach. Isaiah would have to be around all those people with all their regrets, and I would have to be around all those people and all those . . . surfaces. I think about it. A brush against someone's hand here, a touch of a wristband there, it's fine for most people. But not for me. It's a fear I really don't want to face, which means it should work for getting rid of the curse, right? Especially *this* concert, since the money I'd have to use for the tickets would have to come from . . .

Mrs. Gomez.

I quickly navigate to my bank account and find that my pay-check just went through. Four hundred and twenty-five dollars and twelve cents sit in my account. There's a pending nine-dollar Scoop's charge from Talia's and my ice cream yesterday, but otherwise, that's accurate. If I buy two tickets for a hundred and fifty each, I'll have a hundred and sixteen left.

That's not nearly as much as I usually send Mrs. Gomez.

Maybe I've been doing it out of guilt. Maybe I've been doing it because it makes me feel like I have some control over the aftermath of my inaction that day. Maybe I've been doing it because I know I can't replace Shaun, but maybe I can replace his paycheck. Every month, before I do anything else with my money, as much as I can possibly stand gets sent directly to Talia's mother. She hates it, I know. And she'd never tell Talia about it. But eventually, I convinced her to let me. It was better than letting her get evicted, or worse.

"Thank you," she said to me that day, with tears in her eyes. "Alex, you've grown up into an incredible young man. I'm glad Shaun got a chance to know you while he was here. God bless you."

Normally it's something presentable, around two hundred on average. What else would I spend it on, anyway? Aunt Mackie already pays for everything. I've already paid off my car. I have food, clothes, and tons of other comforts around here. I can't let Talia and Mrs. Gomez suffer while I'm over here sitting pretty, but this month, it's going to have to be far less than she's used to. For Isaiah's sake. I make the transfer. An even hundred. I can only hope it's enough.

I know what I'll do. I'll send the rest from my next paycheck in a couple of weeks. She should be okay, right? I'll ask Aunt Mackie for extra groceries when we go to the store next and send Talia home with a bag, no matter how much she protests.

My dad's words ring in my head. I can picture his face as vividly as if he were sitting in front of me, across the kitchen table.

A man's not a man without his paycheck.

Maria is counting on me. *Talia* is counting on me. I can't just spend every dime I have on concert tickets, even if it would be Isaiah's last. I take a long, deep breath and weigh my options. I can either buy the tickets, go to work to make up the money, and hope Isaiah is alive long enough to make it to the concert, or I can pay Maria this money and possibly miss out on the thing that would make Isaiah the happiest.

I'll text Maria tomorrow to apologize.

After work.

It's only opening, after all. What's an hour helping Scoop open the store if it lets me keep my job? Isaiah should be okay for an hour, right? I'll ask Talia to stay at the house and keep an eye on him. I'll probably be back before he even wakes up. Scoop texts me right on cue.

Scoop: I'll take your silence as a no.

Time's up, Alex.

Me: I'll come in.

God, I hope I'm doing the right thing.

Scoop: Yes! Thank you, thank you, thank you. See you at 10.

I hear Isaiah's voice in my ears again.

"Who're you texting?"

"Almost done," I promise. "Sorry. One sec."

I reread the last message from Talia. *I'm sorry I like you so much it scares you.*

Me: Talia, come over again tomorrow, okay? We'll talk.

Talia: I don't want to talk.

Me: Well, I do, because I care about you.

Those little dots pop up, then disappear, then pop up, then disappear. I stare at the phone, waiting. The moments go by, then the minutes. Finally Isaiah's sigh breaks the silence of the room.

"Are you done yet?" he asks.

I toss my phone on the bed next to me. I have to hope she'll reply eventually. For now, I have a dying little brother who wants my attention. I wear what I hope is my most believable happy face, lean forward with my elbows on my knees, and look at him. He's still lying in corpse pose on the bed, staring at the ceiling, until he notices I'm looking at him. He bolts

139

upright and smiles.

"*Finally,*" he says. "What did Talia say?"

"How'd you know it was Talia?"

He shrugs. "Just a feeling."

I remember our conversation from earlier, how she looked at me in the kitchen and said, *I think Isaiah can make his own pizza bites*.

"Exactly how much do you 'feel'?"

Laughter bubbles out of him.

"Wasn't my power this time. Just a hunch. And I can't feel *that* much," he says with an eye roll. Then he grins. "Why? Were you talking about . . . sex?" He drags out the word *sehhhhx* so much. Why does he have to make everything so freaking weird?

"Do you even know what sex is?" As soon as I've asked it, I regret it. "Y'know what? Never mind. I don't want to know."

"Nah, it's fine. I'll explain it. You see, when two people love each other very much—"

"Isaiah, stop it—"

"They come together," he says, interlacing his fingers and shimmying his shoulders, "in a special hug—"

"*Isaiah,*" I snap.

"You know, if you'd just tell me my future," he says, "I *might* stop talking."

I narrow my eyes. He's gone from negotiating with me to threatening me. He has no idea what he's asking me to do.

"Isaiah—"

"And *then*," he says, standing up and balling his hands into fists, "they take their privates—"

140

"Man, *stop*!"

"And *then* . . ." He yanks his fists back against his waist and thrusts his hips forward. "Oh *yeah*!"

I jump off the chair.

"Okay, *never* do that again."

"You gonna tell me?" he asks, plopping back down on the bed, folding his arms and smiling up at me. He knows he's won. But maybe I can play along. Of course, I can't tell him what's actually going to happen, so I put all my chips into outsmarting him. I clear my throat and sit back down in the chair, careful not to touch it with my hands.

"I don't need to touch your hand," I say. "Remember the other night when you fell asleep on the couch and woke up in your room? I carried you there. I saw your whole future then."

Aunt Mackie carried him.

"Oh yeah?" he asks. "What's it say then?"

He doesn't believe me. I'm going to have to work extra hard to make this sound believable.

"Well, it says that tomorrow you'll have pizza bites for lunch."

Isaiah rolls his eyes and purses his lips.

"Wow, man, that's deep. Tell me the stuff I *care* about."

"You don't care about pizza bites?" I ask.

"Oh no, pizza bites are my entire life *now*, but what happens when I get older? Where do I go to college? Who do I marry? Do I have kids?"

"Why do you care about such big life questions anyway? You're twelve."

He gets quiet for a long time, staring down at his feet

swinging off the edge of my bed, and his shoulders slump a bit. I wonder if I've struck a nerve so tender he's not going to answer, and then he surprises me.

"I care because all I really hear about is the past. I've seen some shit, man. I see what happened to Mom and Dad, over and over. I know about our ancestors. You know we used to be kings?"

Kings? One of my eyebrows goes up.

"Kings, man?" I ask. "As in, crown and scepter and subjects and shit?"

"Nah, as in face paint, hair beads, and scents worn by royalty in our tribe."

I pause and stare at him. Is he talking about our ancestors . . . *that* far back? In Africa?

"Whoa, whoa, wait," I begin. "So . . . you've seen four hundred years in the past? In visions?"

He nods determinedly at me.

"Every generation since our family got these powers."

"Whoa, wait, our *family*?" I ask. I try to decide if I want to know the answer to what I'm about to ask. Do I really want to know this? "Did . . . did Mom and Dad have these powers?"

"Just Dad," he says. "He knew he was going to die."

I freeze. My chest gets tight. My head starts feeling like it's being clamped in a vise.

"Dad . . . knew?"

Isaiah nods.

"He could see the future too. Just by being around people he cared about."

142

Dad knew.

He *knew*.

And he got into that car anyway.

"Why did he get in the car then?"

Isaiah sighs. "He won't tell me. And I've asked. Several times."

"Why wouldn't he tell you something like that?"

"No idea," he says, so matter-of-factly it unsettles me. "But he told me he knew. He knew we'd get these powers too. He saw visions of us with them, and he wanted to stop it before it got to us."

I swallow the lump in my throat.

"So, do you want to know how we got them?" he asks.

I sigh.

Do I ever.

I clear my throat and begin.

"You go to college at Sutton University," I begin, launching myself into the hardest string of lies I've ever had to think up. "You get a full-ride scholarship. You don't get married until you're thirty—"

Isaiah audibly sucks his teeth at that part, and I can't help but smile. Little dude is actually looking forward to getting married. And then it hits me all over again. It's not real. It's an illusion. Isaiah doesn't get married. Isaiah doesn't go to college. Isaiah doesn't make it past this weekend.

"Is that enough?" I ask, praying so hard that it is.

"What's her name?" he asks, his feet swinging a little harder. "Is she pretty?"

I stare at him and nod.

"She's fine, man. She's a ten."

"Yes!" he exclaims. "What's her name?"

"M-Mandy."

First name I thought of.

His nose wrinkles.

"Mandy?" he asks. "Isn't that an old-lady name?"

I laugh. My school librarian's name is Mandy.

"'Old' is a relative word, isn't it?" I ask him. "Now, keep your end of the deal. How'd we get stuck with these powers? And do you have *any* idea how we might get rid of them?"

"Well," he says, cracking all ten of his knuckles and flopping his head back and forth to crack his neck, "it started *four* hundred years ago, in West Cameroon. We belonged to the Unguzi tribe, one of the largest groups to settle along the Wouri River. King Takaa was a young king, but he was wise. He knew how to listen, and it served him well. The Unguzi were the best fighters, but they only fought in defense. But one summer a drought came, and the Unguzi were running out of water. King Takaa prayed to the orisha of water, Osun, to give them rain, but none came. One day the neighboring Anaka tribe invaded in search of water that might be in stores in the Unguzi tribe. Takaa insisted they had no water, but the leader of the Anaka didn't believe him. He rained down violence on the Unguzi mercilessly. The fighting was so bad, Takaa had to join the fight himself. When the leader of the Anaka ran him through with a spear, he looked to the sky and called on the orisha of the afterlife to grant him life again. He said he wanted to live. The orisha asked *how* he wanted to live. He thought about the battlefield, about his fear of death, and how it made him

144

ashamed. He felt like a coward. He answered the orisha, 'To live without fear,' and then he just *had* to get greedy. He asked to be able to 'see what cannot be seen' and 'know the unknowable.' The orisha granted him his wish. But it wasn't anything like what he expected."

I gulp, and I have to ask, "How do you know all this?"

"Great-Great-Grandpa Buddy is buried in Elginwood, you know. He had regrets too. And one of them was not asking *his* great-great-great-great-great-etc.-grandfather more questions about what happened in his village. I got curious one day and sat there next to him, just listening. He told me all he already knew."

So Isaiah can hear the regrets of the dead. The regrets of *our* dead.

"So Takaa is our great-great-great—"

"Who's telling this story? Me or you?"

I smile and fold my arms as he continues.

"Takaa lived, and he suffered. Everything he loved showed its true colors. He could see everything for what it really was. He saw every molecule in every drop of water he drank. He saw every bacterium his body killed, and every bug he stepped on underfoot. He saw every consequence of his actions that before had gone unnoticed. Knowing more didn't help him. It made it worse. He lived in guilt. He hated life. And eventually, he jumped off a mountain, never to be seen or heard from again."

I realize my back has been tensing this whole time, and I clear my throat and roll my shoulders.

"Shit, man," I say. "Those are some . . . heavy origins. That's why we have these powers? Because of something our ancestor

145

did four hundred years ago?"

Isaiah nods and shrugs.

"Sucks, don't it?" he asks.

"It's some bullshit," I say. I would've been cool with the first part of Takaa's wish. The *to live without fear* part. "We shouldn't have to live with what happened to Takaa. We didn't even know him. We didn't ask for what he wanted. Why do *we* have to live with this?"

"Because the world remembers what he asked for. What happened to our ancestors is still punishing us, too. In more ways than one."

"Is there a way to get rid of this shit then? Do we have to . . . like . . . ask the orishas or something?"

He shrugs.

"I don't know if I *want* to get rid of mine. It sucks sometimes, but I also like hearing it sometimes, you know?" he asks. "I like hearing Mom and Dad. I don't want to lose them all over again."

A pang of guilt hits me.

"Yeah, I guess I get that. But I don't want to constantly be seeing the future, either. I'd get rid of this in a heartbeat. I didn't even call them powers until I heard about yours. I called it a curse. Feels more like a curse anyway."

"Maybe yours does."

"Yours does too, from what you've told me. At least sometimes."

"At least you can *do* something with yours. At least you can use yours to prepare for what's about to happen. You get warnings. You get time to brace yourself for what's coming. I just get reminded of what I could've done better in the past. What's the

146

point of that?" he asks.

"So you don't make the same mistakes over and over."

He lies back down on the bed and stares at the ceiling again.

"I've seen Takaa. He looks so badass. I wish we still wore face paint like that. Why does America have to be so boring? Just cowboy hats and lassos and whatever else."

"Technically the original Americans wore feathers and face paint and beads. Lots of tribes still do."

"Well, ours doesn't. The Unguzi tribe doesn't exist any-more."

"We're . . . the last ones?"

"No, we've got cousins all over the US. But none of them really know where they came from. How can they?"

"Why?" I ask. "What happened to the Unguzi?"

"Same thing that happened to so many other tribes in West Cameroon. They were invaded by slave traders. Takaa's own family was kidnapped by a man named Tobias Lathan and taken to a slave plantation in North Carolina. His descendants lived there for hundreds of years before our ancestor Daniel Alby bought his own freedom in 1818 and the freedom of his family, and moved north to Maine with his wife and six kids."

"Holy shit, six children?"

"Yup. Eight generations later, you and I are it, bruh."

And after a few days, *I'll* be it.

What the fuck, this is so fucked up.

"Oh my God," I say, leaning back in my chair and staring at the ceiling. "How long have you known all this?"

"I don't know, a year or so? I've been hearing stories like this one since the accident. I remember lying in the hospital bed after the accident, and everything just came zooming at me. I could barely think. I could just *feel*. *Everything*. Hospitals are full of people with regrets, you know. It sucked. But I've kind of learned to control it."

"How?" I say.

"Staying in my room, obviously. No regrets in there but mine."

We sit in silence, and I notice my hands are shaking. This is no way for a kid to live.

"What do *you* do when you feel like it's all too much?" he asks.

He didn't even have to ask me *if* I ever feel like it's too much. He just knows. He knows like I know. Having this . . . curse . . . power . . . whatever . . . it's too much for anyone. It's too much for a *grown-up*, let alone a sixteen-year-old and a twelve-year-old.

"I don't know," I say.

Another *I don't know* for him. I'm the big brother here. I'm supposed to have answers. I'm supposed to know shit. I don't know anything.

"Sometimes," I say, "I just breathe. I just lie here, just like you're doing, right there on the bed, and just breathe, and do nothing, and try to think about nothing. Doesn't always work."

"I bet," he says, nodding. He's focused on nothing, his eyes fixed on the ceiling as I watch his brain work. "Hey, I have another question."

Oh God, what now? I nod for him to go ahead and ask, bracing for whatever. But I'm still not prepared for this one.

"Do I . . . do we . . . ever get rid of our powers? I mean, I thought if you can see the future . . . you might know."

My heart is pounding, and I try not to show my reaction on my face. What's the point in telling him I have no idea how to get rid of this curse? Shouldn't he have some hope in his last days? Some joy? Isn't that what my whole mission has become? Bringing him joy?

"Yeah," I say. "We do."

Peace like a river washes over his face, and he lets out a deep breath of relief.

"How?" he asks.

The question catches me off guard. *Way to go, Alex. How are you going to lie your way out of this one?*

"Uh"—I clear my throat—"I've never been able to tell. I haven't touched the right items to figure that out yet, apparently."

Not the *worst* lie I've ever told.

"Well, we've got time. Let's start thinking! Between my knowledge of the past, and your visions of the future, we should be able to figure this out!"

Before I can cut in, he's off the bed and pacing and jumping headlong into this discussion, a light flickering in his eyes.

"Okay, let's start at the beginning. We both got these powers after the accident. Why?"

I'd always wondered that. Lots of kids—Black kids, even—survive car accidents without inheriting some ancient family curse from an African orisha. Why us? Why *then* of all times? Why weren't we born with this? What does the accident have to do with Takaa's wish?

"What was the accident like for you?" he asks me.

I shrug. "I don't know, man, I don't really remember it. I just remember waking up in the hospital and being a little freaked

149

out that I knew what was going to happen to my IV bag."

"I woke up watching people wheel me into the ambulance. Except, I was lying in the hospital bed. I could feel the covers. I could hear the machines beeping. But I was *watching* the ambulance rattle around me every time I shut my eyes."

"That must've been scary," I realize. "Terrifying, even."

He nods, staring down at the floor again, and then he locks eyes with me. Something's clicked.

"Wait, that's it! *Fear!*"

"Fear?"

"We got these powers after the accident because we were *scared*, dude! Just like Takaa!"

People get scared all the time, and they don't end up with ancient-family-curse twilight-zone bullshit like this. But I take a minute to consider it. If this thing runs in our family, would it be weird to think it gets triggered by near-death experiences, like Takaa?

"Oh, you know what?" asks Isaiah before I can properly process his existing suggestion. "Maybe that's how we get rid of this!"

He's looking at me expectantly, as if what he just said was a complete thought, and now it's my turn to respond, and what's taking me so long?

I shrug. "*What's* how we get rid of this?"

"Maybe we need to face our biggest fears!"

My chest tightens, and alarm bells ring through my head. Of course the universe would put me in charge of preserving this boy and his ultimate life wishes in his last days, a boy who's admitting he's tempted to risk his life to be rid of a family curse. I mean, this is the same universe that gave us this curse in the first place, so I guess this is on-brand of it.

"That sounds like the worst idea you've ever had," I say. "And since it's *you*, you should take that statement very seriously."

He rolls his eyes. "Deadass though! Think about it! Dad won't tell me why he got into the car. Wouldn't it make sense that he got into the car to face his fears? Maybe he was afraid of dying? Maybe he didn't want us to do the same thing?"

Okay, I guess that makes sense. Much to my distress.

"So let's not go doing that then, shall we?" I ask.

"It doesn't have to be anything over the top. What if we went and jumped into the river? I'm afraid of going outside, and you can't swim."

"The *Chicago* River??" I snap. "Going for *facing* our fears here, not dying from them . . . and I can swim just *fine*, thanks. Why don't we go to the gas station down the street and eat some sushi or something?"

"*Hell* no," he says. "Bungee jumping?"

I don't know Aunt Mackie all *that* well, but I know there's no way she'd sign off for us to do that.

"I think you have to be eighteen for that," I say.

We both sit there in silence for a while.

"There has to be something," he says.

Then, after a while, he yawns.

"Sleepy?" I ask. I glance at my phone clock. Eight fifteen p.m.

"Nah," he says, rolling over to his side and pulling his legs up onto the bed. I look up. His eyes are shut, and his breaths are getting longer and more drawn out.

"You sure?" I ask. He doesn't respond at first. "Hey."

"Huh?" he asks.

151

"Come on, sit up," I urge him. "I need your help figuring out where this curse came from. You can't fall asleep on me now."

He yawns again.

"Can't we do it tomorrow? What's the rush?"

A pang hits me for all the instances I've taken my time with Isaiah for granted. All the times we used to play *Smash Bros.* on our couch in East Garfield Park, and I'd hog the controller. All the times I complained after Mom asked me to walk him to the bus stop.

"Yeah," I say, my voice faltering. Because what else am I going to tell him? *No, Isaiah, we have to figure this out tonight, because you may not have many tomorrows left?*

"Yeah," I say again, staring at my hands. "We can do it tomorrow."

No reply. I look up at him and realize he's already fallen asleep, his mouth gently parting about twenty seconds in. God, I hope I'm doing the right thing by telling him all that useless shit about what his future looks like. I hope he doesn't hate me in whatever afterlife he finds. I hope, like I hope for Shaun, that he forgets all about me, and he's happy wherever he is, swimming in pizza bites and Lucky Charms. I hope he's with Mom and Dad. I hope he's with Takaa. I hope he's happy.

I lean back in my chair and pull out my phone and open my texts from Talia.

Nothing. Absolutely nothing.

It reminds me what I decided to do earlier, what I should've resolved to do as soon as I saw Isaiah at the bottom of that hole in the ground.

I'm going to buy the tickets.

My hands are shaking as I click the Ticketwizard and press my thumbprint against the home button to log in.

I breathe a huge breath of relief when I realize there are still Shiv tickets left, but I gasp and hold my breath again when I realize they've skyrocketed to $210 apiece. Jesus Christ, $420.

But I click 2 from the dropdown menu and go to my cart. With tax and everything, they end up being $445.75. Do people really pay this much for one night of live music? I wince as I click *Buy*, and when that confirmation page pops up, I stare at it, thinking, second-guessing myself.

It's rash, it's probably irresponsible, and it's . . . brave? Maybe?

A chill goes up my spine at that, and I breathe and whisper, "Dad? If you can hear me . . . guide me? Please?"

I think of the photo, and before I can remember the sequence of events, I reach inside my pocket and pull it out, canceling the vision I saw of me looking down at it, sitting there on top of his red flowers. The vision I saw last night. I sigh. Time moves on.

~~Lying in bed.~~
~~Graveyard.~~
~~Sitting in my chair.~~
Darkness.
Flickering lights.
Darkness again. Graveyard.
I hope I'm doing the right thing.

7

The News

I GET THROUGH VISIONS of my apron, my visor, and my dishwashing gloves and stand at the sink washing dishes for about ten minutes before I can feel myself getting sweaty from stress. I'm jittery. Washing dishes should be a standard part of *closing* a store, not opening it. But as Scoop said, he was here late last night doing paperwork, and by the time he noticed the dishes, he was too exhausted to stay any longer. I sigh and manage to steady my hands enough to wash, dry, and put away bins and scoops back here, but my brain is spinning in a million directions.

Why am I even here?

I can't focus.

I'm thinking about Isaiah. I'm thinking about what he's doing right now, and wondering if he's safe. I glance at the clock. 10:22 in the morning. He's probably still asleep. Or playing BeatBall, or eating breakfast.

What if he falls off the step stool again trying to get to the cabinet above the freezer?

What if he plugs in his phone to charge it and accidentally drops it into his cereal?

What if he chokes on his food and no one's around to help?

What if he has a seizure?

What if?

If.

I take a long, deep breath. *Cool it, man,* I tell myself. *He's fine.*

And if he's not? my brain hisses.

Then there's nothing you could've done.

I need something.

I need a distraction.

The TV in the corner catches my attention, and I reach for the remote with my gloves and flip it on. Scoop sometimes lets us dishwashers turn it on back here, on the one condition that we leave the sound off. Seems counterintuitive to me, since the only way to enjoy the show is to at least have closed captions on, and does he really want us reading the screen instead of just listening to what's happening? But whatever. It's not like it matters. We get three channels back here. Cartoons, soaps, and the Channel 5 news, which is always showing some kind of murder or robbery happening in one of the bad neighborhoods, or some kid raising money for a good cause in one of the good neighborhoods.

Right now, it's a robbery.

Interesting enough. It's enough of a distraction, anyway. I put down the remote and pick up a silver ice cream bin caked with pink goo stuck in the corners, and I wonder if it's leftover bubblegum or that sickeningly sweet strawberry powder base.

I start scrubbing, and the pungent smell hits me.

It's strawberry.

Still better than sherbet, though. I think of Talia, and I wonder if sherbet and s'mores are really *that* bad of a combo and why I've always been too squeamish to try it and whether she thinks I'm less of a man *because* I'm squeamish, and if I've been giving her other clues into the fact that I'm a spineless—

No, Alex, I force into my brain, *stop it.*

I take a deep breath.

Being a man is more than trying new ice cream flavors. I know this. So why do I let a thought like that spiral into being so hard on myself? I'm employed. I'm pretty athletic. I'm handsome, I'll admit. I've got a gorgeous girl who loves me. Or who loved me. And who still loves me, I hope. And I know my music.

But does any of that really make me a man?

Real men don't run and hide when they find out a friend is in trouble. Real men stick by them. *Leave no man behind,* the saying goes.

I nod determinedly, scrubbing with new fury, hoping to scrub the hour away faster.

"I'm doing it right this time, Dad," I say, as if he can hear me.

Doing it right for Isaiah. Doing what I should've done for Shaun.

I blink a droplet of sweat that's trickled down into my eye, and force myself to look at the TV for filler, anything to take up space where self-loathing would usually be. They're still covering the robbery. I read the words along the bottom. *Break-in at Santiam Estates leaves one dead.*

My whole body goes cold, and everything around me seems

to pause.

I read it again.

Santiam Estates.

I watch the camera pan from that house with the yellow door—the gray one that Talia loves so much, with the pink flowers in the front—to Mr. and Mrs. Zaccari's house with the black door, and down the street to a slew of caution tape and blue and red flashing lights.

I'm through the break-room door, down the narrow hallway, and into the lobby before I have a minute to second-guess myself. Scoop is talking to a man in the lobby, something about a football game, when he notices me.

"Hey, champ," he begins, but when his eyes meet mine, his grin melts into a look of decided concern. "Everything okay?"

I shake my head.

"I'm sorry, sir. I have to go."

I can feel my throat growing tight and my cheeks getting hot. I can't cry here, not until I get to my car. It's happening. It's happening *right now*. One dead, it said. One dead, and I already know who it is.

"I'm sorry," I say, turning and reaching for the door.

"Alex, you just got here!" he hollers, stepping from around the counter and staring at me with his hands on his hips. "I need those dishes done before we open, not to mention the syrups mixed, and the toppings put out."

He sounds like my dad used to when he got angry. His voice is stern and steady, soft, but not to be argued with. I shut my eyes. I can't even bring myself to look at him.

"I have to go. I'll explain everything later, I promise," I say, turning the doorknob and swinging the door open.

Scoop's hand is clamped around my shoulder, and I look up at him, startled. His eyes are flashing with something intense—concern? Betrayal? Both?

"If you leave right now," he says, "I can't let you back."

My eyebrows fly up. He can't mean that. I glance from Scoop to the man who's so engrossed in whatever's on his phone screen that he's not even paying attention to what we're saying. He's a Black man in a navy suit, one that's pressed and looks expensive. And then I notice his hand, which is the same shade as mine, wearing a huge diamond ring, one I've seen before. Looks similar to the one from my vision. Am I . . . am I staring at the man who's going to buy Scoop's eventually? I look back at Scoop, wondering if he already has plans laid out or if these two are just friends at this point, or if they've only just met. I wonder if I'm looking into the eyes of a man so desperately in denial of his company's demise that he's resorted to threatening his only dependable worker into staying.

Whichever reality we're living in, I can't afford to think about it. This place will be gone in a few years, whether I'm here to see it or not. I can't help Scoop. But maybe I can be home to help Aunt Mackie absorb her nephew's absence, if this is really it.

If Isaiah's really gone.

I blink back tears.

Dad's voice echoes in my head.

A man's not a man without his paycheck.

But a man who doesn't protect his family is no man either, I think.

"I'm sorry," I say, to Scoop and to my father, my voice so unsteady it comes out as a whisper. If staying here means letting Isaiah die alone, if it means letting go of whatever idea my dad had about staying employed, if keeping this job comes at the expense of being there for my brother, then fuck it. I yank my arm away and dart outside to my car, where I dry my eyes with my sleeve and pray that however Isaiah went, if he went, that Aunt Mackie didn't have to watch.

A HUSBAND AND WIFE sit at their dining room table one evening, watching a crime report on the news, sipping tea, and lamenting the violent state of the world. They're thankful they live in a neighborhood where crime is rare.

The wife is on the local litter patrol. The husband regularly attends town hall meetings.

The wife is a natural peacekeeper. The husband is a natural protector.

The wife hears a noise outside. The husband gets up to investigate.

8

The Block

IT'S WEIRD TO BE driving through the suburbs toward a dozen flashing police cars parked haphazardly down the block without a *trace* of fear.

For once, I don't have time to be afraid.

I have to get to Isaiah.

The drive home was a blur. I'm sure I thought about *something* along the way, but it just felt like I was in an alternate dimension. I don't even remember watching the road. All I can think about now is that white bag I can already see about twenty feet beyond the caution tape. I park in the middle of the street, just before the small crowd of people begins. A few heads turn to look at me, and I look down at my lap as I fumble for my keys. I don't want their pity. I just want to see Isaiah.

I think of the last thing I said to him, last night. What was it? *Yeah. We can do it tomorrow.*

How was I supposed to know we couldn't?

My eyes are trained on that bag beyond the caution tape as I climb out of the car. Everyone's talking like it's a normal day. It's cold out here for a summer day, overcast and a little windy. I fold my arms against myself and wonder if I'm shaking from the wind or from my nerves. My head is throbbing. It smells like barbecue out here, and I wonder if someone's been grilling this early in the morning, and why it's a strange smell for such a day.

My little brother is probably dead, and people a few houses away are barbecuing.

Everyone from this block is standing out here, most of them chatting to each other and looking on at the scene.

"What happened?" asks someone's voice nearby I don't recognize.

"Robbery, they said," says someone else.

"Is that the Johnsons' house?" asks someone.

"No, the Martins'."

Confusion settles into my head like a cold salve, a welcome reprieve from the guilt and dread that was once there.

The *Martins' house*?

What the hell was Isaiah doing down the street near the Martins' house? How did he end up in the cross fire?

I look between the mass of people, most of whom are taller than me by a few inches. I step forward into the crowd, past Mr. Jabbery, who is holding his wife Marge close, the couple whose lawn Isaiah and I mowed only a couple of times before her nephew came back to live with them and he took over mowing again. I keep my head facing forward, hoping they don't look at me before I pass them.

They don't.

The body bag looks like a bag of anything else. But it's bigger up close.

Too big.

I hear a familiar voice.

"Alex?"

It's frantic, it's squeaky, and it's almost unrecognizable until I match the voice with the owner. Mrs. Zaccari is scrambling down our driveway in my direction, wrapping a cardigan around herself against the cold and glancing between me and the scene.

"Alex, your aunt and I thought you were at work. What are you doing back?"

She throws her arms around me and rests her chin on the top of my head. She's holding me like she would hold a small child, pressing my head against her chest and running her hand along the back of my head. I think the last person to hold me like this was Mom. I close my eyes and take a deep breath. She smells like barbecue smoke.

I look up and spot Aunt Mackie across the scene, right in between two of the cop cars, discussing something important with one of the officers, probably answering questions about the house where the robbery happened. The Martins' house. Maybe the Martins aren't home to answer questions right now and Aunt Mackie is the only one with details about the house.

She's so engrossed in her conversation that she doesn't see me, even though I'm only ten feet away. And then I put two and two together. A body bag that's too big, and an Aunt Mackie who's way too focused on the conversation to also be grieving the loss of her nephew.

"Where's Isaiah?" I ask, feeling a lift in my chest as I look up at Mrs. Zaccari. She seems surprised at my question, and then she looks around a bit.

"I—I don't—" she answers.

"Alex?"

I'd know that singsongy voice anywhere, and my eyes follow its source. There, in the open front door of the house—Aunt Mackie's house—stands Isaiah. Whole. Alive. His eyes lock onto me, and he leaps off the front porch and sprints toward me, and I'm suddenly on high alert again. What if he trips and falls and lands face-first on the concrete? What if a distracted driver barrels down the street and hits him? What if it's been an off day for these officers and one of them sees a suspicious running Black boy, instead of seeing my little brother?

I decide to close the distance, taking on as much of the risk myself as I can.

I take off sprinting toward him, meeting him in the middle of the blocked-off street, and he throws his arms around my neck. I pick him up without thinking, my arms around his middle, my hands against his back. A vision of the gray T-shirt he's wearing flashes into my head, and I blink it away. As I set him down again, his grip on me doesn't weaken. I can feel him shaking, and he sniffs, his face pressed against my pink apron, which I totally forgot I was still wearing.

"I thought it was you," he whimpers.

"Huh?" I ask, unable to piece together what he means.

"I thought you were—" he says.

Oh.

He thought it was me.

"I thought it was you," I say. "On the news. I thought—"

He shakes his head, but his gaze seems to tell me he understands. Either one of us could've become a hashtag today.

"Come here, man," I say, pulling him close, careful to keep

my hands balled into fists. "I'm right here, okay?"

I feel him nod against me.

"I just went to work," I say. "I'm sorry. I asked Talia to tell you I'd be at work and she said of course she'd—"

Then dread settles into my throat.

"Where's Talia?" I ask, pulling his shoulders away from me and looking down into his eyes. They're flickering, like he doesn't know what to say, and I can't tell if it's because he doesn't know where she is, or because she's in the . . .

No, she's not. I saw her in my vision, standing somewhere, with black hair again, in the black dress she bought yesterday, glaring up at me like I'm her mortal enemy. She's fine.

Her voice confirms it.

"Alex?" it calls from somewhere far away. I look up and spot her standing in Aunt Mackie's doorway, in a pair of my gray sweatpants and a loose white T-shirt, with her neon-blue hair pinned up into a messy bun. She's probably been at the house all morning, like she usually is in the summer, spending the night so often the neighbors probably think she lives there. She spots me, and her eyes get huge, and she shuts the door behind her and sprints down the driveway.

"Alex, oh my God, I've been texting you nonstop!" she screams frantically, practically tackling me in a hug. I pull her close, my fists closed against her back. I'm careful not to touch her bare arms.

"Talia," I say. I don't know what else to say to her, and I'm thankful when she fills in the silence.

"I was so scared," she says. "*We* were scared. Someone broke into the Martins' house and there was a gunshot and

167

screaming and . . . I didn't know what to do. I told Isaiah to stay in the house, but when he looked out the window and saw you, he just—"

"I wasn't just going to leave Alex out here," he says.

Something sour settles in my stomach at the thought that Isaiah might have risked falling down the porch steps or getting hit by a car, or shot, just to make sure I wasn't out here alone.

"Isaiah," she begins, pulling away from me and looking down at him with a furrowed brow. "After what happened out here today, I don't think being around all these officers is a good idea."

"Why not?" asks Mrs. Zaccari from behind me.

Oh God. As if today wasn't anxiety-inducing enough, now my little brother's employer is asking me why I, a Black kid, am uneasy with having an army of police parked outside my house.

"Uh," begins Talia, glancing at me before addressing Mrs. Zaccari again. "No reason. Just, it's a lot of men around with guns."

Mrs. Zaccari folds her arms and takes on the tone of a preschool teacher explaining something to her students.

"These guys are here to help," she says. "I promise. I know there's been a lot said about the Chicago PD on the news lately that comes from a place of fear and misunderstanding, but I *promise* you, with them here, we're safe. My husband used to be on the force. And I, for one, think they're here at just the right time, given the event happening tonight. We won't have to worry about any suspicious people trying anything."

I look to Talia, who's looking at me, and I'm sure she's asking the same question I am in my head: How do I explain to this woman that I'm a suspicious person just by looking how I look?

Mrs. Zaccari would bake cookies for anyone on this block. She cares deeply about her family, and all of us who live here in Santiam, but until she spends a day as a Black man, I don't think she'll ever understand why the cops make me uneasy.

Mrs. Zaccari, realizing she's getting nowhere with me or Talia, turns to Isaiah.

"You don't want suspicious people creeping around our neighborhood, do you, hon?"

Isaiah glances at me for only a second, but it's long enough to tell me he's only saying what he has to. Then he shakes his head.

Mrs. Zaccari turns and looks out at the scene beyond the caution tape, and I follow her gaze out of habit. I notice Aunt Mackie staring at me. She's standing alone now, the officer who she'd been talking to directing his attention to another officer farther down the street, right behind where the body is lying statue-still.

It hits me like a truck. Isaiah will be like that before the weekend is over.

I look away before I get sick.

A sharp voice slices through the air.

"Are you Mrs. Karen Zaccari?" it demands, commanding me to look up.

A tall, slender officer with fire-engine-red hair and a chocolate-brown beard is staring intently in our direction, but Mrs. Zaccari looks undeterred.

"I am," she says, stepping forward, unfolding her arms, and shoving her hands in her pockets. Seeing the pockets thing startles me, because a move like that might get me killed.

"Ma'am, we have some questions for you and your husband. Would you mind stepping under the tape and joining us?"

He beckons with his hand and steps forward to pull the caution tape up so she can crouch under. I can't hear what they're saying anymore, but I'm half-shocked and half-impressed at how calm she was the whole time he was addressing her. I'm standing here trying not to shit my pants, and all he did was look in my direction. But I guess she doesn't really need to be afraid. For her, the police are the good guys. For me? It's different every day, depending on what I'm wearing, where my hands are, and how lucky I am.

"So," I ask Talia hesitantly, unsure whether I want to know the answer. "Who's, uh . . . I mean, who . . . was it?"

Talia sighs and folds her arms against her like she's suddenly uncomfortable.

"Apparently that guy," she says, motioning toward the body with her chin, "was staying at the Davidsons' down the street through a vacation rental app, and while they were off at work, he broke into the Martins' house next door."

"Why?" asks Isaiah, looking up at her. His hands are in his pockets, and I wish he wouldn't keep them there while we're out here with all these officers. Talia shrugs and shakes her head.

"I'on know. People just *do* things sometimes, Isaiah."

"So," continues my little brother, "how'd he end up . . ."

Talia looks at me as if to apologize for what she's about to tell him, and I don't even have a guess as to what it could be. Did the guy fall on a freaking chain saw or something?

"Mr. Zaccari shot him."

I freeze. Mrs. Zaccari's husband?

The ex-cop?

A chill goes up my spine, and I scan the crowd for him.

"Where is he?" I ask.

"They've got him in the back of the car. They're taking him in to ask him some questions."

"Mr. Zaccari *killed* somebody?" asks Isaiah. I'm as shocked as he is. Mr. Zaccari is super quiet. He's barely said a word to me or Isaiah in all the times we've been over there. Mrs. Zaccari does all the talking for both of them. We used to sit in their living room and watch cartoons if we finished mowing their lawn early. He was usually asleep in the armchair across the room from us, but he'd always wake up to hug us goodbye before we left and helped us smuggle away extra white chocolate macadamia nut cookies into our backpacks.

Mrs. Zaccari's words from last night bubble up in my head again.

There's so much crap out there in the world, MacKayla, outside Santiam. I want to make sure all our kids are safe.

Apparently, so does Mr. Zaccari.

But I guess it could've gone way worse. The robber could've chosen *our* house to rob. He could've stolen some of my vinyls. He could've taken Aunt Mackie's jewelry.

He could've killed Isaiah.

But then, that's assuming this guy was actually dangerous. What if he was lost? What if he went out to breakfast and came back to the wrong house, thinking he'd locked himself out? What if Isaiah had accidentally kicked his soccer ball over the Martins' fence this morning?

Sure, the "robber" could've killed Isaiah.

But under the right circumstances, so could Mr. Zaccari.

I take a long, deep breath. Better this guy than my little

171

brother, I guess. Anything to keep him around for even a little bit longer. I'm suddenly feeling dizzy, and a cold breeze raises goose bumps on my arms.

"Come on," I say, motioning to the house. "Anyone else hungry? Let's order something."

"Actually," says Talia, her eyes trained on mine, "Alex, I need to talk to you about something. Isaiah, why don't you go inside and watch cartoons? Aunt Mackie brought home the new double rainbow Lucky Charms for you today—"

"Yes!" he exclaims, and he's racing up the driveway to the front door before I can say anything. God, I wish he wouldn't run so fast like that, especially across concrete, where he could bust his head open. I know he's itching to face our fears, but do we have to face so many *before* the concert?

Shit.

"Hey," Talia says, her voice breathy as she folds her arms and stares up at me with an expression that's hard to read. "Mind if we take a walk?"

It's *really* cold out here.

"Yeah," I say. "Sure, okay."

We turn away from the blockade of flashing red and blue and meander down the sidewalk together. She doesn't say anything at first, and I wonder if she expects me to start the conversation. The birds are whistling like crazy out here, and I wonder if this is one of those the-birds-know-some-shit-is-about-to-go-down situations where I should actually be at home in the house with Isaiah. What if he burns down the house trying to turn on the oven or something?

"I owe you an apology," says Talia, snapping me back to now.

172

I look over at her, and she shakes her head.

"I shouldn't have tried to pressure you into having sex until you were ready. It's just, these things usually go in reverse, you know? I didn't want to be one of those girlfriends who can't keep up, or is scared to."

I guess I know what she means. I don't talk to many people at school, but from the conversations I overhear in the halls, in hetero relationships it's always the girlfriend who's pressured into giving up the V-card first. None of the guys in my class seem to have apprehensions. Then again, none of the guys in my class seem to have weird premonitions induced by touching things, especially their girlfriends.

"It's okay," I say.

"No, it's not," she says. "It was wrong to expect you to be ready, and I'm sorry."

It should bring me comfort, but it doesn't. I'm the one who should be apologizing to *her*. I'm the one who's been keeping her in the dark about this whole situation. I've been lying by not telling her about my power, and I can't ever. Her apology just hurts, because I know it's going to keep happening. She's going to keep asking, and I'm going to keep turning her down, and eventually, she'll get sick of me, or find a guy with some notches. And probably more muscles than me. And more inches.

"I appreciate it," I say.

I *do* appreciate it, in the same way adults appreciate a small child bringing them a flower that's actually a weed—it's a nice gesture, but it doesn't really fix anything. Eventually, the weed's going to grow back.

"Hey," she says, reaching for my arm. I instinctively flinch

173

at her touch, forgetting I have nothing to worry about since my hands are in my pockets. Her face is full of questions. "You good?"

"Yeah," I lie, my heart racing. "Yeah, I'm good."

"What do you say about . . . just . . . spending time together instead? No sex, no pressure. We can just . . . talk? We don't even have to kiss if you don't want to."

That's the thing. I *want* to. She means, without knowing it, *if you can't*.

I try to swallow the lump in my throat. Why am I still shaking inside? Why are my hands still sweaty? She just said no sex. I take a deep breath and wonder if I'm afraid of the physical, or something else.

"That . . . sounds like fun," I say, hoping it doesn't sound as unsure as I feel.

Am I . . . am I really afraid to spend time with her at all?

And why?

"Awesome. In that case," she says, immediately perking up to her normal self again and hopping in front of me. She turns to face me and stops, reaching for my hands. But I'm quick with the reflexes. I loop my arms around her waist instead and pull her against me, careful to close my hands into fists behind her so I don't actually touch anything. Her face is only inches from mine, but now I don't care. We're at least three blocks from my house. Out here, ain't nothing happening between us. Nothing I have to worry about anyway.

I look down at her, at her big brown eyes. She's not wearing any makeup today. Her lips are only slightly pinker than the rest of her face, and her eyelashes are thinner, and more brown than black, but those deep brown eyes are still mesmerizing, and they're still smiling up at me.

"I have a surprise for you," she says, folding her arms behind her back and wiggling her shoulders. "Guess."

The last time Talia had a surprise for me—well, besides her recent blue hair—she bought a new sky-blue bathing suit with a built-in push-up bra, and I'm hoping for the sake of *all* my sanity that this surprise is nothing in that vein, especially right after that apology.

"I don't know, Tal," I say with a shrug. I don't like all these *I don't know*s I've been doling out lately, so I toss out an absurd guess. "A puppy?"

She rolls her eyes, and I smile. There's nothing I love more than making her cringe at my jokes. I love that look on her face that's both amused and disgusted with herself for being amused. I love her.

And then it hits me.

I'm not afraid to spend time with her.

I'm afraid to *lose* her.

That night next to the road, whenever she dyes her hair back to black, after whatever I do to earn her hatred. Whatever I do to make her look at me like that, I might lose her. But is keeping her away really keeping that night from happening, or am I just not enjoying the time we have together before it happens? She replies, bringing me back to the present, in which she's grinning up at me without a trace of anger.

"No, but that's a fantastic idea!" she exclaims, jolting me back into right now. "I'm sure Aunt Mackie would *love* to have puppy-piss yellow-splotched carpet in the living room."

"Good point," I laugh. It feels like I haven't laughed, truly, like this, in days. Somehow, Talia's company is exactly what I've needed all day. She's the only person I can trust. If I lose her . . .

My eyes are stinging as I look from her eyes to her lips, and I really don't want to cry right now. So I lean forward. She rests a hand on my chest and presses herself against me, kissing me softly. When she pulls away again, she rubs her nose against mine and says, "Guess again."

"A kitten?"

"Kittens also pee, weirdo," she giggles.

"A fish?"

"Bruh," she laughs, "I think those pee too. This surprise doesn't eat food, doesn't breathe, and doesn't pee."

I pause for a second, trying to suppress a laugh as I give my next guess.

"A dead fish?"

She pushes herself away from me and points in my face.

"Something's seriously wrong with you," she laughs. "No, it's not a dead fish."

"Okay, I give up," I say. "What's the surprise?"

"You *really* give up?" she asks.

"I really, *really* give up."

She smirks and glances down before reaching into her pocket and slipping out her phone. I try to think of anything I might've hinted that I've wanted lately. It's nowhere near my birthday, which isn't until December. Our six-month anniversary was two weeks ago, when we took our ice cream to the park and just talked. Nothing fancy, nothing expensive. I guess—by necessity or by preference, I don't know—that's just our style. Talia swipes her finger across her screen a few times, and finally she turns the phone to me. I see the familiar Ticketwizard site, and my heart skips as I realize she bought me event tickets, somehow. I glance up at her with a smile before taking the phone in my hands, canceling the vision of me scrolling down, and scrolling down. I arrive at the name, and my heart sinks.

Talia bought two general admission tickets to see Shiv Skeptic.

Shit.

This couldn't get any worse.

Isaiah, and even I—just a little—are hoping this concert breaks the curse. Isaiah is hoping to face his biggest fear, leaving the house, and I'm hoping to get into this concert, hang out in the back, face my fear of huge crowds and seeing the future and overspending from my bank account. Maybe a speaker will burst twenty feet away and we'll both be terrified but just fine, and Isaiah will get to enjoy even a *little* bit of time without this curse before whatever happens to him happens.

Now Talia wants to go?

This is wrong. All of this is so, so wrong.

I look at her.

I'm supposed to be excited about this. She's *expecting* me to be excited about this. I *want* to be excited about this. But I'm terrified. I'm jumpy. I'm suddenly shaking.

"Talia," I begin, my voice unsteady. I swallow and try to find the right words to say next, but I don't have to.

"My mom bought them for us," she says. "Before you ask where I got the money for these. She said it's to thank you for everything."

"For everything?" I ask, hoping Talia is going in the direction of *thanks for taking care of my daughter* and not in the direction of *thanks for sending me a chunk of your paycheck every few weeks*. I'm hoping to God that Maria didn't tell Talia the extent to which I've been "helping" her out since Shaun passed. The last thing I need is to have to explain to Talia that I'm sending the money because I want to help, and not because I see her and her mother as charity cases, or worse, having to admit that I knew about Shaun in advance and did nothing about it.

"Everything," she says, her eyes studying mine. "For everything . . . thank you."

Shit. She knows.

"Talia, I meant to tell you at some point," I say.

"I'm sure you did," she says. "I don't blame you for *not* telling me. I know myself. I'm too proud. Now that I'm sixteen, I'll be making my own money soon, and I'll find a way to pay you back, but until then, I'm just grateful we have groceries at home. So . . . pride aside, ego aside, thank you."

She leans forward and kisses me, looping her arms around my waist and pulling me against her. She's warm, and she smells like soap and shampoo, and my arm brushes against hers and I feel how soft her skin is. Pleasure pistons in my brain are firing at lightning speed, and I can feel my hands getting clammy inside the fists they're still balled into behind her. Then, mid-kiss, my eyes fly open at the realization that she's kissing me under the assumption that I'm going to say yes to the concert.

"Hey, uh," I say, pulling away. "You're welcome and everything, Tal, but I was actually hoping to spend time with Isaiah tonight."

The light in her eyes goes out. Her smile falls. She lets out

178

a single, sharp chuckle of disbelief.

"What? Does it have to be tonight?"

"I . . . ," I begin. "I promised him—"

"Alex, I know how much you adore music. And you've never been to a concert because you've had to work, or because it was too expensive. This is *Shiv Skeptic* we're talking about. If there's ever been a day for you to take a rain check on hanging out with Isaiah, this is it."

"I'm sorry, Tal," I say. I can't even look at her as I lie to her face. "I *want* to go."

I do *not* want to go. I'd rather stay home tonight and stand behind Talia in my room with my arms around her waist, vibing to the music, exploring her as much as she wants me to, kissing her neck, rapping along with her to all the songs she knows. But the reality is, every single moment I have with Isaiah is precious. If there's anything that would make his last days memorable, it's being able to live without his visions, and that means—hopefully—going to this concert. And if I went with Talia, my attention would be divided. I'd be distracted while Isaiah was surrounded by thousands of loud, drunk, high strangers. What if he's kidnapped? What if he's dragged into a nearby alley and mugged and stabbed? What if he bumps into the wrong drunk guy and he takes it as a hostile act and punches his lights out?

I take a deep breath and remember my dad's words. . . .

A man's not a man without his paycheck.

And what I said to myself as I left Scoop's . . .

But a man who doesn't protect his family is no man either.

And I let my mind wander a bit. . . .

But one man can't protect everyone.

If I look away from Isaiah for even a *second* tonight, and something happens, I'll never be able to live with myself. So, as I look into Talia's doe-like eyes, full of disappointment, with one eyebrow trembling like she's about to cry, I know I'm doing what I must, even though it breaks me.

"Wow, Alex," she says. "Wow."

"I really am sorry, Tal," I say again. "Please know that. I really, really want to go."

She lifts her arms and snaps at me, "Then fucking *go*. God, Alex, take some risks once in a while, like you used to! You've changed!"

Have I? Since the accident? I remember that day at the pool. I was afraid then. Afraid of losing Talia. As afraid as I am today.

Does she know I'm afraid?

"Talia, I can't . . . ," I say. "I can't do that anymore."

"Why not?" she spits. "You used to. You used to talk to me. Tell me what's going on. What's going on, Alex? Is there someone else in your life? Are we growing apart? Are you mad at me for something?"

"No, of course not!" I hurl back. "I just . . . have something I need to do tonight! It's for Isaiah. It sounds ridiculous, but . . . I really just need you to let me stay with Isaiah tonight. Just for tonight. I promise if it were *any* other day, I'd be there in a heartbeat."

"Why can't you just tell me what's going on?" she hisses. "Why can't you just be honest with me?"

"Tal, this is the *one* time you can't know specifics, okay? You

180

think I need to be more open? Maybe you need to grow up—"

I catch myself.

"Talia, I'm sorry—" But it's too late. Her eyes are flashing.

"*I* need to grow up?? I'm the one who understands that we only have three years left as teenagers before the *world* will expect us to grow up. I'm not going to waste those years trying to be an adult! Can you just be sixteen with me? For once?"

When you lose both your parents at twelve, your best friend at thirteen, and your little brother at sixteen, you don't get to be sixteen. Not if you're a man-in-training. Not if you're the oldest. Not if you have an example to set. Not if you're constantly fighting for a future.

"Talia, I don't get to be sixteen," I hiss. I'm angry now. Rage is racing through my veins like a drug. "You think any of these people see a *kid* when they see me?" I gesture to the dwindling crowd gathered around the body bag in the distance. "You think any of these people see a kid when they see me or Isaiah run out of our front door? Either of us could've been the one in that body bag today. I don't get to be sixteen, because people judge me like a twenty-year-old! I've got a job, I've got a car, I do okay in school, and when I come home, *that* shit is still staring me in the face. Don't tell me to be sixteen, Talia. Don't you *dare*." My eyes are burning. My cheeks and neck are burning.

"Alex, I've lost people too," she offers. "I've lost my dad. I've lost my brother. My best friend. I can't lose you, too."

Wait, is she afraid I'm going to leave *her*? No, she can't be. She'll never lose me. If and when we come to the end of this, she'll have to abandon ship first.

"You won't, Talia," I say.

She pauses, and I just look at her in silence. It's not as simple as she wants it to be. How do I explain to her that it's *way* more complicated than that, without explaining *how*? How do I make her see what I say, and feel what I feel? How do I explain to her that I'm doing the best I can? I can feel my jaw tense and my eyes brimming with tears. It feels like I'm being stabbed in the chest right now.

"It already feels like I have," she hisses, and turns and walks away. Several times in the next few moments, I consider opening my mouth to speak, to say something, anything. But I hold on to a picture in my head that I hated at first. A sad smile plays at the corner of my mouth at the realization that the vision I've been wishing I'd never seen has now become my only assurance that there's more to *us*.

One day Talia will stand in front of me, enraged, in the black dress she bought yesterday, after her blue hair is brown again, long after I turned down a magical night with her at the most perfect concert in the world, after both our wounds have healed from today.

I shut my eyes and play that picture over and over in my head.

This is not that fight.

I've seen us together after this fight.

I walk home alone.

9

The Talk

I FIND ISAIAH PASSED out on the sofa in the living room. There are pizza bite crumbs all over the silver tray on the coffee table and all down the front of his shirt. In the thirty minutes it took me to make Talia hate me, he's eaten pizza bites on the sofa instead of the table like we're supposed to, and passed out right in the open, covered in incriminating evidence.

"Hey, man," I say, my voice gravel in my throat, before Aunt Mackie finishes giving whatever information the cops need beyond *a man broke into a house, and the next-door neighbor shot him*. Isaiah moves a couple of his fingers and sniffs as if something's tickling his nose in his sleep. He drags an arm across his crumb-covered mouth and rolls away from me onto his side. "Hey, man, we've gotta get this cleaned up before Aunt Mackie comes inside."

He looks over his shoulder at me and shakes his head groggily.

"But I'm sleepy," he says.

I hear keys at the front door and snatch up the tray, brush the coffee table crumbs onto it, and dart into the kitchen. The last thing Isaiah needs in his last couple of days is to be grounded.

If Aunt Mackie sees that he was eating these greasy pizza bites in here again and getting crumbs all up in her sofa, there's going to be a tiff. If I can prevent even one of those, I'll be doing good.

"Boys?" comes her voice, just as I turn on the faucet to rinse off the pan. I slip it into the dishwasher and hear the sound of Aunt Mackie's short heels being shuffled into the coat closet in the foyer. I've forgotten to take off my Vans. I quickly kick them off and toss them into the pantry, where she won't see them. Again, no need to stir up conflict, especially now when time is precious.

"We're both home," I reply. No response from Isaiah. He's probably asleep again.

Aunt Mackie steps into the kitchen and slides her black Sherlock Holmes–looking designer trench coat off her shoulders with the deepest sigh I've ever heard.

"Everything okay out there?" I ask, watching as she slumps onto one of the barstools and buries her face in her hands. The tip of her nose, peeking out from between her hands, is red from the cold outside. Even the weather knows today is no ordinary summer day.

"Yes, baby," she whimpers.

Baby? Aunt Mackie has called me Alex, or on bad days, Alex Matthew, since the day I was born. Something's terribly wrong. I could, and probably *should*, wake Isaiah up so we can talk more about how to get rid of these powers. The concert starts in only nine hours, and we're walking to the Wall, so that'll eat into even more of our time.

Against my better judgment, I decide to stay. Isaiah needs me, but so does Aunt Mackie.

184

I slide onto the barstool next to her, gripping the back of the chair, canceling the vision of me hoisting myself up onto it, and then hoisting myself up onto it. I try to settle my shaking hands. It doesn't work. I rest my arms on the ice-cold marble countertop and stare at her, and I realize her hands are shaking too. When they come away from her face, her eyes are red and puffy, and her cheeks are wet. My throat closes. Aunt Mackie is a fortress. *Nothing* rattles her. I've never seen her cry. I never even knew she *could* cry.

"Aunt Mackie?" I ask.

She glances at me and flashes a smile before reaching for a napkin from the cast-iron African napkin holder statuette in the middle of the island. She presses it into her eyes, and her chest and back swell with a deep inhale and sigh.

"Everything's fine, Alex," she says. "I've just been through a lot today."

Aunt Mackie didn't cry at our parents' funeral. She stood there like a statue, with her eyebrows knit together in a determined stare as she said goodbye to her sister and her sister's husband. I always thought she got by with substituting duty where sadness would be.

"I'm sorry," I say.

"Don't," she says. "Don't be sorry. You don't have time to be sorry. You're a kid. You should be focused on kid stuff. Not . . . *this*."

Not . . . *what*?

A murder down the street? We live thirty miles from downtown Chicago. Murder is as common on the news as the daily weather segment. Aunt Mackie pushes herself out of the chair and goes to the pantry door, swings it open, and gives me a smirk.

"Sorry," I say, getting up to put my shoes away.

"Don't worry about it," she says. "I think we've both had a hard day. Sit. Here."

She holds out a tall bottle of white wine to me, with little bubbles dancing up the inside of the glass, like soda. I look from the bottle to her face, and back to the bottle.

"Go on," she says. "Did your mom ever let you have any?"

I'm still staring at the bottle as I shake my head, reading the label.

Connaissance le Blanc Brut, 2003.

"What's Connaissance le Blanc Brut?" I ask, although I'm sure it's French for some type of white wine.

"Champagne," she says, pulling two tall, clear glasses out of the corner cabinet Isaiah and I aren't allowed to go near.

Champagne? Isn't that usually for weddings and birthdays and stuff? What's the occasion? Or did Aunt Mackie run out of wine and now she's had a hard enough day to go for the good stuff in the back that's been there since we moved in? The bottle's all dusty and everything. Clearly, I'm staring at her like I'm confused, because she laughs and sets the bottle and both glasses on the counter in front of me.

"You don't have to be scared of it," she says.

I'm not scared of it. I'm just confused.

"What's the occasion?" I ask.

"The occasion," she says with a smile, "is that you've become a man."

Now I freeze. What the hell is she talking about? I've heard that milestone represented as a lot of different things—voice

186

cracking, growing a mustache, and, most often of all, losing your V-card. *Please* don't let her try to give me "the talk" at sixteen. She's about four years too late trying to teach me how it all works. The internet and post-PE conversations have taught me all I've needed to know so far. I'm staring at her weirdly enough for her to erupt in laughter again. She unwraps the foil from the bottle top and twists the corkscrew into it.

"I don't think I'm talking about what you think I'm talking about," she says, as the bottle releases the cork with a loud *pop!* She pours the clear bubbly elixir into my glass, then hers. It smells warm and sweet, like those hot toddies my dad used to drink every Christmas. Just once he let me try it, thinking I wouldn't like it. But before he realized it, I'd downed a few swigs. Minutes later, I was out like a light.

I watch the mountain of bubbles dissolve from the top of my glass, and I wonder what criteria Aunt Mackie is using to determine that I'm "man enough" to handle alcohol now.

She takes her glass between her index finger and thumb and sinks back down onto her barstool. Her eyes are still red and puffy, but they're calm, and her mouth is pressed into a happy, proud smile as she raises her glass to me. I glance at my glass, and she motions to it with her free hand.

"Go on," she coaxes.

I take hold of the stem hesitantly, blink away the vision of our glasses clinking together in a toast, and then tap my glass against hers. She takes a swig and sets hers down.

"Sweet as I remember," she says.

Sweet? Since when was wine sweet?

I sniff at my glass, and that sour soda-y smell swells strong

187

in my nostrils. I bravely take a sip, and the intense tangy sweetness and fizz dance on my tongue. Forget whatever I said about wine being bitter and miserable.

This shit is *good*.

"This is the champagne your parents drank at their wedding."

I look at her and then back down at the champagne. Suddenly it goes sour in my mouth.

"Oh," I say, setting the glass down and staring at it. I wonder if it tasted just like this. I wonder if it was Mom or Dad who picked it out. Probably Mom. She was the one with the sweet tooth.

"Katie was already pregnant with you, so she asked me to make sure the chefs knew to put sparkling cider in her glass."

Mom was already pregnant with me?

"I was the only one who knew," she says between sips. "I kept that secret all these years. I figured you should be the first to know."

"Never knew I was an accident."

"Oh," she says, downing the rest of her champagne before reaching for the bottle again, "you were no accident. Your parents knew they wanted kids before they knew they wanted to get married."

I don't even know how to feel about that. I guess I should feel special, that they were trying to have me, that they threw caution to the wind and decided *fuck what Grandpa Jack and Grandma Georgina say Jesus says*. At least that's how I like to imagine how they felt about what Jesus says.

"Oh," I say. "Cool."

I'm sure it sounds sarcastic, but I don't mean for it to. I genuinely think the history is cool. I wish I could've been there. I'm still kinda jealous that Isaiah can just *go* there—to the past—whenever the universe wants him to have a vision. But I guess he'd say the same thing about my powers. Curse. Whatever this is.

"Why are you telling me this now?" I ask. Aunt Mackie pours the champagne into her glass until the bubbles run slightly over, and then splashes a little more into my glass, as if she hasn't noticed I only took one sip.

"Because," she says, reaching over and wrapping her long-nailed fingers around my hand, "I want to thank you for being such a good kid. When I signed the papers to be legal guardian for you and your brother at the hospital when you both were born, should something catastrophic happen, I never thought I'd actually have to do it."

There's a lump in my throat as I put myself in Aunt Mackie's shoes. I can't imagine losing a sibling, even though I know I'm about to, but I *definitely* can't imagine inheriting that sibling's kids all of a sudden, especially if I were the face of Chicago's real estate market.

"Sorry," I say. I feel her hand tighten around mine.

"Don't you *ever* apologize for that. You and Isaiah are the *best* thing that's ever happened to me."

Does she mean that? Does she really?

I don't know what to say. I just nod and stare at my glass.

"You boys," she continues, "give my life meaning. And you keep me laughing. You constantly impress me. And *you*, Alex, have been a stellar example to Isaiah of what it means to be a man. Even when it's scary."

That shocks me. I feel like I haven't said a word to Isaiah since we moved here, not unless I had to. I haven't done a good job. I haven't included him in anything. I've hardly driven him anywhere since getting my license. If I were a *real* big brother, Isaiah would know how to ride a bike by now. He'd know how to throw a perfect spiral—well, maybe not that, because I can't even do that—he certainly wouldn't have to drown his boredom in BeatBall, and he'd probably be more open to vegetables instead of trying to build muscle out of fried cheese, pepperoni, and rainbow marshmallows.

"Nah," I chuckle. "I'm not as brave as you think I am." I reach forward and take the glass in my hand again, and blink away the vision. I take a bigger sip than last time. I can minimize the number of visions I have to have of the glass if I can drink this down faster. I take a swig and set it down on the counter again.

"You absolutely are," she says. "Think about all the laughs you have with Talia, and how you smile when you have your headphones in across the room and think I'm not paying attention. Joy in the midst of oppression is its own kind of bravery."

And I guess she's right.

"I know you two don't talk much, and you may not think you've had an impact, but he's watching. He sees the way you go to work every day, how you're responsible with your car, and the way you treat Talia."

I've just been fired, my car is going to kill a married businessman one day, and Talia's heart is broken because I can't give her a good reason why I'm not going to see Shiv with her tonight. And because I'm scared to get close to her, to let her see the real me, for all my visions and all my fears.

I take a deep breath and think.

Responsible. I guess, on paper, I am. But why do I still feel so . . . lacking? Is it really enough to be a good example for Isaiah? Is it really enough to show him how to live life by the manual? What good has that done him in the face of his regret about the past?

"Hey," she says, leaning back against her barstool. "Wasn't there a barber you used to go to in East Garfield Park that you were close with? Do you ever see him much anymore?"

"Galen?" I ask. I remember so many times, sitting in his chair and shutting my eyes against the tufts of hair falling around me, and telling him about my worries in school. Telling him about Talia and how excited I always was to see her, even before we were dating, and about how much I missed Shaun.

I smile and chuckle a little, sadly. "That was forever ago."

Aunt Mackie shrugs.

"Couldn't hurt to call and make an appointment. We all need someone to talk to now and then."

I would've done better to spend less time following the rules and more time just *being* there for Isaiah. Talking to him. Letting him know it's okay to talk to someone about what he's going through. Letting him know he's not alone. Like Aunt Mackie is doing for me now.

"Thanks," I say. "I'll think about it."

Maybe that's what Isaiah needs from me most. To know that he's not alone.

"Anyway, all I'm saying is, you could've turned out a lot worse," she says. I can feel her eyes on me. "That kid who broke into the Martins' house today was your age."

My blood runs cold.

"Mr. Zaccari killed a *kid*?" I ask before thinking.

"It's not *quite* that simple," she says. She breathes deep and taps her nails on the counter before continuing, "This boy was staying with Eric and John—you know, the Davidsons down the street?"

I nod.

"They rented out the guest wing of their house this weekend, and while they were both away at work, he went next door to the Martins' and hopped the fence. He was too young to even *be* on that app by himself, but I guess he must have lied about his age. Mr. Zaccari saw him across the street and went to investigate—"

"With a gun?" I ask.

"He wasn't armed at first. He saw the boy prying open a window in the backyard and went back for his pistol."

I have *so* many questions. Was Mr. Zaccari just peering out his front window like a bulldog all day? Is that what it means to be on neighborhood watch? How did he know this guy wasn't actually staying with the Martins? Maybe he'd locked himself out of the house and was trying to get back in while they weren't home.

Aunt Mackie explains further.

"He says he told the boy to put his hands in the air and"— she pauses—"the boy lunged at him instead."

"Was the kid armed?" *Always* my first question when another person joins the roster of people shot over petty shit.

"It doesn't appear so."

"Was he particularly tall? Aggressive? Within punching distance?"

"We don't know," she says. I can hear the hesitation in her voice.

I can feel my blood pounding through the veins in my neck, and my cheeks are burning. I think back to every name that turns up on the news with the hashtag #sayhisname, #sayhername #saytheirname, all the times news reporters have announced that another kid who looks like me has been killed before seeing the inside of a jail cell, let alone a court-room. I know the stats. I know what the news tells me my future is. And in this case, I know the past.

"Was he Black?"

She goes quiet. I hear a car roll by on the street outside, and the ticking of the clock in the hall. It's *that* quiet in here for what seems like forever, until I finally decide to answer my own question.

"Never mind," I say, downing the rest of my champagne. "I already know."

My mouth liked the champagne, but my stomach didn't. I turn the knob on the door to my bedroom just as I realize I see a vision of myself darting into the bathroom next door. I follow suit, flip up the toilet seat, and empty every last drop of what I drank into the toilet.

After I swish out my mouth with water and head back to my room, I'm surprised to find Isaiah sitting on the edge of my bed, where he was yesterday, when I told him a whole twenty-minute lie about how he's going to grow up, get married, and live a long and healthy life.

"Hey, man," I say. He's quiet. His forehead is still covered in lines from sleeping with his face smooshed against the leather sofa. His eyes are focused on his hands. His thumbs are dancing around each other, and his feet are dangling in concentric circles off the edge of the bed.

Anxious habits. I know them well.

"What's up?" I ask, sinking down next to him. He doesn't look at me. He just shakes his head and asks in a raspy little voice, "Why'd you quit your job today?"

Okay, I thought I understood his powers until now.

"What makes you think I quit my job?"

"Well, now it's the fact that you didn't immediately deny it."

"I don't have to deny it for it to be false," I say.

"That's still not denying it."

"Fine. I deny it."

"Denying it doesn't make it not true."

Smart-ass. I roll my eyes and wish I could lock my arm around his neck and give him a good old big-brother noogie. But since touching him would mean seeing what happens to him, I keep my coward hands at my coward sides. I sigh and look at him. He's already staring at me.

"How'd you know I quit?"

"I knew it."

"Come on, man, tell me."

He shrugs and shakes his head.

"I can't really explain it. The whole time you were gone at work, I could just *feel* something different. I couldn't sit still. My stomach hurt. I felt like, *really* tired, and my heart wouldn't stop racing. I knew something had happened. Something recent. And when you showed up outside ten minutes later and I ran out to meet you and saw your face, I saw a vision of you running out of Scoop's in tears."

"You knew specifically that I had quit my job?"

He shrugs. "I mean, I put it together. I saw a vision of you because you were regretting going to work in the first place today. Plus, nobody runs away from where they work in tears in the middle of their shift. I don't know how else to explain it to you. It's something you have to live with to understand."

I remember my conversation with Mrs. Zaccari this morning, having to explain why the cops make me nervous even though I don't have so much as a parking ticket on my record.

"I feel that," I say.

"So, why'd you quit?"

I sigh. I quit because I thought I saw on the news that Isaiah was dead like I'd seen in my vision, but there's no way I can *say* that. So I dodge the question.

"You can see that I quit my job, but you can't see *why* I quit my job?"

He makes a weird gurgling sound, and my paranoid ass looks at him in a panic, thinking maybe he's choking on something or having a heart attack. But he's giggling. Hard. Until it bursts out of his open mouth into all-out laughter.

"What?" I smile.

"You sound *just* like Grandpa, overthinking everything."

That's super weird to hear, considering both our grandpas died before Isaiah was born, when I was too young to remember. All I have are pictures of Grandpa Harold holding me at the hospital, and Grandpa Jack holding me at my christening, which he and Grandma Georgina insisted my parents go

195

through with regardless of their lack of religious affiliation. Aunt Mackie once told me his exact words were, *Just because you don't believe in the Lord doesn't mean the kids should have to suffer for it*.

But Grandpa Jack was *Mom's* dad. *Dad's* dad—his whole lineage, apparently—had whatever curse Isaiah and I have. I might believe when the Bible can explain *this* shit.

"Which grandpa?" I ask.

"Dad's dad," he says.

"Grandpa Harold?"

He nods. "He overthinks everything and asks way too many questions, just like you."

I smirk at first, but what he says next surprises me. "He had the same power as you."

He did?

"He told me he knew Dad was going to die, and he regretted not making the most of the time they had."

I don't know what to say, I really don't. I could ask if he did anything to try to stop it, but if his power was exactly like mine, I already know the answer. By the time he was old enough to have Dad, he would've known he couldn't do anything to prevent his son's end. I know already and I'm only sixteen.

At least Isaiah and I are getting started brainstorming a solution together, while we're both young. But then, I guess, if we have to face what scares us most, maybe . . .

The realization hits me sharply.

"Did . . . did Dad get into that car because . . . he was trying to face his fear?"

Isaiah goes silent and then manages in a helpless voice, "Of dying? Yeah."

"He was . . . trying to end the curse before it got to us?"

He nods.

"Before we experienced fear so bad it triggered the curse in us?"

He nods.

Fuck. I take a long, deep breath. Dad really got into the car that day for *us*. He . . . he loved us that much. My eyes are burning and my mouth feels dry. I clear my throat and try to keep from crying.

"Do you . . . know that because he regretted doing that at the last second?"

"No," he says, "I know that because he regretted not telling us more often that . . . he loved us."

My chest tightens. Dad regretted not telling us that he loved us? But he *did* tell us, didn't he? I think back to when he came into my room to kiss me good night. I remember all those Sunday evening drives we used to take, laughing and cracking jokes as Mom held her face in her hands in shame at how bad they were. But then I wonder when I heard him say it. When he really sat me down, looked me in the eyes, and said it.

And I realize I can't remember.

Isaiah continues before I can say anything. "Our *great*-great-grandpa had the coolest powers, though. Buddy Lyons."

We have a great-great-grandpa named . . . Buddy Lyons?

"Sounds like the name of a baseball player," I say.

"Eh, he was a batboy for the Montreal Royals a couple of times, and he shook hands with Jackie Robinson once, but the *coolest* thing about him was that his powers were a combination of yours and mine."

"Wait, our ancestors all have *different* powers? Why are they all different?"

Isaiah shrugs. "You said yourself anxiety is different for everybody. So why can't our visions be different for everybody?"

Something tightens in my chest. He's absolutely right. I nod, a smile tugging at the edge of my mouth. This goofy BeatBall-playing kid in front of me might still be a kid, but he's wise when he wants to be. My mind drifts back to Buddy Lyons.

Some kind of weird combination of the past *and* the future? Poor dude.

"He could touch anything and see *all* potential outcomes of his next decision."

"Holy shit, that sucks," I say. "I thought my powers were stressful enough. I'm . . . kinda thankful I don't have that, honestly."

Then a thought crosses my mind.

"Isaiah, have you talked to our ancestors who were . . . taken from Africa?"

"Yeah," he sighs, pulling his knees up to his chest and making the bed sink a bit lower. "I mean, not directly of course. Not all of them are buried in Elginwood. But the ones who are have passed on the stories to me. I've seen a lot of . . . stuff." I immediately wish I hadn't asked. He's clearly uncomfortable.

"Y'know what? Forget I even asked that—"

"No, it's okay. You should probably know. His name was Kando. He was the son of Takaa. The guy who asked to 'know the unknowable,'" he says with air quotes, "or whatever bullshit."

Under normal circumstances, I'd tell him it's not good to swear, but I have to agree with him on this one: Takaa was kind of a jackass.

"What happened to his son, though?" I ask.

"Kando? He married the prettiest girl in the village," he says, his eyes lighting up as he recalls the story. "Her name was Ursa. Our great-great-great-great . . . and lots more greats . . . grandma. Takaa saw that they'd be invaded by huge slave ships, and Kando and his wife were going to be kidnapped, so he moved the village away from their coastal settlement, farther inland, where he thought they'd be safe."

I'm fascinated now. Isaiah tells everything so straightforward, but since he chooses simple words, I can easily imagine them. Our family. I can see Takaa standing like the king he was, looking out at the ocean from the shores of Cameroon, maybe doing something dramatic and badass like picking up a seashell and foreseeing the slave ships coming for his people and refusing to go down without a fight. I see him raising his spear into the air and letting out a battle cry so loud his whole village can hear it and knows to move out.

Then Isaiah's words sink in.

"Where he *thought* they'd be safe?" I ask.

He nods and pushes himself off the bed, his feet meeting the floor with a thud.

"A *huge* storm rolled in," he says, lifting one hand into the air and moving it fluidly over his head. A deep rumbling begins, low at first, from somewhere behind me. I glance over my shoulder and look at the window, blinds closed, and I wonder if that's *actually* thunder I'm hearing, on a summer night in the middle of Chicago. Isaiah continues.

"Takaa, Kando, Ursa, and the rest of the village packed up and hiked into the mountains through the rain."

A sharp explosion cracks through the whole house, startling me off the bed. My heart is racing.

"What was that?" I ask Isaiah, not expecting an answer.

"You can hear that?" he asks.

Our eyes meet. His are wide with awe and fascination, but I'm sure mine look as freaked out as I feel.

"Is that . . . from the story?" I ask. This can't be real. Isaiah shrugs and chuckles.

"Guess you're hearing what I hear all the time," he says.

"Dude, this is badass."

"Not always. Close your eyes."

I give him a look that I hope says *you better not try anything funny while I'm not paying attention.*

"Come on," he says.

I do as he asks. I welcome the darkness. I take a deep breath, smelling the musky scent of my room, feeling the soft carpet under my feet.

"Ursa was pregnant," he says.

Behind my eyelids, it's still dark, for a while, until a faint yellow glow flickers to life in the distance. It grows and expands, warping into an egg shape, darkening in the center, forming a face wrapped in pink cloth. It's a woman, with one hand over her belly, staring at me with the most intensely dark eyes I've ever seen. My breath catches as she smiles at me, and then turns to leave. She takes a hand in hers from the darkness, and everything else flashes to life, as if someone's flipped a light switch in my head.

"It was a treacherous climb," says Isaiah. "Falling rocks were a constant danger."

I'm standing on a four-inch-wide ledge fifty feet up a mountain face behind the woman in pink. I look down at my feet, and they barely fit on the ledge side by side. I swallow the temptation to open my eyes and look straight ahead as I feel the floor shake beneath me. A huge boulder slams into the ledge just a few feet in front of us, sending two men careening off the side, with rocks and mud falling behind them. The woman, who I know is Ursa, screams and grabs hold of the man in front of her. I catch a glimpse of a man in front of both of them, tall, with a long staff and a red cloth wrapped around his waist. He looks over his shoulder in my direction and says a single word: "Âwámsɛn."

"Ah-wam-sen," I say out loud.

And somehow, I understand what he's saying to them.

Hurry.

Before I can think, the ground beneath me melts, my stomach skyrockets into my throat, and I go tumbling down the mountain. My eyes fly open, and I'm back in my room. I touch my chest, my shirt, just to make sure I'm actually here and not about to fall to my death.

Isaiah sits down next to me, his eyes closed, his palms up.

"Scared?" he says with a grin.

"What happened to them?" I demand. "Ursa couldn't have fallen to her death, could she? What about Kando?"

"Kando broke both of his legs in the fall," says Isaiah. "Takaa continued up the mountain, but Ursa wouldn't leave Kando. The rest of the tribe continued up the mountain with Takaa.

201

Ursa and Kando were taken aboard a slave ship called the *St. Lucia* and taken to North Carolina, where they were separated. Takaa watched the ships leave from the mountain, couldn't take the shame and the pain, and jumped off."

My mouth hangs agape. I'm at a loss for words. That's it? That's . . . how their story ends?

"What about the baby?"

"You don't want to know, man."

I don't want to know? How can he say that? That's our great-times-whatever-grandma or -grandpa he's talking about. Of *course* I want to know.

"Yeah, I do," I say.

He glares up at me. "Fine. Ursa had the baby. They told her it died."

"And . . . ? What happened?"

"They sold her to a family in South Carolina. Her name was Sadie."

"Our great-times-whatever-minus-one-grandmother."

He shakes his head.

"Great-times-whatever-minus-one-*aunt*," he says. "Our great-times-whatever-minus-one-*grandmother* was the daughter of Ursa and a man named Isaiah Matthew Weidner. A slave owner."

Fuck.

I feel my neck getting hot, and I look down at my arm, at the color, a dark brown the same color as Aunt Mackie's mahogany dining room table. Medium tone. A few shades lighter than Ursa's.

"Come on, man," says Isaiah. "You *had* to know that, right?"

I guess I should have. Every time Black History Month rolls

around, the details about how plantation owners treated their slaves, what they did to them. You don't hear much about the beatings, the rapes, the murders, the illegitimate children who were taken in as house slaves. I've always known in the back of my mind that there's a slew of undocumented crimes against my family that will never see justice. Being Black in America means being constantly reminded of the darkness you come from, without knowing *details* about the darkness you come from. But to *see* Ursa's face, and *know* what happened to her, to see firsthand what I'm a product of, makes me physically ill.

I might throw up again.

"And," I say in realization, "his name was Isaiah?"

Isaiah nods. "I hate it. Dad named me after him."

"*Why* would he do that?"

He scrunches his nose in disgust.

"I don't know. He said it was to 'right the wrongs of history' or something. I swear when I grow up, I'm changing my name, especially if I blow up."

I spot the perfect segue into a new subject that won't upset him so much, and I take it.

"What name would you pick?"

He shrugs. "I guess it doesn't really matter. I'm not blowing up anytime soon. I can't even leave this room without being scared of everything and everyone. How am I supposed to get on a stage one day?"

"I'll protect you," I say.

He raises an eyebrow. "You gon' follow me up onstage every time I perform?"

"Nah, I didn't say that," I laugh. "But I could at least *be* there. In the audience. You could just look at me and know that ain't *nobody* gonna laugh at my brother as long as I'm there."

His mouth curves into a smile, and he folds his arms in defiance.

"Izzy."

"Izzy? That would be your name? Like the pizza place?"

"No, Izzy like Izzy Rufus, BeatBall wizard and king of the synth."

"Or Lord of the Synth."

His eyes get huge.

"That's *genius*! You wanna come on tour with me? Izzy Rufus, Lord of the Synth has a ring to it!"

I chuckle. "What would I play?"

"You can rap!"

"I can rap *other* people's words."

"If you can think up something wicked like 'Lord of the Synth' just like that, you can freestyle," he says.

"Can *you*?" I ask.

"Yeah, duh."

"Then do it."

"Well," he says, swinging his arms and sucking his teeth, "I can't just *do* it. I have to be *inspired*."

Exactly what I thought.

"Well, I've got some inspiration for you," I say.

He looks at me so skeptically, I have to laugh.

"What is it?" he asks.

"I'll show you. Get your shoes."

"Huh? Are we going somewhere? It's getting dark out."

"We'll be sneaky."

Isaiah looks up at me like I've lost my entire mind, and I'm pretty sure I have. But I have to convince him somehow.

"I know the *perfect* thing to do that scares us. Wanna know what it is?" I ask.

His eyes grow wide and he nods excitedly. *Please, let this be a good idea.*

"You sure?" I ask, pulling out my phone, canceling the vision of me unlocking it, and unlocking it. He nods again. "You have to promise not to freak out, and not to ask questions."

"You didn't . . . kill anybody, did you?"

"Yeah," I say. "I need your help burying the body."

His eyes are wide as saucers until I look up at him and smile.

"Asshole," he giggles.

"Still think so?" I ask, holding up the phone screen to him. His eyebrows meet in the center of his forehead, and he squints at the screen before taking it in his hands. One of his fingers brushes against the back of my hand, and I thank my lucky stars I can only see the future based on what my palms touch. That was way too close.

"Oh my God, are we going to see—" he squeals before I can shush him.

"Yes."

"But how did you afford—"

"No questions, remember? You can either have answers, or a trip to see Shiv."

"Wait, but how are we going to go without Aunt Mackie? There's no way she'll let us."

"We'll sneak out," I shrug, with the confidence of someone who's sneaked out before—i.e. not me.

"Wait, just one more question?" he asks.

I roll my eyes. "Fine."

He glances at his lap before continuing.

"How is the Shiv concert going to make us face our fears?"

I take a deep breath and sigh. "I'm kinda secretly hoping it won't. I'm . . . scared, Isaiah," I admit. I think it's the first time I've ever admitted it. "I think if we're meant to get rid of this curse tonight, maybe we *have* to be afraid? Maybe being afraid of something *maybe* happening will be enough to cure us?"

"Mrs. Zaccari thinks it's scary enough," he giggles.

I have to smile at that. And then he admits something of his own.

"I'm . . . scared too, Alex."

I swallow the lump in my throat and nod. I can't imagine. Isaiah's still just a kid. His feet dangle off the side of my bed, and his small frame is drowning in one of dad's T-shirts, the collar hanging lopsided off his bony shoulder. He looks up at me and nods determinedly.

"But I want to be normal," he says.

"Me too." I nod, although who's to really define what "normal" even is? Especially when it comes to brains. Neurotypical, though? Can't help but feel like that'd be . . . nice.

"No, I mean . . . I want to go out and *do* things, and hang out with people and . . . not be scared when I leave my room."

"This is perfect then, right?" I exclaim. "You're facing your fears by going to this concert, and I'm facing my fears by . . ."

By being around Isaiah until it happens.

" . . . quitting my job to hang with you all day. Including this concert."

"Quitting your job scares you?" asks Isaiah.

I shrug. "Well, yeah."

"Why?"

Oh, how do I explain this?

"Remember when Dad took us to volunteer at the dry-goods donation center for the homeless? And . . . he told us to get good grades and work hard so we don't end up . . . you know . . ."

"He never told *me* that," says Isaiah. "He just told me I was doing a good job helping people."

"Well, he told me," I say. "And I never forgot it, and I never forgot that a house like the one we had in Garfield Park would be in my future unless I kept a good job. So quitting one feels . . ."

"Scary," he says. "I get it now."

"But it's okay to be scared," I add. "That's what Takaa didn't realize, right? That it's okay to be scared? That it's okay to regret the past?"

He smiles. "Yeah."

I stare at him for a long moment, hoping, praying, that whatever ancestors can see us from wherever they are right now keep him safe tonight. Whatever exists, let it protect us, let it protect *him*.

Let Takaa protect him.

Let Shaun protect him.

Let Mom and Dad protect him.

"Race ya!" he yells suddenly. He darts for the door and sprints down the hall to his room.

"Isaiah, where—?"

"Getting my shoes!"

I smile. For once in my life, despite my fear, I'm pleased with myself. A warm feeling settles in my stomach, and I take a deep breath. I remember King Takaa. I remember his face as that huge boulder came tumbling down the mountain and his son fell with it. And I know that whatever happens, however Isaiah goes, I'll have done the right thing. We're not going up the mountain. We're making the most of the time we have left.

No matter how terrifying.

With trembling hands, I get through visions of my jeans, my T-shirt, my socks, my shoes, my jacket, my keys, my wallet, my phone, and my phone charger, and Isaiah and I push open the window to my room and climb out onto the driveway.

10

The Lights

ISAIAH AND I WALK the whole twelve blocks, since I know parking will be a nightmare, and since the fresh air does wonders for calming nerves. The sky is black. No stars. No moon. Just the whitish-yellow glow of streetlight after streetlight above us. The storefronts here are all closed. We walk past a coffee shop that Talia swears has the best hot chocolate in Chicago, and the only coffee shop I've ever seen that carries tayberry syrup.

Hecho con tayberries reales, she says.

I picture her face, and something cold and unwelcome settles in my stomach. Isaiah looks up at me, but I keep my focus on my feet.

"Did you two break up?" he asks. It drives a spike straight through my chest.

"You readin' minds now?" I ask, half-joking.

"Nah." He shrugs. "I just know you don't feel this strongly about many things. Music, and Talia. I know you don't usually get so worked up over music, so that just leaves Talia. Is she okay?"

I remember the last words she said to me.

It already feels like I have.

She thinks she's lost me. And I guess, in a way, she has. I already know we're going to break up at some point, when her hair goes dark again, so what's the use in opening up to her? What's the use in telling her how I feel? I've already lost *her*.

I shake my head, wishing it was that simple. Wishing *I* was that simple.

"Yeah, she's fine."

He sighs, and I'm sure he doesn't believe me.

"You can tell me, you know," he says. "I won't tell."

No way. Why would I dump all my issues onto him when we're already scared to death, and *supposed* to be out here trying to get rid of this curse so he can have peace?

"It's okay, Isaiah," I say.

"Are *you*?" he asks.

"Am I what?"

"Okay."

I look down at him. He's got his hands in his pockets and his eyes on his shoes. He doesn't look at me when he says, "It's okay if you're not okay. But . . . you should probably tell someone you're not. And, I guess, since we're brothers . . . you could tell me?"

My heart swells at his words, at the hope that I might confide to him my biggest secret—the thing that weighs me down every morning when I try to get out of bed, the thing that makes me feel guilty for getting to exist while one of my best friends doesn't. I could tell him about Shaun. I think of how good it would feel, what a relief it would be to tell someone. And before I catch myself, I say it.

"I'm not okay."

My eyes prick with tears. Isaiah looks up at me and I look him dead in the eyes.

"I'm not," I say again, dragging my sleeve across my eyes. "Sometimes it feels like my brain is too full. Like my thoughts are moving too fast and I can't keep up. And . . . Talia doesn't know about the curse. And I don't really want to tell her, because this shit sounds crazy. Know what I mean?"

He nods up at me.

"I know," he says. "I feel like no one would really *get* this. Not even Aunt Mackie. I'm glad I can talk to you."

It melts me.

"And I'm glad I can talk to you," I say, deciding to do something brave. I reach my arm around his shoulder, my fist balled for my own protection, and pull him against me as we walk. He's warm, and as he wraps his arm around my waist, I soak in the feeling. I forgot how good it feels to hug someone. Not romantically. Just because.

"Do you think Cobra Katjee and Leviathan will be there?" he asks.

My heart skips at the thought of being among so many people in such a huge crowd, but I reply with a straight face anyway.

"Course!" I say, surprised he's changing the subject back to Shiv. "He never goes anywhere without the Dragons."

"Do you think Cobra will do his drum solo from 'The Rush'? That's my favorite part."

"Maybe." I shrug. We keep walking, and I spot a poster on the front door of Mikkelson's Bokhandel, a Swedish bookstore.

It's Shiv, front and center, screaming into the camera with his eyes shut tight and his fists clenched. Sweat is flying all over the place, like he's just run a marathon, and the veins in his neck are so strained, they look like they could pop right through his skin. Leviathan is to his right, a monster of a man with a big bald head and a glare so menacing even the poster is terrifying, and he's not even looking at the camera. Cobra Katjee is on the left, with that sharp jawline of his, red bandanna around his forehead, and his huge black-and-silver sweatshirt hood pulled over his head in the exaggerated shape of a cobra hood.

Isaiah sees me staring as we walk past, and he stops to look. "I wanna be like him when I grow up."

When. I. Grow. Up. What a privilege it is to be able to say those words. I quietly promise myself I'll never take it for granted again.

"Like him, how?" I ask.

He doesn't take his eyes off the poster as he says, "I want friends."

I didn't expect that.

"You don't have friends?" I ask. "You've got me, don't you?"

"Yeah," he says, his voice almost a whisper. "But I want to leave my room and stuff. You know. Like we used to. I want to play basketball. Like, outside. With friends."

I nod. I get it. I shouldn't have assumed that Isaiah was holing himself up in his room because he wanted to. I should've checked in. I should've *been* there.

I sigh and try to cheer him up now.

"Come on," I say. "This is no time to be sad. We're about to see *Shiv*! Aren't you excited?" I wrap my arm around his neck and pull him close, careful to keep my fist closed.

"I mean," he says, "kinda? But also, this is scary." He reaches up to pry my arm from around him. "Do you think there will be a *lot* of people there? Like, *hundreds*?"

I sigh and move my tongue around nervously inside my too-dry mouth.

There will *definitely* be a lot of people there.

"I don't know," I say, "but if you stay close to me, I promise you'll be okay."

We keep walking until we turn the corner to the venue and spot the line of cars at a standstill, waiting to get in. Only a few people are on foot, many carrying foldable lawn chairs and blankets. The Wall is an outdoor venue, and Chicago nights can get cold, even in the summer. I'm already wishing I'd packed at least a sweatshirt. But I wanted to wear the only Shiv memorabilia I own—a black windbreaker with a holographic black dragon in the middle that flickers silver when it catches the light just right, and gray smoke climbing up toward the collar.

But damn, it's chilly.

I look down at Isaiah and ask, "You good?"

He nods, but his arms are folded, and his bony shoulders are scrunched up around his neck. At every turn, I'm spotting things I could do better, ways I could be a better big brother. Aunt Mackie would've made sure we brought something warmer, just in case.

We walk past a huge map of the parking lot, and I smile. If you're new to Shiv Skeptic, if you've only heard his top singles, if the words *The Rush* mean nothing to you, the *first* thing you should know about him is that he doesn't do small. He doesn't

213

do subtle. He doesn't do soft.

And he doesn't do anything by accident.

The map of the parking lot is a huge spiral, with an exit leading out the way cars come in. It's arranged in the shape of the dragon glyph, the symbol of the Dragons. It's on every album, it's in the middle of the dragon's forehead on every piece of merch, and it's in the middle of Cobra Katjee's bandanna.

"Hey, look!" cries Isaiah suddenly, grabbing my wrist and shaking it. His finger brushes against my palm, just under my thumb, and a vision flashes in my head and I panic. No, no, no. It's as strong as the ones I get with Talia, sucking my brain into a vacuum, making my whole body tense up, my teeth clench. Everything hurts. Everything's in sepia. I see Isaiah turning around where we stand, rows of headlights behind us as cars find the dwindling open spots in the parking lot. And then this vision blends with a familiar one—one I've rearranged my whole life to avoid. Talia, standing with headlights behind her, arms crossed, hair dark, eyes glaring. He lets go, and I suck in a breath. I blink away the vision, and we're back. I yank away my hand.

No way. That can't happen. Talia's hair is blue. And she's not here.

"Man, be careful!" I snap. He looks up at me, startled, his eyes wide with something I immediately recognize. Fear. The *last* thing I wanted for him in his last days on earth. "Hey," I say. "I didn't mean—I mean, I'm sorry. You touched my hand, and it triggered a weird vision."

"Oh. Sorry, Alex."

One of only a few times he's called me by name. He says it so sweetly, like he's genuinely sorry for causing me that pain.

214

He should know. He sees things too.

"Now, what am I supposed to be looking at?" I ask. A familiar voice answers my question, but it's not Isaiah's. It's behind me.

"Alex?"

I turn to look, paralyzed when I see Talia behind us. She's wearing that black sundress and black combat boots with silver buckles that go all the way to her knees. Her lips are jet-black, and her hair is suddenly dark and curly again, the blue gone. Her face is flawless—makeup done so well she looks like a doll, and her eyes are framed in heavy, sharp black eyeliner. My blood goes still in my veins. Time stops. I can't breathe.

It's really happening.

Now.

"Talia, you look . . . *different*."

I already knew she'd get rid of the blue hair and go back to dark. But I didn't think it would happen this fast.

"What the hell are you doing here?" she hisses, her eyes narrow. She glances at Isaiah, who's looking at her, and then up at me, with fear. I know I have to defuse this situation. I know how this must look to her. I decline her invitation to see Shiv, and then suddenly I'm here with Isaiah.

"Thought you couldn't come tonight," she growls, folding her arms and cocking her hips to one side.

Oh God, now I've really done it.

"No," I say, a little too fast. "Talia, I just wanted to hang with Isaiah tonight. I—"

"Sure," she says. "And we couldn't all go together? Why didn't you want me here, Alex? What's going on with you?"

"Talia," I say, stepping forward and pressing my hands together in front of my lips. "On God, there's nothing wrong. I just—"

"You've been acting weird. First you won't hold my hand, and now you're making excuses to avoid me? I thought you'd just been grieving ever since . . ." She lets the rest of the sentence evaporate before moving on. "All those times you said you just wanted to stay home. That you were too tired, too anxious. All those days you skipped out on visiting Shaun with me. The times when I needed you most. You know why I fell in love with you, Alex? You used to *care*. Now it feels like you're a million miles away."

"Talia—"

She holds up her hand for silence so sharply I flinch, thinking she's going to slap me, but then she glares at me and says, "It's over, Alex. I can't take this anymore."

Over?

She can't mean that. I have to stop this.

"Talia, *please* let me explain. There's a good reason for this, I swear."

That physical response I get—the urge to do something drastic and probably reckless to save this situation, like I did that day at the pool—wells in me like a tidal wave, and I consider the unthinkable. I remember all the times I've had to dodge Talia's touch and explained away all the gloves I've worn with some excuse about an infected cut on my thumb or just a general fear of germs. Am I really about to throw all that away? All that effort? All my lies? All my secrets? I know what I have to do. I glance down at Isaiah in a silent apology, because this secret that he and I have each kept to ourselves for almost four years now, the thing that's bonded us closer in the last few days than anything else in the world, is about to be Talia's secret too.

Another couple walks past us, hand in hand—one guy is wearing plaid flannel and the other is in a black leather jacket. They both glance at me and Talia, and I realize we're probably making a scene. Heat floods my cheeks, but I try not to look too flustered as I weave my biggest secret into easily digestible words.

"I can, uh," I begin. Her eyebrows fly up and she purses her lips, as if she's waiting for news she knows isn't going to convince her of anything. "I can, uh, *see* things."

"See things?" she asks, the sarcasm dark and biting on her tongue.

I nod.

"Yeah, uh, like . . ."

Come on, Alex, think of an example.

"If I touch things, I can . . . kinda see what will happen to them . . . in the next few seconds."

She's silent for a long moment before she rolls her eyes and sighs. "What are you talking about?"

"Ever since the accident," I say. "I swear it's true. And I predicted something that made me *have* to say no to you, no to going to this concert with you tonight."

"How do I know you're not lying about *that*?" she asks. "You've been dishonest enough with so many other things already."

"I *swear*, Talia, it's true!" I'm raising my voice now, but I don't care. "Why do you think I freeze up whenever I get in my

217

car and touch the wheel? Huh? Why do you think I'm afraid to touch you anymore? Do you really think it's because I don't like you?"

It's right on the tip of my tongue.

I love you.

Say it, Alex, you coward. This might be your only shot.

It hangs there in the air, an empty space where my words should be. But she's staring at me like she would stare at a stranger, sizing me up, trying to figure me out. I swallow, praying she believes me.

"All this time I thought you just had anxiety," she says, shaking her head. Her eyes are glossy, and a tear falls black from her eye, leaving a stream of gray down her airbrushed face. "This is . . . this is . . . something else."

It hurts, how she's looking at me. Like she's afraid of me.

"Talia, no," I plead. "No, it's not like that."

I have to find something to prove to her that this is real. All I have is my shirt, my keys, my phone, my wallet, and my charger. Then a vision swells to life. And I see a mosquito perched on beige skin, up close, with its stinger sunk deep, and I blink away the sight and notice the tiniest tingle in my left ring finger, just below the second knuckle. I keep my eyes on Talia and say, calmly, "There's a mosquito on my left ring finger, just below my second knuckle. When I lift my hand up, it's going to fly off, just past your face, and you're going to try to swat it away, but you'll accidentally hit yourself in the face."

Isaiah lets out a chuckle at that, and I have to smile. "It's true," I say, raising my hand in front of my face. The tiny black sucker with the swollen red belly takes off, zooming straight at

Talia, who squeals and swats at it, and sure enough, slaps herself in the face. She almost stumbles into the road, where the line of cars is still at a standstill, and I reach forward instinctively to grab her, but then I realize I can't—or am too afraid to.

Luckily, she catches herself before that happens and brushes her curls out of her face, somehow angrier now than she was before. Her forehead is burning red as she says, "That doesn't prove anything."

"It's true, Talia," offers Isaiah. "Ever since the accident that killed our parents, we *both* see things."

I look down at him gratefully. Coming to my rescue with his biggest secret laid bare for her to see, just when I needed him most. I don't deserve him. She looks questioningly down at Isaiah, whose cheekiness and affinity for playing practical jokes is now working against our credibility. But it looks like his word is having *some* effect. Her expression is softening.

"You can see the future?" she asks.

I nod.

"Of anything you touch."

"Yes."

"Of . . . me."

"Of us."

"*That's* why you won't get close to me? You're afraid to see our future?"

"I mean, kinda?" I ask. Is it really that far-fetched? I've been afraid to touch her because I've been afraid of *this*. This very moment, when she's looking at me like I've become her worst enemy. And for the first time . . . I have no idea what happens next.

No idea.

I clench my fists, stepping into the future unknown, with Talia.

"I guess . . . I saw this moment coming, and . . . I didn't want it to?" I venture. "So I didn't get too close. I didn't want . . . I don't know." *Come on, Alex, get your words together.* My eyes are brimming with tears, and I look up at her. "I knew after tonight I was probably going to lose you, because you don't trust me anymore. And I didn't want to make it harder than it had to be."

Isaiah's eyes are huge when he looks up at me again and says, "I'm going to go do . . . something . . . somewhere else. I'll see you inside, Alex."

"Uh, no?" I demand. "You're twelve. You're staying right here with me."

"Wait," says Talia, her voice suddenly shrill. "If you started getting these visions after the accident that took your parents, then . . . did you see . . ."

Oh God, please don't.

I'm sending every telepathic wave I can, every silent plea for her not to bring this up here. Not in front of Isaiah. Not tonight. *Any* other night.

She swallows, and for a minute I'm hopeful she catches my drift, but she asks it anyway, in a pathetic whisper. "Did you see . . . Shaun's accident . . . before it happened?"

My cheeks are hot. It's suddenly hard to breathe. I stare at my shoes as I clamp my jaw shut, breathing against the tears I know are forming. Fuck. I'm afraid to talk. I'm afraid to *not* talk. I don't know which I'm more afraid of. I knew. Of course

220

I knew. I knew, and I ran anyway.

"You *knew*?!" she screams. Her voice cuts through the air like a whip, echoing through the night air, cutting deep. A young woman leans out the window of the car next to us, but I think I'm too broken to be embarrassed. "¡Sabías que iba a morir y no me dijiste nada!" shrieks Talia, stepping back from me. Two more tears stream down her face. "¡No me dijiste nada! You *knew*, and you didn't even tell me. I could've stopped him from getting into that car that day! We could've tried to stop it! Shaun may have been your friend, but he was *my* brother!"

My eyes are burning, and I press my fingers into my eyes and say, with as much strength as I have left, "I wanted to tell you."

"I don't give a *fuck* what you *wanted* to tell me! You should've just been honest with me, Alex! You should've told me!"

"Hey!" hollers a voice from somewhere nearby, probably a driver of one of the cars that's already agitated at having to be stuck in traffic on the way to see an outrageously expensive Shiv Skeptic concert. "Shut the hell up!" he yells.

Talia turns her rage toward where the voice came from.

"¡Me cago en tu puta madre!" she fires back without missing a beat. I don't know what exactly she said, but I know what "puta" means, and I know what "madre" means, and I can piece it together.

"Talia, please," I say. I can't tell her to calm down. Not without making things much, much worse. "Can we talk about this?"

"I have nothing to say to you," she spits, marching past me in the direction of the concert. I watch her go, with the huge

221

white strobe lights lighting up the sky beyond her. The silver buckles of her boots jingle quieter and quieter and quieter as she goes. And I'm left standing here, next to Isaiah, who I'm sure doesn't know what to say any more than I do. I take a deep breath and press the heels of my hands into my eyes, and I feel like I'm going to break.

This is too much.

This is all just too fucking much.

I just want to stand here and cry.

I feel a tiny tug at the corner of my shirt, and I look down at Isaiah, who I'm surprised to find smiling up at me.

"Thanks," he says.

"For what, man?" I croak. I clear my throat and try again. "For what?"

"You didn't tell her what I did."

Now I'm confused.

"What did you do?"

"You know," he says with a shrug, "You saw it."

"Saw *what*, man?" I ask. I might sound a bit frustrated, but I don't care. I *am* frustrated. I'm frustrated and tired and cold and wounded. "Just say it."

He gets real quiet for a minute and looks down at the pavement.

"You saw how Shaun died."

I freeze, connecting the two. What Isaiah did. How Shaun died.

"What did you do, Isaiah?" I ask.

"It was an accident," he pleads, taking a step back from me and holding out his hands like I'm about to fight him. "I didn't mean—I mean, I . . ."

"Look, Isaiah," I huff, "I don't want to get any madder than I already am, okay? I'ma need you to start speaking in complete fucking sentences *real* soon."

"I . . . ," he says, and sniffs. His voice is squeaky and scratchy, and he buries his face in his hands and admits, "I shouldn't have left my ball outside. I left it. I was at Shaun's house kicking it around and it landed on our roof and I . . . I left it."

He left his ball outside.

Shaun's mother Maria crashed their car.

I'm not following.

But he's sobbing now, with his hands over his face, and I realize I've made a horrible mistake. I've kicked him when he's down. I really am the worst big brother in the entire world. I lean down in front of him, careful to keep my hands off the pavement, and look up at him.

"Isaiah, *please* explain," I say. "I'm sorry I yelled, okay? But it sounds like you've got something to get off your chest, and that's what I'm here for, okay?"

His shoulders are trembling, and he drags his elbow across his wet face, and I can't take it. I reach forward, fists closed, and pull him against me. He wraps his arms around my neck and buries his face in my shoulder.

"It's okay to cry, man," I say. "It's okay."

I don't care that we're in public. I don't care that all these cars and all these drivers are around. I don't care who sees. If Isaiah wants—needs—to cry, to get this out, who am I to stop him? I hold him for as long as he needs me to, which ends up being a few minutes. Every time I relax my arms like I'm about to pull away, he holds me tighter. Finally, when more and more people begin having to walk around us, and we become a certifiable traffic obstruction, I try to loosen the paralyzing fear again.

"You can tell me whatever it is, Isaiah. I'm listening. No yelling, okay? Promise."

I decide that even if he doesn't tell me, he needs to tell *someone*. I think we could both use a trip to the barber to talk to Galen when all of this is over.

If there's even time.

I feel him nod against my neck, and then he pulls away. I straighten back up and crack my knees, which have begun to fall asleep from bending for so long. When his voice comes out, it's almost a whisper.

"I left the ball in the gutter. When it rained, it pushed the ball off the side of the house, and it rolled into the street. I . . ."

Oh God.

"Isaiah," I say, "you can't think that's your fault, okay? You left your ball outside. Normal kid stuff."

There's no way he should have to live with that. He was just a regular kid being regular. He was eight. He shakes his head in silence and presses his hands against his cheeks.

"No . . . ," he says simply. I think he's out of words for this, so it's my turn to take over.

"Isaiah, I saw Shaun die," I admit. It hurts. God, it hurts to admit it out loud. It cuts open the wound all over again. "I knew he was going to die, and I didn't do anything to stop it."

"Could you have?" asks Isaiah.

"Well, no," I say. "But I didn't have to just *leave* him.

I could've stayed with him. I could've played with him, could've hung out with him, could've done whatever would make him happiest. I could've promised I'd take care of his mom and sister. I could've promised him all kinds of things."

He wipes away his tears and sniffs.

"Listen," I say, "I'm sorry you had to carry this alone. You should've been able to come and tell me. *I* should've made you feel like you could come and tell me. I'm sorry I didn't. And I want you to know that if you ever have anything you want to talk about, I'm right here for you. I'm right here."

Isaiah's face suddenly goes from all contorted from crying to even keel. Everything levels out. The tension is gone from his eyebrows, the cold gone from his eyes, the tightness gone from his mouth. His eyes drift away from my face as if he's realized something. Something's clicked in his head, and I realize that might've done the trick.

"You mean that?" he asks.

My heart is pounding at the gravity of this question. I'm not leaving him. There's no way. I would walk through whatever I need to, just to keep him safe. And if I can't keep him safe, because I'm only a man, keep him company.

I nod.

"Okay," he says.

"That's it?" I ask with a smile. "Just okay? Not '*Spittin' grit, too legit to quit, we lit, we Black Dragon*'?"

That gets a smile out of him. He even chuckles and dries the last of his tears.

"I know you not gon' leave me hanging," I say, shrugging my shoulders up and down and sticking my lips out like they do in

225

the music video.

"Slayin' demons they be screamin' mercy Jesus, white-flaggin'."

"That didn't sound like demon slaying to me."

He grins determinedly and leans into a Renegade with that attitude I know so well, the one that's been smothered by so many tears and so much pain in the last couple of days, I'm surprised it's not extinguished entirely.

"Slayin' demons they be screamin' mercy Jesus, white-flaggin'," he raps, throwing in an exaggerated *ayyyyy* at the end for flair.

"All right, that's the Isaiah I know and love," I say, tucking him under my arm and walking forward with him. The arena gets closer and closer, and the roar of the crowd is so strong and so loud, it shakes the ground under our sneakers. That feeling I always get when I'm watching live footage of a concert, that energy that radiates from the venue, from all hundred-something-thousand concertgoers all there to show love to the artist you love, swells in my chest so strong I feel like dancing. I glance down at Isaiah several times before we reach the front gates and I scan in our tickets, and as his smile grows with every step, I feel more and more assurance.

But the sight of so many people here, all wandering into the same arena, makes me nervous. I think about how many of them must have regrets. Maybe they paid too much for tickets, or they're here with someone they're having an affair with, or they skipped work to be here, or—

"Alex, look!" cries Isaiah, pointing through the throngs of people, who all stand about a foot taller than him. I follow his finger to the merch wall, where there's a whole rack of glittering

LED lights. "Rave gloves! Can we get some?"

Rave gloves, like they had in the music video.

I have to admit, they're dope. I see a few people walking around with them, their fingertips aglow in purple, blue, yellow, and green lights. I squint up at the merch sign, looking for a price tag, and I see it.

$39.95.

Per pair.

I blow air through my lips and say, "Man, that's a lot of money."

"Please?" he asks.

I shake myself out of it.

Come on, Alex, this is ridiculous.

But then I think: What would it mean for Isaiah to feel like he's in a Shiv music video? How much is it worth to me? I have to think about every decision I make as if I'll have to think about it for the rest of my life, because given my situation, I probably will. In thirty years, when I'm making millions of dollars as a stockbroker because—duh—name a better career for someone who can see the future, will I wish I'd spent another $39.95 on gloves for him?

Can you just be sixteen with me?

I stop and take a deep breath. Talia's right. Wouldn't it be a relief to get to be a kid for once? For Isaiah to get to be a kid for once? Just for one night? What would I do if I were a regular sixteen-year-old kid? Would I spend forty bucks on rave gloves?

What if we're forty bucks away from getting rid of this curse?

I pull out my phone, open my bank account app, and

navigate to the most recent payment.

$100 to Maria Gomez, it says. *Transaction pending*.

"I'm sorry," I whisper, as I click *cancel*.

I can't wait.

I touch my shirtsleeve and my heart sinks deeper into disappointment when I see myself take my hand away. I end the vision. I take my hand away. I look down at Isaiah, who's still looking up at the gloves, starry-eyed and obliviously happy.

We buy the gloves. One pair for him, and one pair for me.

We get matching red sweatshirts, too, with Cobra Katjee's insignia huge across the front, because the Wall is an outdoor venue, and it's damn cold out here.

Isaiah puts on the gloves and Milly Rocks to whatever beat is booming from the speakers inside the stadium, and for the first time in way too long, I see joy bursting from him like I did in the photo.

I hope I'm doing the right thing.

I hope we're a hundred and twenty dollars closer to the cure.

We're running out of time.

11

The King

THE OPENING ACT IS a rapper named DeNola, who I've never heard of before, but he spits *fire*. I'm not surprised he's opening for the Dragons. He's leaping all over the stage like a damn tree frog, holding the mic so tight it's like he thinks it's a weapon. I can't make out a word he's saying, because we're way too close to one of the speakers and the bass is pounding through my brain like the wheels of a freight train if I were trapped underneath it.

But I *live* for this shit.

Everyone around us does too. I'm short for my age, and the people directly in front of me are at least six feet tall, but they're relatively still, and the stage is so high that I can see it through the gaps between them.

I look at Isaiah, who has his arms folded and is looking off to his right at nothing.

"Hey," I say, leaning down to him. He looks back at me, startled. "You good?" I ask.

He nods, but I don't believe him.

"What's up, man? You don't like the gloves?"

"No, they're great!" He has to yell to make sure he's heard

over all this noise. "It's just really loud!"

"That's what you wanted, right?" I ask. "It's a concert!"

"No, I mean," he says, looking around again like a trapped rat, "it's *really* loud in here, Alex."

Again he's called me by name. Our conversation from earlier rises to the surface.

Do you ever feel like the world is screaming at you?.

I look at him, wringing his hands together under his sweatshirt sleeves, shoulders hunched around his ears as his eyes dart around.

"You sure you're up for this?" I ask him. He pauses for a moment, and then looks up at me and nods.

"Yeah, I'm having fun anyway. I can't wait to see Shiv."

Suddenly the music cuts out. Dead silence for a moment before the crowd erupts in hollers and applause. Then DeNola, with his light-up sneakers flashing red on the stage, raises a Black Power fist firmly into the air and yells with the force of a thousand grown-ass men,

"CHICAGOOOOOOOOO!"

I'm quiet as everyone else goes nuts with the cheering. I'm saving my voice for when the king comes out on stage. DeNola sprints to the left side of the stage and stops sharply with one leg in the air. The whole arena gasps as if he might fall off into the general admission section and start crowd surfing, but he stops himself. All the hands that flew up at the anticipation for him sink back down. He raises the mic again.

"Who here from the West Side?" he bellows.

Scattered cheering rings out through the arena, some from voices near us. I smirk. If only Mrs. Zaccari knew about all the

West Siders—people from *her* neighborhood—who are here tonight. Isaiah and I exchange glances, and he rolls his eyes with a smile. I like to think we're thinking the same thing.

"*A'ight, who here from the South Side?*" he hollers.

There's the volume. The whole arena comes alive with roars and screams, including mine and Isaiah's. I remember our house—our *old* house in East Garfield Park. Every inch of it. I remember the creaky wooden stairs with the carpet strip down the middle that Isaiah and I used to race down on our bellies, and how he always won because I didn't have enough baby fat on my belly anymore and that shit hurt my ribs. I close my eyes and remember how it smelled. I remember the taste of the toaster waffles Mom used to make for dinner when she ran out of ideas or was too tired to make anything else. She always apologized for having to make them, but they were my favorite. I remember how the freezer always smelled like banana pudding after Dad spilled a whole bowl of it while snooping around trying to sneak ice cream. I can feel the ground rattling in my chest as the cheering thunders around me.

God *damn* there are a lot of people here.

"Ah, *there* my people go!" hollers DeNola with a deep, earthy chuckle into the mic. He skips across the stage and catapults himself into a forward flip, both feet cracking loudly against the metal of the stage before he leans into the mic and hollers.

"*AAAAAAAAHHHHHH,*" but he finishes that *ahhhh* into a high A, letting his voice trail off into a delicate vibrato that hums through the space like a flock of doves.

Holy shit, I'm adding this guy's whole discography to my phone. I pull out my phone and blink away a vision of me unlocking it, and unlock it.

I have a new text from Aunt Mackie.

MACKAYLA KAPLAN: Where are you?

There's no way I'm answering that. I'll explain everything to her later. I find DeNola in my music app, click download on all four of his albums, and slide my phone back into my pocket. I look down at Isaiah. He's on his tiptoes, craning his neck to see through the gaps under arms and between legs.

"Hey, man," I say, leaning down to him. "When Shiv comes out, I'ma put you on my shoulders, okay?"

He nods without looking at me, still focused on trying to see DeNola better.

The man's voice explodes through the room again, and I jump.

"WHICH ONE O' Y'ALL BEEN FUCKIN' WIT ME?"

What the hell kinda question . . . ?

I look around at everyone. Nobody else seems flustered. The crowd erupts in hollers, and arms fly up in droves. Then he hollers it again, stepping across the stage in long strides, crouched down like a praying mantis.

"I SAID WHICH ONE O' Y'ALL BEEN FUCKIN' WIT ME?"

Half the arena says it with him this time. I grin, realizing those must be the opening lyrics to his next song. He goes corpse still on stage, takes hold of his white snapback, and sliiiides it down his face in one smooth, slow motion. The crowd is loving this, and I wonder what's coming next. The lights fade to black. I can't see a thing, but I've seen enough concert footage to know to shut my eyes and brace for impact. Bass explodes through

232

the place, rattling the floor, the speakers, and my eardrums, and I open my eyes to see light bursting from the stage like someone set off twenty firecrackers around him.

"I AIN'T COME OUT HERE TO FUCK WIT CH'ALL! YOU SAY—"

He extends the mic out to the crowd, which responds perfectly on beat with,

"WE AIN'T COME OUT HERE TO FUCK WIT CHOO!"

Ohhhkay, this guy might tear up some trills, but his lyrics are a little . . . flat. A woman in front of us and to the left turns to the woman next to her. They're dressed alike, so I assume they came together. She yells in her friend's ear, "What's this song called?"

And the friend yells back, her words strung together into a slurred mess, "It's called 'I Ain't Come Out Here to Fuck wit Ch'all!'"

Laughter comes bubbling out of me, and I shake my head. At least the man's direct with the song titles. I look back up to the stage while this man sings the same. Lyric. Fifty. Times. Mental note: delete this song from my downloads later. I cross my arms and look around absentmindedly.

It takes me way too long to realize Isaiah's gone.

I panic. I look everywhere.

"Isaiah?" I call into the mass of bodies jumping up and down and waving arms and hollering up at DeNola, but there's no answer. I begin to weave, keeping my hands close to me as I move, but I forget once or twice and catch a vision of this random guy I apparently touched reeling his head back and yelling, "We ain't come out here to fuck wit choo!" I cancel the vision just in time to reorient myself before I bump chest-first into a woman and accidentally let a finger brush against her arm. I see a vision of her hand reaching up, and her face contorting into a scowl, and it looks like she's about to bring the back of her hand down straight at me. I cancel the vision and duck, narrowly missing the blow.

"What the *fuck*, dude?" she snaps.

"I'm sorry," I say, darting away and vanishing deeper into the crowd. My heart is pounding. My eyes are frantic. Where is he?

So many red sweatshirts. It's like *everyone* in here bought one. Nobody under five feet tall, though. I keep my eyes down as I run into person after person, cancel vision after vision, and issue apology after apology. I think of the worst. My brother being snatched up by some stranger, who hauls him off in his car and does whatever he wants with him. All I saw in my vision was that white casket with the inscription at the bottom of that hole in the ground. My vision never promised Isaiah would go painlessly, or even while he's with me. My cheeks burn and my eyes tingle with tears as I realize the very real possibility that the next time I see my brother, he could be lying dead in a field somewhere, his last moments spent in sheer terror, lost. Alone. Watching a vision of what would've happened if he'd been more careful and stayed by his brother at that concert.

And then I spot his little red hood. Without thinking, like I did that day at the pool, I reach forward and grip his wrist. His sweatshirt sleeves are pulled low over his hands, so I catch a vision of his sweatshirt and cancel it easily.

"Isaiah!" I snap. He looks up at me with huge eyes,

mouth agape.

"I—I—"

"You *what*?" I demand. "Have you lost your damn mind wandering off like that?"

"I was just—"

"Just *what*?"

His eyes are flickering with something, and then he looks just past my face. I look over my shoulder to see a boy about my height, standing with his hands in the pockets of his black leather jacket. His red hair is frizzy and dead, fried straight. I'd know that look anywhere. Talia used to do that to her own hair back in middle school. But this guy looks like he's older than me by a few years. He's smiling at me like I should know him.

"Alex?" he asks. His voice is surprisingly calm, for how harsh his gaze is. Thick black lines have been traced around his eyes, less like eyeliner and more like Sharpie.

"Have we met?" I ask, rising to my feet and stepping in front of Isaiah, who I now realize was looking past me in fear. Something about this guy—the way he looks at me, the way he glances down at Isaiah with that tongue-between-the-teeth smile of his that scrunches up his eyes—scares my brother.

And puts me on high alert.

"Uh," he breathes, the implied *duh* heavy in his voice. "Yeah. Our parents are neighbors."

He's so jittery as he points from his face to mine. His head bobs slightly unnaturally. I hold out my hand beside me so Isaiah knows to stay behind me. He rolls his eyes and blows air through his lips, finding it hilarious that I still don't recognize him.

"Eli?" he offers. "Zaccari?"

I look closer at his face, at his high cheekbones and chin that ends in a sharp V like Mrs. Zaccari's, and his thick red eyebrows like Mr. Zaccari has.

"Eli?" I say.

He nods, and then a laugh spills out of his mouth.

"Yeah," he says. "Long time no see, on Facebook anyway."

He steps closer to me, and my first instinct is to lean back and get away from him, but he's so close now, leaning in and looping his hands around my arm. I can smell the cigarette smoke on him now, and the body spray.

"I just need to tell you something," he says. His hair sweeps against my neck as he leans in close to my head and whispers, "You're not like these other people. *You need to leave. Now.*"

He shoves something crinkly and plasticky into my sweatshirt pocket and whips around so fast I don't have time to answer him before he slips between the rows of screaming people and his red hair vanishes. I'm standing here stunned, trying to process what the hell just happened. Of course, the first thing I do is reach into my pocket to figure out what that thing is, and when I pull it out, I find a small plastic baggie with three tiny discs inside—one blue, one orange, and one neon yellow, pill size. The chalk is wearing away in spots, and the powder coats the inside of the bag. Each of the pills has a tiny smiley face stamped on it.

I see a vision of me turning the baggie over in my hand.

"What is it?" asks Isaiah.

I've heard of so many things being offered at so many different concerts that I recognize them immediately. They're

236

Smartees. E-bombs. Egg Rolls. Scooby Snacks. Dancing Shoes. Ecstasy.

"Nothing," I say. "We need to find a trash can."

Now.

Whatever Eli meant by *you need to leave*, I don't know. Maybe he was too strung out to realize what he was saying, or realize he was handing me some valuable product. Maybe he meant to hand me something else?

Whatever the case, I want this shit off me and as far away from both of us as soon as possible. I've never tried any kind of drugs, not even cigarettes, but if I get caught with this in my pocket, security will treat me like I have, meaning Isaiah and I could get kicked out of this place and arrested, or worse. I fully realize my position as a Black kid with this baggie. If I'm caught, if Isaiah is caught, we could both be dead.

This guy just handed me a live grenade.

And I realize he might not even know it. I realize he was probably trying to get us to leave. For what reason, I don't know. Clearly something's about to go down. Something he doesn't want us here for. My throat closes as I realize this is definitely where it's going to happen. Tonight has to be the night. We'll get that worst-fear experience we've been looking for after all. I try to reach for any shred of hope that I'll get to go home tonight. I remember my vision of looking down at Isaiah's grave, and I wonder if those were *my* shoes in the grass, with me looking down into the hole, or if, like my vision of my car sinking into water one day, I was someone else.

And I remember Shaun.

I remember his face. I remember when I realized there was

237

a real possibility that I'd be with him when he met his end, and I remember running. I remember saving my own ass at the cost of his security, and I remember that the last thoughts to go through his head might have been wondering what he did to lose me. And I *won't* do that to my brother. We're not leaving this place until we've faced enough of our fears to get rid of these visions, whatever's about to happen. Isaiah deserves a chance at a life without being weighed down by the past, however short. After all the shit he's been through in just twelve years, he deserves this joy.

Joy in the face of oppression is its own kind of bravery.

We're staying right here, and I'm going to live the rest of my life knowing I did everything I could to make him understand that he's not alone.

Even if the rest of my life is only a few more minutes.

"Come on, man," I say, guiding him between the cheering, screaming bodies that smell of sweat, fragrances, body odor, and hot breath. Someone with a shrill, screechy voice lets out a sharp *whoooo!* in my left ear, and I can't tell if it's by accident or to intentionally punish me for having to squeeze past them. Don't they see I have a kid with me? Can't they just assume I have to take him to the bathroom and be a bit kinder?

We reach the aisle and walk the whole thirty feet up the ramp, where there's a big black trash can waiting for us. I'm glad it's so dark in here. The stage lights are flashing like lightning, and between the bass line that pulses with the lights, I yank the bag out of my sweatshirt pocket and toss it into the bin.

Crisis averted.

But now we've lost our spot in the crowd, a spot that was

close enough to the stage that we could see the sweat on DeNola's forehead and the individual LED lights in his shoes. I look over my shoulder at the stage. Now we can barely see whether he has dreads or braids. But it's comfortable back here. This is how I'm *used* to seeing concerts. From a distance. From behind my phone screen until now, but this is the next safest thing. Where it's comfortable and easy not to touch people or things, where I can stand next to Talia in peace, where the crowds are sparser and the seats are cheaper, and I can take up as little space as possible.

It's safe back here.

"Are we going back down there?" asks Isaiah.

Guilt sinks in my stomach like a stone. If we're supposed to be here to face our fears, to face *whatever* Eli may have planned tonight, then we have to go back into the crowds. Back into what scares us most. Just as I'm about to answer, DeNola finishes the song and raises his mic into the air, and the lights all shut off.

Perfect chance.

"Go!" I urge Isaiah, grabbing his wrist around his sweat-shirt sleeve, canceling the vision of him darting forward into the crowd in his sweatshirt. "Go, go, go!"

We race through the darkness, barely making out where the seats end and the aisle begins. I follow close behind him, watching his glowing fingertips in the dark. We reach GA again, where everyone's morphed into a single flailing entity made of heads, arms, flashing cameras, cell-phone lights, glow sticks, glow bracelets, and hands with glowing LED finger-tips. Slowly, we reenter the fray, carefully, weaving past bodies again. I layer my apologies.

"Sorry, excuse us, sorry, excuse us, sorry, excuse us."

And finally we get near the front again, just as the stage comes to life. Several strobe lights are on, turned directly to DeNola.

"Y'all my family," he says, breathing heavy into the mic, "and I appreciate you."

He kisses two fingers and raises them to the crowd, and everyone erupts in cheering all over again. I glance down at Isaiah to make sure he's there. His face looks indifferent. He's not looking at the stage. He's looking around.

But then . . .

"Y'all ready for the *king*?"

Hysterics like I've never heard before in my life swell around us. Voices are cracking now in protest of the volume demanded by their owners. I let out a yell myself.

"*Haa!*" I bellow. Isaiah looks up at me and grins.

The Dragon's roar.

"*Haaaaaa!*" he yells, his voice higher than mine, but just as powerful.

Hell yeah, we're ready.

What if a bomb goes off? ask my deepest, darkest thoughts. *What if it's anthrax? What if the stage collapses? How fast a death would each of those be? A bomb would incinerate us in seconds. Anthrax would have us coughing up blood for hours. One of these amps could fall and crush us immediately, or it could leave us gasping for air under rubble for days before we asphyxiate under layers of bodies.*

There are tears in my eyes. I remember Aunt Mackie's words.

240

And you, Alex, have been a stellar example to Isaiah of what it means to be a man. Even when it's scary.

"Even when it's scary," I whisper to myself. I'm definitely scared. I'm fucking terrified. I look around me at all these faces. Any one of these people could be the catalyst. What if the guy behind me happens to be bored with life and decides to stab us in the back? What if we *both* get kidnapped and thrown in the back of a van and driven to some field somewhere?

Breathe, Alex. Remember your anxiety steps.

I take a deep breath.

I hold my breath and count to ten.

I don't have time to count to a hundred.

I can't lie in corpse pose here.

I can't get a glass of water without losing our spot again.

I can't get fresh air. This is an outdoor venue. This is as fresh as the air is getting.

I stare up at the ceiling, which is actually the night sky, starless, full of smoke from the pyrotechnics.

This helps a little.

I can't see them, but I know the stars are up there, somewhere, and even though I don't believe in God, I like to believe Shaun is up there too.

I curl my index fingers and fold my middle fingers, weaving all of them into the letters *S-H-I-V*. I'm not going anywhere this time.

"I'm staying right here," I whisper to him.

The lights go dark. The whole place goes black. I reach down and find Isaiah, pressing my hand against his back to make sure he's there. I brave the vision of the stage exploding

241

in blinding white light, which illuminates his face, his mouth open in anticipation of what's to come, and expanding into a smile as he sees him up there—the king himself. In my vision, Isaiah's sitting with a perfect view of the stage, a few feet higher than anyone else in the crowd so he's looking through flailing arms instead of around torsos. His pupils dilate. His eyes close, and he throws a fist into the air as the recognition of his favorite song settles into him like hot chocolate on a cold winter's day.

Bangin'.

Ballin'.

Bobbin'.

Bouncin'.

Bumpin'.

Black.

Dragon.

I know that face. That gleam in his eyes. That look of longing, wishing, hoping. The look that says *that could be me one day.*

And I know I have to give him a view he won't forget.

I end the vision, reach down, scoop him up under his arms, and hoist him onto my shoulders before he knows what's happened, before anyone else knows what's about to happen. And then it happens.

The stage is so bright, and the voice is so loud, deep and raspy.

"CHICAAAAAGOOOOOOOOOO!"

I catch a glimpse of the king between two people's shoulders. He's facing the back of the stage, mic raised in a fist. He's wearing his classic black tank top with the black harness all over him, and silver chain-mail shoulder pads. He's got black skinny jeans that are ripped at the knees, all the way around. I don't know how he keeps the shin parts of those from slipping down. They must be attached somehow, but the optical illusion is freaking cool. If I were a millionaire, I'd have a pair of those in my closet for every day of the week. He looks like a badass, ripped-out-of-his-mind Michael Jackson, and when he turns around to face us, as if we're all unexpected guests in his house, we *all* respond in kind. I can hear the cheers around me melding into a low, rhythmic "Black Dragon, Black Dragon, Black Dragon, Black Dragon!"

I squeeze my arms tighter around Isaiah's shins and bump him higher on my neck to alleviate some of his weight sitting right on my upper spine. I'm feeling the weight of every single one of those pizza bites he's eaten in the last month. But I'm happy. So happy that my heart is racing. So overwhelmed that my hands are tingling. So mesmerized that I can't take my eyes off the stage.

Shiv walks out to the front, saunters even, super casual. He's close enough that I can see the insignia on the chain around his neck—a silver medallion with the dragon glyph, covered in glittering diamonds. I'm sure it costs more than everything I have to my name. It's perfect. *He's* perfect.

He sinks down low into his knees and launches himself into a six-foot vertical leap, yanking his knees up to his chest at the highest point. When his feet come back down and connect with the ground, the stage erupts in fireworks, and the screen behind him flashes to white. Two black silhouettes now block the screen, maybe thirty feet high. One, a skinny

243

man with his hands tucked inside a baggy sweatshirt with a hugely oversize cobra hood, stands casually on the left. The other, a mammoth man with a round bald head and huge hands—one hanging at his side, and the other holding the neck of a guitar—stands to the right of Shiv. *There they are.* Cobra Katjee, Leviathan, and Shiv, the Black Dragon himself. I can't believe this is real.

Wherever Talia is in this arena, probably somewhere in GA like us, I hope she's loving this as much as I am.

However she feels about me.

Shiv raises his hand to the screen, which flies up, revealing Cobra and Leviathan, who bound down the backstage stairs to the front of the stage. Leviathan leaps off the last step and lands next to Shiv with a thud that shakes the whole place. Katjee darts forward, sinking to his knees and sliding all the way to the front, so close I can see the silver insignia on his red bandanna. He's looking straight out at the crowd, but if he looked down *right now*, he could see us.

The whole arena is glittering with flashing cell phone lights and glowy finger gloves.

And then I remember.

~~Lying in bed~~

~~The morning in the graveyard.~~

~~The evening I spent sitting in my chair.~~

~~The whole next day in darkness.~~

~~The evening lights flickering through my jacket pocket.~~

This concert must be the lights, flickering through my jacket pocket right now. It *has* to be. That just leaves . . .

More darkness. The morning in the graveyard.

Isaiah rests his hands on my forehead for support, and I wonder if his abs are getting tired from sitting upright like this on my shoulders. I bump him up again as the three gods on stage launch into the song I already know is coming—the song everyone in this place probably knows by heart.

> *"Bangin', ballin', bobbin', bouncin', bumpin'*
> *Black Dragon.*
> *Got them bottles poppin', yeah we hoppin' in*
> *the station wagon."*

God, they're wicked live. Isaiah is bouncing himself up and down on my neck now, his thighs so heavy on my shoulders I'm afraid I might break my collarbone. But I adjust one of his legs, and I keep going. I can't put him down, not when we're in the middle of the first Shiv song we rapped together.

> *"Bitch, yo' Lam ain't paid off, made of money?*
> *More like made o' debt. Bet.*
> *Call me when yo' credit score is set like*
> *Aquanet. Yeh."*

What other rapper out there finds a way to make money management sound hella tight? I read in *Rolling Stone* once that he owns exactly two cars—a 2014 Tesla and a white Range Rover SUV, which were a combined $150,000. When other rappers are out here driving half-million-dollar Lambos and multimillion-dollar Bugattis, dropping a hundred Gs on a single piece of jewelry, modest is a tragic understatement.

> *"Let my crew find out you slingin', bringin'*
> *Crissy to my shows, bruh.*
> *Shit turn you a zombie, leave yo body for the*
> *crows, bruh."*

At this lyric, Leviathan drops his huge ass into the Harlem Shake—the *real* one. He's from Harlem, actually. Born Leon Hamilton, he had his own stint with crystal meth that landed him in prison for twelve years, and he's been clean for as long as he's been a Dragon. My chest swells. This is more than just a Harlem Shake for him. This—what he's doing right now, with his mouth open wide as he swings his arms and shoulders wildly—is a victory dance.

I wonder if Mrs. Zaccari even knows what Crissy is. If she knew Shiv was out here, damning everyone who brings crystal meth to his concerts, she might feel differently about him. She might even relax her paranoia about these people around me—several of whom are actually white people in their twenties—staying in our neighborhood.

> *"Niggas think they'll catch me slippin', sippin'*
> *on this juice, mayne.*
> *Cobra got my keys cuz had enough to get me*
> *loose, mayne."*

Cobra Katjee, the short, spry guy who I'm pretty sure has never said a word out loud, slinks up behind Shiv and swipes a literal pair of keys out of his back pocket, holding them up to the audience and jingling them, before tossing them out into the crowd, sending them flying over Isaiah's head and mine. Laughter overwhelms me, and I wonder how many of these people think those are his real keys. There might very well be a bloodbath behind us over some plastic silver baby teething keys. That jingling sound effect was just part of the song.

Shiv steps forward, crouching down at the edge of the stage and looking down into the sea of arms with glowing finger gloves and faces lit up by the stage lights. He reaches an arm down into the crowd and a rainbow of arms rises to meet him, like anemone tentacles. They're so wild I'm surprised they don't yank him down into the audience. I'm sure security is losing their shit at how intimate he's being with them. That's Shiv—big. Real. Authentic.

Calmly, as if he's sitting in a library somewhere, and not standing onstage with hundreds of thousands of eyes on him, he slips something out of his pocket and into his mouth, his chest slowly expanding as the crowd erupts in even more furious screams. He stands. He clasps his fists. He breathes out through his nose.

Smoke plumes from his nostrils, cascading a strawberry scent down over the crowd. We're close enough to smell it.

The Black Dragon has arrived.

"Y'all ready for a twist?" he asks, as the beat goes on. A twist? Like what? New music? Lava rising from the floor? New collab? Wait . . . is he going to bring his grandmother out onstage? Shiv's grandma has been rapping since the eighties. The Rappin' Granny, they call her. An absolute legend. I know that whatever Shiv's got planned, it's going to be big. I look around the stage, waiting for a plume of flames, or synthetic

247

hail, or fireworks. But Cobra is beckoning to the crowd with his hands, his unnaturally long tongue hanging out of his mouth, walking forward like he sat on a horse for a tad too long. Leviathan has his Shaq-size hand raised into the air.

"Y'all been asking me to bring her on tour wit me, and she hella busy and all that. *But*, just for tonight, are y'all ready for the sovereign of strings? The oracle of orchestra? The high priestess of hair ties? Y'all know who I'm talmbout!" The whole arena erupts in screams and shrieks of delight, although I'm not sure I even know who it is. Oracle of orchestra? Who the hell?

Suddenly Shiv, front and center, runs straight backward into the darkness and smoke, which comes rushing off the front of the stage like a waterfall of clouds.

A new sound comes ringing through the speakers. A familiar *whee-ooh-whee-ooh*, and then silence. My heart pounds as I recognize it, and I feel Isaiah's whole body tense and his glowing gloved hands pat the front of my forehead.

"Alex!" he cries. "It's *The Rush*!"

I smile, wondering how many of these people are going to know this song as well as we do. It's so old. It's so underground. This album isn't on Spotify. It's not on iTunes. It's not on YouTube. If you don't have the original CD, or the vinyl, or an illegal download from 2006, good luck. I squeeze Isaiah's ankles as if we're about to go to battle, as if this is a competition. *Whee-ooh-whee-ooh* comes the sound again. But it's different this time. It's not a synth anymore. I know this instrument. Strings. It sounds like strings.

Violin?

A *pat-pat-pat-pat-pat* roars to life all around us, the sound of helicopter blades. Light pours out of the sky. Gasps ring out around me, and we all look up. Wispy blue fabric flaps in the wind like a jellyfish overhead, and I squint against the blinding light until I can make it out. I see pencil-thin legs, and slender arms, one holding a large, shiny violin the color of Aunt Mackie's dining room table. A huge black bun sits at the crown of her head. Cobra, Leviathan, and Shiv all stand in a line at the front of the stage with an arm extended out toward the girl, and she turns, takes hold of Shiv's hand, and leaps off the helicopter ladder onto the stage. When she turns to face us all, her cheeks are glowing rosy pink, and her eyes are a deep brown. Her lips are a faint pink, and her skin is ghostly. Jaws drop, including mine. Her blue dress is like a cloud around her, fading into the smoke that's still pouring off the stage. She looks like an angel.

I tap the back of my hand against Isaiah's thigh, and he leans his face down so he can hear me better.

"That's Nyein Chen!" I yell to him. He nods, and I hope that means he remembers the name.

Nyein Chen, the twenty-year-old award-winning concert violinist whose concerts are supposed to have "a much different clientele" than, say, a Shiv Skeptic concert. The girl whose music is supposed to be for people who are "less likely to get drunk and high than people who attend a Shiv Skeptic concert."

Looks like America's perfect classically trained princess is an honorary Dragon.

Whee-ooh-whee-ooh goes her violin siren, which sounds *just* like a cop car.

The crowd loses their minds over that one, as many connect for the first time that the violin made that sound, not a computer. Nyein's mouth curves into a grin as she looks out at the arena, and she freezes just like that, with her violin pressed against her neck, and her other arm raised in front of her face with her slender fingers on the bow. She walks slowly, fluidly, to the side of the stage where Cobra is standing. She steps in front of him and guides the bow into another *whee-ooh-whee-ooh*. And then she runs to the other side of the stage, like a delicate blue feather, and releases another *whee-ooh-whee-ooh* into the arena.

I would *pay* to see Mrs. Zaccari's reaction to this.

Nyein reaches up, rips a hair clip out of her bun, lets all her long black hair down her back, secures the clip to the top of the violin neck, and rips that bow across the whole instrument like a mad scientist into four sharp, squealy *whoop-whoop-whoop-whoop*s before Shiv launches into the first lyrics of *The Rush*. The song "Black Gold."

> *"I was born in '87 to a cheater and a liar,*
> *Mothafuckin' Uncle Sam and his greedy Golden*
> *Eye."*

I grin at the video game reference. Both of Isaiah's hands come away from my forehead as he raps along, swinging his arms along with Shiv. Nyein is still tearing up that violin. At her own concerts, she's careful to keep a neutral face. Not a smile. Not a determined stare. Just a flat-mouthed, open-eyed, relaxed gaze. But now, she's almost unrecognizable. She's gritting her teeth as she plays, commanding sound from the strings. She brings that *whoop-whoop-whoop-whoop* of cop sirens front and center, and I wonder how many people here are hearing "Black Gold" for the first time, and how many understand the lyrics. Shiv doesn't do anything by accident. *The Rush* has six references to a concept called the "black gold rush," the spark of mass incarceration in the nineties, before I was born. I learned things from that album that they won't teach us in school—about Uncle Sam's greedy Golden Eye, and how people make billions of dollars incarcerating the poor, people on the South Side, like me. Like Isaiah. They saw money to be made off locking up Black people, and Reagan, Bush, and Clinton were happy to oblige with legislation.

Greedy-ass, triflin'—

Before I can finish my thought, I notice Cobra looking down at us. Not just at the sea of people in GA. His dark eyes are huge, trained directly on me.

On Isaiah.

Like Jesus reaching out to Peter on the boat, Cobra reaches out his hand, covered in his signature silver rings and black snake tattoos wrapped all around his fingers and wrists, to us. He ignores the screaming fans in the front, arms reaching up to grab him, and beckons in our direction. People around us start looking up at Isaiah.

"Go on, little dude, he wants you up there!" yells a man behind us.

Wait, what?

I panic. How is this happening? Cobra wants Isaiah onstage? Like, for real? I pat Isaiah's leg and yell to him, "Do you want to go up—?"

"No!" he screams, before I can finish my sentence. But

251

there's hesitation in his voice, and I don't know why. Isn't this what he's wanted for years?

"Why not?" I ask.

"What if they laugh at me?" he whispers shakily, tightening his arms around my head. "What if . . . I . . . I can't, Alex. I'm . . . scared."

"Is this what scares you most?" I ask, the pieces connecting in my head.

Maybe this is *his* cure.

"Y-yeah," he says. I don't blame him.

"You don't have to," I say. "But what if it's . . . you know . . . the *answer*."

Cobra is still reaching out to him. People in front of us start glancing over their shoulders and making way for us. Suddenly, because we have the attention of Cobra Katjee, we're kids again to them. I feel hands on my arms and my back, guiding us forward. Everyone's screaming. Shiv is on the other side of the stage, rapping the next line, my favorite.

> *"12.5 percent of the US population makes up 62 percent of US incarcerations."*

It's true.

And with stats like that, one has to believe either that Black people are more prone to crime, or we're being targeted unfairly.

We reach the front of the stage, and Isaiah's whole body has tensed. Cobra looks so much older than twenty-seven up close. There are creases at the sides of his eyes and lines in his forehead. If I met him at a cookout, I'd default to "Uncle Katjee" before "Cousin Katjee." But his eyes are kind, and his smile is warm and sure. He looks me dead in the eyes and says, "We'll take care of him."

We'll take care of him.

I realize the full weight of what that means. Isaiah and I came here looking for a near-death experience, and once I let Isaiah go up there onstage, he'll be so far away from me. At least a dozen feet. I won't be able to protect him.

I'll be helpless again.

Unless.

My heart starts to race as I realize what I have to do. I think back to our grandparents. To Buddy Lyons. To Ursa and Kando and Takaa, and I remember the thing that connected us all—*fear*. Deep, paralyzing fear that runs all the way through every man in every generation of our family. And I think of my dad's hands gripping the steering wheel as he drove headlong into what he thought was the cure. It was brave, what he did. But it wasn't what scared him most.

And as I stand here looking up at Cobra Katjee's out-stretched hand, I realize I'm doing the same thing.

Being at this concert with Mrs. Gomez's money makes me feel uneasy.

Letting go of Isaiah makes me feel helpless.

But there's only one thing that absolutely terrifies me right now.

I take a deep breath, plant my feet firmly on the ground beneath me, and prepare to do what I should've done when I first saw the vision of him lying at the bottom of that hole in the ground. What I should've done in the graveyard yesterday when we decided to go looking for trouble in the hope of kicking this curse. I look at Isaiah's leg, hanging over my right shoulder, and I wrap my fingers gently around his ankle. And *this* time, I don't let go.

The vision begins, sending my heart rate into the stratosphere.

I'm sucked into a whirlwind of light. Isaiah is standing on the stage between Cobra and Leviathan, with Shiv crouching a bit to talk to him. Isaiah is looking Shiv Skeptic right in the eyes, only feet away from him, and I know I have to let him go. This is what we came for. *This* has made it all worth it— sneaking out, taking the money back from Maria, even my fight with Talia.

It's time Isaiah and I did what's best for *us*. I watch the joy on Isaiah's face, his mouth open in a huge smile. But it sinks. His eyes go wide.

Everything goes red.

Isaiah kicks his leg away from my hand, snapping me back to the present. His hands are on my forehead, and I can hear him whisper, "Alex . . . I'm scared."

"It's okay," I whisper up to him. There are tears welling in my eyes as I step forward. "It's okay to be scared, Isaiah."

"I . . . can't do it by myself."

"You're not by yourself," I say, knowing it's about to happen. "I'm here. I'm right here."

I close my eyes and think of Shaun.

"I'm right here, okay? I promise. I'm not going anywhere."

There's a long pause where Isaiah goes quiet, and then I

feel something that surprises me beyond anything I could've expected out of today. I feel a tiny, soft kiss on my forehead, right at my hairline.

"I'm right here too, okay?" he says.

I nod and kiss his knee, since it's right next to me.

"We've got each other. No matter what."

"No matter what," he says.

"Okay," I say, stepping forward. He extends his arms out to Katjee, who's still patiently reaching for him. "Ready?"

Katjee's smile grows wider as he says again, "We'll take care of him."

I believe him. I have to. And before I let Isaiah go, I yell up to him, "Knock 'em dead, Izzy!"

Cobra locks his arms around Isaiah's and pulls him up onstage like his hundred-pound body is nothing. A literal weight is off my shoulders. He looks so small up there, a tiny copy of Cobra wearing a red version of his sweatshirt. The whole place erupts in cheers, those glittering cell-phone flashes lighting up the arena for him. If I wanted to make this the night of his life, I've done it. I hope that wherever Talia is in the audience, she sees Isaiah now, living his dream of being Izzy Rufus on stage before a crowd of hundreds of thousands. And I hope, after it happens—whatever *it* is—that she understands why this was so important.

I slip my hands into my jacket pockets and brace for the vision of my jacket, but . . .

Nothing.

Nothing happens.

"What?" I ask out loud. Holy shit, wait, is it gone? Can . . .

can it really be . . . gone? Just like that? I pat my chest, expecting a vision of my jacket. Nothing. I touch my jeans. Nothing. I kick my leg up and touch my shoe. Nothing.

Nothing.

Just here. Just now. Just this place, and the lights, and the music, and Isaiah walking to the middle of the stage with Cobra Katjee on his arm. He squints against all the lights, raising an arm to shield his eyes. And then he finds me, and I stare up at him, hope flaring in my body like a fever. And I hope, or pray, with every fiber of me that Isaiah's power is gone too. I raise my eyebrows at him to ask.

Well?

He stares at me for a moment—in disbelief—his mouth hanging slightly open, eyes wide. And then his lips curve into a smile, and he nods and steps in place like a giddy six-year-old on Christmas morning.

Yes!

We've done it!

I've never cried from joy, or relief, or the slurry of emotions I'm feeling right now, but my vision is blurry, and I choke back a sob that gets drowned out by the hollering around me.

We've got each other. No matter what.

I nod up at Isaiah proudly in return and hope that maybe whatever thing Eli was trying to warn us about will just . . . not happen. That maybe since we're rid of this curse, the orishas will skip out on the danger part of tonight. That maybe we'll both get to go home, and maybe my vision about Isaiah will be wrong.

Shiv turns from his spot on the other side of the stage and

256

holds up his arm. The music shuts off as if someone zipped it up into a soundproof bag. I'm so close, I can hear his shoes as he crosses the stage. He towers over Isaiah, who takes a step back from him, probably overwhelmed at the sight of him.

Shiv is a *huge* dude.

But he bends in front of Isaiah, drapes a big sweaty arm around his shoulders, and asks in the kindest voice, "What's your name, li'l red?"

He hands Isaiah the mic.

"Isaiah," he says sheepishly. His voice is shaking, and my heart is pounding. *Come on, Izzy, make it count.* He's probably so scared up there.

"Isaiah, everyone!" hollers Shiv to the whole place. More screams and cheering. A voice rings out in my ear next to me.

"Nigga, that's your brother?" it asks. The voice belongs to a slender Black woman standing to my left, who's my height, with hoop earrings the size of my hands and eyelashes as long as my pinky finger. I nod at her.

"He's lucky," she says.

"He's *adorable!*" cries an overly spray-tanned lady to my left, who has her arm on my shoulder.

"Thanks," I say.

What the hell else do I say? I look up at my little brother, at the boy hundreds of thousands of people are watching in adoration, who just a few minutes beforehand was being hissed at because we needed to get back to our spots just a few feet behind where I am right now. *Now* they love him.

I still can't believe I'm really watching Shiv talking to my brother, and then I remember I should probably be getting

257

this on video. I pull out my phone, vision-free, and unlock it. Another series of texts from Aunt Mackie.

MACKAYLA KAPLAN: Alex Matthew, I need to know where you and Isaiah are right now. You know to be home by the time the streetlights come on.

MACKAYLA KAPLAN: Talia's not answering her phone either. Are you all together? Are you okay? Please text me back.

MACKAYLA KAPLAN: Alex, call me back right now or I'm filing a missing persons report.

What the fuck?

That'll get the cops involved. They'll send out Amber Alerts and whatever else, and the cops, plus Isaiah and me, tonight especially, could spell disaster. I've seen too much shit on the news. Too many hashtags. I already know how that story often ends, and of all the ways for Isaiah to go out, I refuse to let it be that.

I text her back.

Me: We're fine, Aunt Mackie. I'll explain everything when we get home. Promise.

I hurry and send it and open my camera. I hit record just as Shiv turns back to Isaiah and says, "You know *The Rush*?" he asks.

Isaiah nods.

"S'far as I'm concerned, that makes you a Dragon, Isaiah."

The whole arena roars to life again. Holy shit, this is beyond what I could've dreamed up for him. Just *going* to this concert was enough. Hearing songs from *The Rush* live was enough. Getting Isaiah on stage was *more* than enough. Getting rid of these visions was *beyond* more than enough. Getting him

258

initiated as an honorary Dragon? One of the greats?? *Hell. To. The. Yeah.*

"Now, I'll ask you again, li'l Dragon," says Shiv, leaning over before him again. "What's your name?"

Isaiah's eyes flicker as he looks out at all the eyes staring back at him, and he takes the mic in his hand and says with newfound fire in him, "Whaddup, y'all. Izzy Red is in the house! The Red Dragon! *Haaaaa!*"

His *haaaaa* comes out like a baby lion cub on stage with three kings of the jungle and a mighty queen. Nyein has been standing calmly on the other side of the stage, and she claps along with the rest of this place, watching Isaiah like a proud big sister, even though she's just met him. Her eyes are warm, and she nods her approval at the name.

"That's dope, li'l man," says Shiv. "A'ight, Izzy Red, the Red Dragon, as an honorary Dragon, you'll need some official gear." He nods Cobra Katjee and Leviathan over. Leviathan unclamps his silver wrist shackles, which he wears to remind him where he came from, and leans down in front of Isaiah, smiling at him as he holds them out. Isaiah rolls up his huge red sleeves to reveal his chicken-wing arms, accepting the cuffs with the biggest smile before throwing his arms around Leviathan's enormous neck. I laugh and smile along with everyone else in this place, intermixed with a collective *awwwww* that fades into applause. Leviathan stands and picks up little Isaiah like he's nothing, twirling around with him before setting him back down on the stage floor. Isaiah wipes off the side of his face all casual, but I laugh, realizing Leviathan must be sweaty as hell up there.

Cobra comes forward next, ceremoniously sliding both his

hands under his enormous cobra hood and pulling it back, revealing his short black hair, untying his bandanna from around his head, and offering them out to Isaiah. Cobra ties it securely around Isaiah's forehead, that silver dragon glyph glittering proudly between his eyes. His grin is *huge*, and so is mine.

My eyes start tearing up again at the realization that Isaiah gets to experience all of this vision-free. My God, I'm glad we came.

"Go, little bro," I say.

"You play video games, Red Dragon?" booms Leviathan.

Isaiah nods.

Cobra slides a mic out of his sweatshirt pocket and holds it out to Isaiah. He takes it in both his hands as carefully as if it's the Holy Grail.

"You wanna start us off with 'The Game'?"

"Hell yeah," he says.

Scattered laughter ripples through the arena, including mine. He's such a clown sometimes.

Isaiah lifts the mic to his mouth and lets out the biggest, deepest *Haaaaaaaaa!* he can manage. His free hand is in the air as the lights shut off and the stage sizzles to life again. And then the bass drops. The crowd around me starts jumping, the energy around me pulsating as arms and heads start bobbing to the music. Shiv launches into the first lyrics, but I can tell he's holding back so he doesn't overshadow Isaiah's voice.

"Goin' down to the corner store armed with my hatchet, machete, grenade, and my gun."

They rap it together—the lyrics Isaiah and I sang in the car on the way to see Mom and Dad. I remember looking over at him as he rapped the next part back to me with pride like I'd never seen from him, and now I scream the words along with both of them.

"Just to have company, someone to talk to, but I make it look like I play this for fun. That's the game."

The beat drops out, and Nyein's violin sings to life in a low G. This song, "The Game," was the first one I heard by Shiv. It's also off *The Rush*. Someone like Mrs. Zaccari, who seems to miss the forest for the trees when it comes to song lyrics, might zero in on the hatchet, the machete, the grenade, and the gun. But this song is a reference to video games as an out-let for a desperate need for social interaction. Shiv says they taught him to play the game of life, and although I've never really been a hardcore gamer, I can respect the lyrics. Isaiah sings my favorite part so sweetly it makes me want to cry.

"So many lives to live. So many ways to die. So many ways to play. So many ways to say goodbyyyyye."

That *goodbyyyye* has a trill in it, and Isaiah does his best to make his voice do what Cobra's does in the song, dancing along each note in the chord. Nyein's violin sings behind him so he's not up there alone. She steps closer to him until she's right next to him. He looks up at her as he sings it again.

"So many lives to live. So many ways to die. So many ways to play. So many ways to say goodbyyyye."

Everyone in this auditorium is pouring their voices into the air, and somehow, they're all impressively on-key. I can *feel* the force of it in my stomach, the hum of all few-hundred-thousand of us singing as one, with my brother onstage leading us all. That

261

silver medallion in the center of his forehead catches the light just right as he launches into the next repeat of the bridge.

"So many lives to live."

His free hand is still in the air. I can see his fingers trembling.

"So many ways to die."

His hand closes into a fist above his head.

"So many ways to play."

He shuts his eyes, and I think I catch a glimpse of reflectiveness on his face. At first I think it's sweat.

"So many ways to say . . ."

He looks right at me and opens his hands to the sky again as he sings, straight to me,

"Goodbyyyyye."

My chest is pounding. I feel a single raindrop on my forehead. Rain. Shaun saying *hello*. *Well done*, maybe. I think of the photo in my pocket and wonder when I'll take it out, the last thing that has to happen before . . . before . . . and my chest tightens. The hum of the audience fades into a hazy ringing in my ears. And then, *pop-pop-pop-pop!* The stage pyrotechnics don't match the sound, and I wonder if something's malfunctioned.

It takes a few seconds for me to crawl back into the recesses of my deepest memories from four years ago, from our house on the South Side, 1121 Alabaster Road, Chicago, with the cracked sidewalks and the black iron on the windows and the cars that drove through neighborhoods like ours and picked houses at random for initiation drives. But I remember. I know that popping sound. It's not fireworks. It's not stage pyrotechnics.

It's gunshots.

12

The Rain

TWO THINGS GO THROUGH your head when you find yourself in the middle of a sudden public disaster, natural or unnatural. First: *Is this really happening?* It's like you're watching a movie of yourself watching everything going on around you—the sounds don't sound real. The screams don't sound real. You think you're imagining things. The denial is paralyzing. You stand still as you try to process whether you're actually here or if you're dreaming, and how you can force yourself to wake up. Second: *Where is it coming from?* Once I'm out of the denial stage, and my eyes lock onto the faces around me, the flailing hands, people grabbing hold of other people—people they love—and yanking them to the ground, purses flying, hair flying, I frantically look for the source of the barrage. Where are the bullets coming from? Where's the shooter? I look up and around at the millions of vantage points all around us. Every chair in here is a candidate, along with all the buildings towering around us.

It's an outdoor venue, after all.

And for me, there's a third thing—wondering how the hell to get Isaiah up out of here. I look up at Isaiah standing on the stage in his red sweatshirt, mic still in hand, backing away from the edge, his eyes darting around the stadium in search of what he needs to run from. But Shiv knows this sound. Cobra knows this sound. Leviathan knows this sound. Shiv grabs Isaiah's wrist, Cobra grabs Nyein's, and they all sprint into the shadows at the back of the stage and up the stairs. Isaiah's red sweatshirt fades into the blackness, and that fight impulse in me bubbles up.

That third thing swells all my adrenaline into my legs, and I sprint forward, leap up onto the front of the stage, and hurl myself across the set to the stairs in the back. A booming voice from behind me hollers, "Hey, you can't be up here!" I don't have time to deal with security. I have to find Isaiah. What if he runs too fast back here and runs straight into a pole or trips on a loose wire, or falls down the other side of the stairs? His clock is ticking, and I can't see him. I can't live with that setup.

A huge silhouette is ready to meet me in front of the stairs, and I try to dodge him, but he clamps his huge muscly arms around my chest, clamping my arms to my sides. I kick furiously and scream, but one of my hands finds his shirt, and as I turn, I get a good look at his face, just before he yanks me to the ground, his hand pressing into my back with both my arms pinned behind me. I feel the cold of the dusty metal floor slam against my face. A strange warm buzzing hums through my head and into my neck, and for a second, I wonder if I've shattered my skull.

The screaming that's now ringing out through the auditorium fizzles into several high-pitched wails, and I realize it's the emergency alarms. I have to get out of here.

"That's my brother!" I holler with all the breath in my lungs.

"Let me go! Isaiah is my brother!"

Tears prick my eyes, and I squirm, but he pulls both my arms behind my back and yanks them up into my shoulder blades.

"Fuck!" I yell. The stinging pain that's shooting through my elbows and shoulders is indescribable. I squint and try not to scream again. "Stop!" I whimper. "Please! I have to find Isaiah! Where's Isaiah?!"

Pop-pop-pop-pop-pop!

I suck in a breath at the sound. Where's the shooter? If they're somewhere in the nosebleeds, I'm a sitting duck up here on the stage. It's just me and the security guard. I peel my eyes open in search of flashing yellow lights in the arena. It's huge from up here, and I realize why Isaiah was so scared to speak at first. From where I'm lying, it looks like there are millions of seats here, now millions of people clambering over each other like ants escaping a sinking log.

Pop-pop-pop-pop-pop!

Something wet speckles my face and neck.

I feel the grip around my wrists relax.

The floor explodes in a thunderous *boom!* and I look behind me.

There's the security guard, sprawled on his back, blue eyes wide open, transfixed on nothing.

A hole the size of a dime sits just above his left eyebrow.

I don't recognize the shriek that comes from my own mouth. I turn and take off sprinting into the darkness backstage, dodging hanging cables, pushing curtains out of the way, jumping over boxes, and ducking under clothes racks.

"Isaiah?" I yell. My voice is shattered into a million pieces, and I hurry to wipe away the tears clouding my vision. My already red sweatshirt sleeve comes away wet and even redder with the blood of that innocent man I just watched die. "Fuck," I whimper again. "Isaiah!"

Come on, where are you?

A woman in a short black dress flies past me from behind, and at first I wonder how she can run right past a kid at a time like this, without asking if I'm lost, or if I need help, or if I'm safe. But then—thank God—my logic kicks in. I take off after her.

"Isaiah!" I call again. No answer. Somebody screams from deeper backstage, *"Oh my God oh my God oh my God!"* And it sets off all my panic receptors. My stomach is doing somersaults, and I suddenly feel like throwing up. That security guard back there, the one with the hole in his head, was a target. *I* was a target. Death struck just a few feet above me, as I lay there helplessly on my stomach, and in another timeline, I would've been a few seconds late to jump on the stage, a few seconds late falling to the ground. I suddenly regret ever being jealous of Isaiah's power. I don't want to be able to look back on this night in twenty years and wonder what *might've* happened.

"Isaiah!" I yell, my voice skyrocketing into the upper register and echoing through the place. "Goddamn it." I can't help it. My eyes are still cloudy. I can't wipe away the tears fast enough. I brace for the worst. I just know I'm going to pull back one of these curtains or turn one of these corners and find my little brother lying dead on the floor with a bullet in his head, just like that security guard, with his eyes open and wild and scared, probably looking for me just minutes earlier.

And then I hear the best sound I could pray for.

"Alex!"

His arms are clamped around my torso before I have a chance to look for him, and I reach down and pull him into the tightest hug I've ever given. I want to keep him here for the rest of the night and let him cry against my chest like he is now. I want to tell him everything's going to be fine and it's all over now.

But it's not over.

Pop-pop-pop-pop-pop!

"Come on, man, we gotta move!" I urge him. His arms come away reluctantly and he looks at me with his tearstained face and whimpers, "What's happening?"

"There's someone here with a gun, and we're leaving," I explain, grabbing his wrist, which I realize too late isn't covered by his sweatshirt, and then I remember—no visions. Isaiah takes off suddenly, deeper backstage, and I run after.

"Isaiah, wait!"

"Where do we go?" he screams, refusing to slow down.

I spy a green exit sign above a door at the end of the dim hallway to our left and throw my shoulder against the crash bar across the middle. It's a pitch-dark stairwell, and I guide Isaiah in and down the stairs, to a big red sign above a door with red-and-white-striped caution tape marked EMERGENCY EXIT. My hands find the door, vision-free, and Isaiah and I step out into the empty alley and are peppered with rain.

"We're not safe yet," I say. He looks up at me with wide, scared eyes. "Follow me. We're going home."

We throw our hoods up and run. We sprint through the alley and turn the corner down Armistice Avenue, the yellowish-white glow of the streetlights the only light to guide us. My shoes slide just a bit on the freshly slicked sidewalk as we turn the corner, and I warn Isaiah to be careful not to trip. He's wearing Vans just like I am. The rain is falling in sheets around us and running down into my eyes. The screams and sirens from the Wall shrink quieter and quieter behind us as we escape the chaos and fly past Mikkelson's Bokhandel, but something catches my eye. There's a face in the window, on a poster. A face I haven't seen before with piercing eyes boring into my soul in black and white. Electric candle flames flicker from below the poster on the wall just inside the bookstore, lighting up the paper to just under his chin. The boy can't be much older than me, and the candles beneath indicate he's probably . . . gone . . .

And then I wonder.

Am I staring into the eyes of the man—the boy—who was killed at the Davidsons' house? Is this . . . him? He looks so . . . young. I mean, I knew he *was* young, but I didn't expect his eyes to look so bright and full of hope. And promise.

"Alex, come on!" I hear Isaiah holler from further ahead. I glance in his direction through the rain and then look back at the boy. It feels so strange just leaving his poster here. I wish it wasn't the middle of the night so I could leave a candle or something. I know in another world where Isaiah had been in his shoes, it could've been him.

I nod out of respect in his direction, wishing I could do more, and then run past the coffee shop that Talia swears has the best hot chocolate.

A memory appears in my head as vividly as one of my visions. I'm sitting at our four-person kitchen table, coloring a drawing with crayon, poorly. There's color all outside the lines and in the most unnatural of spots. It's a torn-out coloring-book page of a cartoon hot-air balloon, but it might as well have been a blank page to me. I had drawn a picture of the four of us—Mom standing there holding her favorite mug full of coffee, Dad with his arm around her, Isaiah poking a bug with a stick off on one side of the drawing, and me swinging myself high into the air on the tire swing we had in our backyard, at our house in East Garfield Park. There are blue lines where raindrops went, all over the top half of the page. Dad looks down at my art from where he sits across the table from me, and I hope he likes it. But instead of giving a verdict, he gives me a factoid.

"Did you know," he says, scooping another teaspoon of sugar into his healthy adult cereal, "they say if you run in the rain, you actually end up wetter than if you'd walked?"

This catches Isaiah's attention. He looks up from his coloring page in outrage.

"Nah-uh," he protests, in his squeaky eight-year-old voice.

"Yah-huh," says Dad playfully before spooning cereal into his mouth. His mustache swishes as he chews, and he hurries to swallow so he can explain further. "Saw it on TV once."

Isaiah rolls his eyes.

"Not everything you see on TV is true, Dad."

I smile, because it's weird hearing that from Isaiah to Dad instead of vice versa.

"We'll just have to test it out then," says Dad, scooping

another spoonful of cereal into his mouth.

We never got the chance to do that experiment. As I run through the rain with Isaiah, I wonder if he remembers that day. I wonder if he's asking himself whether we'd get less wet out here in the rain if we walk than if we run. The way I see it, with how hard this rain is coming down, we'll be dripping wet by the time we get home no matter what we do. Some things are avoidable. Some things aren't. And yet, here we are, sprinting anyway.

"Alex!" cries Isaiah. My name explodes out of him as if he's completely out of breath, and he stops suddenly and doubles over, hands on knees, face turned to the ground. He's breathing so hard he's starting to wheeze, and I stop and turn to him.

"You okay?" I ask, realizing my lungs are burning too. The adrenaline only carried us so far, and now my hands are tingling. My body is crying out for rest. But he doesn't look hurt—no blood soaking through his clothes anywhere. A car flies past us, the wheels licking up rainwater from the ground as it goes. The headlights disappear once it's past us, and we're left alone in the dark again. The silver insignia in the center of Isaiah's red Cobra Katjee bandanna catches the light of a nearby streetlamp as he looks up at me, and I have to smile.

"Did it . . . work for you, too?" I ask.

A smile curves at the corner of his mouth, and he nods and straightens, brushing his hands off on each other.

"No visions," he says, "No worrying. No noise. All I can hear now is . . . the rain." He looks up at the sky and blinks away the drops as they pepper his face. "It's so quiet out here." And then he wipes his eyes with his soaking sleeve and smiles at me.

"Did you have fun up there?" I ask.

He nods, raising his hands to either side of his forehead and shutting his eyes against the rain as if he's soaking up a warm shower. "It was . . . everything I dreamed it would be. Thanks, Alex."

I smile.

I've always known I'd never get a do-over after what I did to Shaun. I'll always have to live with that guilt. But at least I can say I've learned. At least I can hold on to Isaiah's face, right now, at the joy in his eyes. His silver wrist cuffs are so oversize they've slid down his slender arms to his elbows, and the dragon glyph on Cobra's bandanna takes up his entire forehead.

But he's happy.

He has joy, for once.

For once, he's not afraid.

He has me.

Impulsively, since I feel the urge, I reach out and pull him close, squeezing him in a freezing-cold, soaking-wet hug. I don't even care that we're getting drenched by the rain. All I care about is that he's squeezing me back, his little arms around my shoulders. I rock back and forth gently.

"We did it, man," I say.

"Yeah," he whispers, and then, after a long, deep breath, he says, "I love you, Alex."

I kiss the top of his head and squeeze him tighter, that feeling like I could fly seeping back into me. I don't want to let him go.

"I love you too, Isaiah," I whisper.

Joy in the face of oppression is its own kind of bravery.

Even if it wasn't the thing that got rid of the curse after all. Even if all it took was being there for each other, while we faced our *true* worst fears. I take a huge wad of my soaking-wet sweatshirt sleeve into my fist, just to remind myself I'm really free.

I feel him relaxing his hold on me, and reluctantly, I let him go.

"Come on," I say, looking down the street at the huge black iron gates of Santiam Estates. "Let's go home."

A mischievous grin spreads across his face.

"Race ya," he says, taking off before I can protest.

"Isaiah!" I yell, sprinting after him.

He's off into the darkness like a bullet, and I laugh, securing my hood tighter over my head. The rain is pelting the ground so hard now there's a solid half-inch of water up here on the sidewalk. Water is snaking along curbs and disappearing into storm drains. Isaiah's red hoodie turns the corner up ahead into the black iron gates and under the security check-in bar, and for a split second, I panic at the realization that Talia was somewhere in the arena.

I check my phone, scroll past Aunt Mackie's seventeen missed messages to Talia's.

I'm out. You good?

I fire off the quickest text I've ever sent.

I'm good. And I'm sorry.

I turn the corner up the hill into Santiam, hoping she didn't worry too much, and that she didn't stay in that place any longer than she had to, that she didn't see me spring onto the

272

stage after Isaiah and disappear into the huge black curtains. I hope she didn't watch that security guard get shot on top of me. I know she made it out physically unharmed, but I shut my eyes and hope to God she got out before it did anything to her mind.

If tonight did anything to give her anxiety like I have, I'll never forgive myself for not texting her as soon as Eli slipped that baggie into my pocket. Then it dawns on me.

Eli implied that *something* was going down tonight.

He even warned us to leave.

My heart is racing at the possibility that Mr. and Mrs. Zaccari's son wasn't at that concert tonight to watch Shiv or the Dragons, or Nyein, or even to sell X. Maybe he was there to make sure a mass shooting went off without a hitch. By proxy, the son of the woman petitioning to instate background checks on our neighborhood may have just helped murder several people tonight.

The minute we get to the house, I'm telling Aunt Mackie *exactly* what I saw, and then Isaiah and I are going into a self-initiated witness protection program until Eli's at least questioned.

Isaiah's getting tired.

I can see his little red hood getting closer and closer to me as I close the distance.

We run past Talia's favorite house—the humble one between its flashy neighbors, gray with the bright yellow door. The only house with any color.

We'll have a house like that one day, says her voice again in my head.

I still don't know if we will.

We run past Mr. and Mrs. Sanderson's cream-colored house with the black shutters, and the Zaccaris' house with the grass that still looks overgrown. My lungs are on fire and my jeans and sweatshirt are heavy with rainwater, but at this point, I'm just happy to be back in our neighborhood. I'm just glad we made it out of there alive.

"Ay, wait up!" I holler to Isaiah, slowing my pace. We can walk now. But he keeps running.

"Yo, Izzy!" I yell again, but he's a solid hundred feet ahead of me now. *Goddamn it.* I force more strength into my legs and take off down the street again. The roads are empty, so when he bolts across the street, I don't panic. I don't hear any cars, and Aunt Mackie's house is right around the corner.

In the distance, somewhere far behind us, a vehicle roars to life. I wonder if Mrs. Sanderson is off her diet and back to her late-night Taco Bell runs. Or maybe it's Mr. Davis off to the store to pick up something at the 7-Eleven. I keep my eyes on Isaiah, squinting to see him in the dark distance. The vehicle behind us lets out an increasingly loud *vrooooom!* and the tires *squeeeeal!* and my heart starts pounding. I look over my shoulder at the pair of headlights barreling down the street like an angry bullet, straight for us.

I remember all those times Mom would tell us to be home before the streetlights come on. I remember all the *pop-pop-pop-pops* I heard outside our door, sometimes close enough for us all to look up at each other as we ate dinner. The headlights grow and blind me, and I expect the car to stop any minute.

Any minute.

But the lights get brighter, and the tires squeal louder, and I reflexively throw myself off the sidewalk and onto someone's lawn. The lights follow me, and I scramble to my feet and book it down the sidewalk. I'd be safe from this maniac on the lawn, but I have to get to Isaiah.

Whoever this guy is, he doesn't want us red-hooded kids anywhere near him or his vehicle.

He's driving like he's murderous, drunk, or both, and Isaiah and I have to get out of here.

"Isaiah, *run!*" I holler as I watch him turn the corner up ahead. I hear the vehicle gaining. The headlights light up the pavement under my shoes like I'm walking on gold. I reflexively dart right, onto the grass and up the hill across the Davises' front lawn. If I can cut this corner and meet Isaiah on the other side, I can catch up to him. But the Davises have a vegetable garden along the side of their house, with a huge ivy trellis in the way. I run all the way around it, slipping in the grass. I fall on my side and haphazardly push myself back to my feet, trying to catch my breath as I run down the other side of the hill.

I can't see him.

"Isaiah!" I holler. I sprint across the side yard, and soon I can see the street.

The truck growls as it turns the corner, and I catch a glimpse of that red streak along the side—this is the truck that's always parked on the left side of the Zaccaris' driveway. My heart skips, and my eyes lock onto Isaiah sprinting down the sidewalk just thirty feet in front of me. Those yellow lights glow through the trees, and they grow, and they grow, until the sidewalk under his feet is yellow.

It's too close.

No, it's *too close*.

"Isaiah, run!" I holler.

In a split second, everything changes.

He hears me.

He looks for me.

His red hood is still pulled over his head.

The truck screeches.

A HUSBAND AND WIFE sit at their dining room table one evening, watching a crime report on the news, sipping tea, and lamenting the violent state of the world. They're thankful they live in a neighborhood where crime is rare.

The wife is on the local litter patrol. The husband regularly attends town hall meetings.

The wife is a natural peacekeeper. The husband is a natural protector.

The wife heard a noise outside. The husband got up to investigate.

13

The Past

THIS WASN'T THE WAY it was supposed to go. I mean, it was, I guess, according to my vision. And according to the laws and fabric of space and time, this was *always* how it was supposed to go. But if I had a say in it, I never would've chosen this.

I look across my bedroom at Isaiah. His legs are dangling off the edge of my bed, and he's swiping his finger across his phone to make that BeatBall jump across the screen. Shiv's lyrics are blasting loud and proud from my laptop behind me, and the ball bounces with every pound of the bass line. He looks up at me and opens his mouth. He's talking, but I can't hear anything.

"What?" I ask.

But I can't hear myself talking either.

"What?" I ask again, louder this time.

I realize I'm lucid dreaming. I know this isn't real. Isaiah isn't really here. I'm not really here. I'm asleep. I stand up and close the distance. I sink down next to him on my mattress, and undeterred by visions, I wrap my arm around his shoulders and pull him close. I feel the fabric of his shirt under my palms. He wraps his little arm around my waist and I feel his jaw move against my chest. He's talking again, but I still can't hear him.

"Isaiah?" I ask. Even though I can't hear myself, Isaiah can. I know, because he looks up at me with wide, questioning eyes.

"Isaiah, I love you."

He opens his mouth to speak.

I blink my eyes open to the blinding white lights overhead and feel a tear roll out of the corner of my eye and down my temple, then disappear into my hair. My head is laid back against this cloud-soft pillow, but I know if I keep sleeping with my face tilted to one side, I'm going to wake up with a sore neck. I look around. Everything hurts, like it does when you've been lying in the same position for way too long. My mouth is dry, and I realize I probably had my mouth open while I slept.

Another tear rolls out of my eye, and I reach up to wipe it away. Something papery and soft is tied around my wrist, and when I look at it, I realize it's a bright orange hospital bracelet. I freeze, at first remembering the headlights. The rain. The screech of tires. And I wonder if I'm still dreaming, reliving that day Isaiah and I lost our parents.

And then I remember Isaiah.

It's like all the air is being pulled out of my lungs. I press my fingers into my eyes and clench my jaw against the burning pain of tears. But it's no use. I cry. I sob into my hands. I roll to my side and curl up into a little ball and I slam my fist against the bed.

It's happened.

Breathe, Alex.

"What the fuck?" I whimper.

I thought I was doing something right. I thought the concert was a good idea. We got rid of our powers, didn't we? That was the whole point of going. So Isaiah could have time without them.

Not ten minutes without them only to have to run for his life after a mass shooting. I shut my eyes and picture Cobra's face as he knelt on the stage, reaching out to Isaiah, beckoning us.

We'll take care of him, he said.

And I take relief in the fact that they did.

When the shots rang out, Isaiah was first on their mind. They snatched him backstage when they could've just left him out there in the arena with all the other "fans." They protected him. Shiv protected Isaiah like he was his own brother, and I'll never forget that.

I swallow again. Every inch of me is weak. Every muscle is crying out for rest. We must have sprinted a whole mile last night. Is it still night? I look over at the wall of windows, hidden behind blackout curtains, and wonder. It still *feels* like night.

A squeaky groan rings out from across the room, and I see I'm not alone. Aunt Mackie is slumped in an armchair, and I wonder how many people have sat in that chair awaiting the birth of a new family member, and how many have sat there awaiting the death of one. That chair has probably seen some shit. Even more than I've seen. I sniff back tears and dry my face with my hospital gown. I look at Aunt Mackie again. She fell asleep with her glasses on. Her mouth is hanging slightly open. Her hair is still braided up into a bun, but her black satin bonnet is tied haphazardly around her head. Her lips aren't their usual burgundy. She's wearing her blue silk pajamas and long black bathrobe. I wish I could let her sleep like that forever, at peace, for a moment unaware that Isaiah's gone.

I wish *I* could sleep like that forever, peacefully oblivious. The door creaks open, and an unfamiliar face appears in the doorframe.

"Alex Rufus?" asks a slender woman with skin the same shade as mine, and large, dark eyes and long, straight black hair with a silver streak in the front. She's holding a tablet, and her smile is gradual and genuine. I'm instantly inclined to believe she's happy to see that I'm awake, and not smiling at me out of pity. I nod at her and sit up straight again. This bed moves a lot more than I expected a hospital bed would. I don't remember them being this rattly when I was last lying in one.

"My name is Priya," she says, stepping around the side of my bed and looking at a few of the weird colorful beeping machines next to me. "How are you feeling?"

Like *I* was hit by a truck.

"Where's Isaiah?" I ask. She's careful to keep her face even and expressionless as she turns her attention to her clipboard. If he wasn't dead, she would've looked me in the eyes and smiled as she said, "He's just in the other room, playing on his phone."

I knew it.

I hate myself for being so weak that I can't even wait for her to answer before falling apart. I press the heels of my hands against my eyes and swallow as best as I can around this dry-ass tongue of mine. I don't even wait for her to answer.

"Can I have some water?" I ask.

"Sure thing," she says, her voice almost a whisper now.

She turns and makes her way back to the door, and I can't help it. I have to know. I have to hear it myself.

"He's gone," I say, catching her. "Isn't he?"

She stops at the door, her hand on the knob, uncursed by visions all her life, while I've only just recently begun to live mine. She looks back at me, and she takes a huge breath in before answering. I feel a tear fall from each eye and roll down my cheeks.

"I think we'd better wait until your aunt wakes up."

Why? Because I'm not "man enough" to handle the news? Because it would be too much for me? As if I didn't fucking know this would happen and I've been living with it for the last two days, suffering alone with that knowledge?

Priya leaves.

I expect the door to close behind her.

But instead, a familiar face replaces her. A face that on any other day would make my heart do flips, and today stirs up a whole string of emotions I'm not ready for.

"Alex?" asks Talia. The black makeup around her eyes has smudged so much that she looks like she's been through a war zone.

"Talia," I say, my voice cracking under the weight of her name. I break down all over again. God, why the fuck can't I stop crying? *You knew this was coming, Alex.*

But I feel like I can't handle this.

Even knowing beforehand didn't ease this pain. I can't do this. I need help.

Her arms are around my shoulders before I realize what's happening, and I feel her rain-damp hair against my cheek. She's wearing that black hat I bought her at the fair last year, the one that now smells like her mother's lavender essential oil. I close my eyes, and I'm at Maria's house again, sitting on the sofa between Talia and Shaun, and her embrace brings more comfort than I could've hoped for. And then I remember the curse. The fact that I'm free. That I can touch her again. I wrap

283

my arms around her and pull her against me, as best as I can in this hospital bed. I hold her tight, sobbing into her shoulder, falling apart in her arms.

And I feel relief like I can't believe.

"Alex," she whimpers. She takes in a sharp breath, her shoulders trembling, and I realize she's crying too.

The feel of her chest against mine, the warmth of her, even her being in this room right now, tell me all I need to know.

"I'm sorry," she cries. "I'm so, so sorry."

I don't know what to say. Sorry for what? If anything, *I* should be the sorry one. Sorry for being so distant. Sorry for taking six months to tell her what was really going on with me. Sorry for waiting so long to tell her *why* I'm scared to touch her, sorry that she thought I didn't love her. That I didn't want to be close to her every waking moment. What was the word she used?

Disgusting.

The opposite of everything I've ever felt for her. The opposite of enamored. The opposite of captivated. Is there a word for "full of desire"? Because if so, that's me. I don't know what to do except hold her tight against me.

"I shouldn't have jumped to conclusions," she says, pulling back from me and wiping her eyes with her sleeve. "I shouldn't have gotten mad at you for saying no to the tickets, and I shouldn't have left you at that concert. I should never have left you. . . ."

Her voice trails off, and I just stare at her. She buries her face in her hands. God, I hate seeing her like this. Hopeless. Helpless.

"Talia?" I ask. She doesn't look up at me.

"Yeah," she says, clearing her throat and folding her arms.

"*I'm* sorry."

Just saying those words to her lifts a weight from my back that I've been carrying for four long years.

"I should've told you about my power." It sounds stupid even as I say it. "I should've told you why I'm so weird when it comes to . . . y'know. Everything. I should've trusted that you'd believe me. I should've just been honest."

"No, Alex—"

But I'm not done.

"I should've told you about Shaun," I say. I haven't said his name out loud in so long, and certainly never to her. "I should've told you."

She looks up at me now, and her eyes are red and brimming with fresh tears. She reaches up and presses her soft hand against my cheek. She wipes away a tear from my face.

"As long as you're with me, Alex," she says, "I don't want you to regret anything."

Oh, but I do. These visions were going on for so unbearably long, I was beginning to think it was a permanent fixture of who I am—Alex, afraid of the future. Alex, ashamed of the past. Now, I realize, it's okay to be afraid of the future. It's okay to be anxious. Men get anxious. Men are afraid sometimes. I remember the concert.

Cobra, Leviathan, Nyein, and Shiv all *ran* when the gunshots rang out. They *ran* and they were *scared*, and I don't think any less of them for it. Who would?

"I'll tell you the truth," I say, squeezing her wrists and raising her hands to my mouth to kiss her fingers. "I'll be honest with you from now on, about how I'm feeling, about what's

285

going through my head, about . . . everything. Okay? You have my word. And . . . if you ever catch me slipping . . . please . . . tell me. I can't do this anymore, Talia. I can't live all bottled up, keeping everything to myself. I've been through so much."

I think Talia can see it in my face. She blinks a few times and opens her mouth, but before she can say anything, the chair on the other side of the room creaks again and Aunt Mackie is pushing herself up out of it like a woman forty years her senior.

"Aunt Mackie," says Talia, stepping back from me and looking up at her.

Aunt Mackie's arms are folded around herself and her shoulders are hunched as she approaches my bed. Her eyes have lost their light completely, and her face looks dull and ashen, like she's been crying, or like she's sick, or a little of both.

"I'll leave you to talk," says Talia, heading back to the door and taking one last glance at me before disappearing into the hallway and clicking the door shut.

Aunt Mackie sits on the edge of the bed and stares straight ahead toward the windows. I can hear the ticking of the clock on the wall across the room, and the steady hum of the machine to my left with the big green 6-0 on it and the EKG that's connected to the sensor gently clipped to the tip of my left index finger. Soon, after the silence becomes too much for even her, she clears her throat and rests her hand on my ankle behind her. I swallow the lump in my throat. Aunt Mackie is an unscalable fortress on any day of the week. She's the strongest person I know. And she's sitting in front of me looking like she could crumble into dust at any moment.

I can't take it.

"I remember what happened," I say. "You . . . you don't have to tell me."

I meant for it to sound less flippant than it did. I wanted to spare her the misery of delivering the news herself, but now I'm afraid I just came across as an asshole.

"Alex," says Aunt Mackie, her voice a croak in her throat. For a minute I think she'll be angry at me about the concert. I wouldn't fault her if she blamed me for this. In her mind, if I'd been an obedient kid and done as she said, Isaiah and I would've never been at that concert. We would've never been out late enough to tip off the neighborhood watch—

And then I remember.

Mr. Zaccari.

All the fear and paralyzing, aching sadness that rippled through my body a moment ago like an uneasy tide goes up in smoke in the presence of rage.

"It was Mr. Zaccari's truck, wasn't it?" I ask. My heart is racing. I'm mad as hell. So help me, if that man is in this fucking building, I'll kill him myself. I ball my hands into fists and push myself up straighter against the back of this bed.

"Mr. Zaccari hit him, didn't he?" I demand.

Aunt Mackie is still staring off into nowhere, and this somehow makes the rage race through my blood even faster. I remember the look in Talia's eyes as she stood there and told me to my face that Mrs. Zaccari's husband had shot a man—a *kid*—point-blank, in broad daylight, in the name of protecting the neighborhood. I should've known then what else he'd do for the neighborhood. I should've put the pieces together. They were all there.

The concert.

The "types of people" to be *at* the concert.

The "types of people" who aren't welcome in Santiam.

I guess as two Black kids fleeing a mass shooting, we *looked* enough like the "types of people." We had our hoodies on. Our hoods were up. I should've known. I should've fucking known. And I think I'm mad most of all, not because they turned on me, but because I feel wronged. I feel betrayed. And they say that for there to be betrayal, there has to be trust first.

So I guess I trusted Mr. and Mrs. Zaccari.

That's what pisses me off.

I trusted them enough to live next to them.

I trusted them enough to mow their lawn and eat their cookies and let them *hug* me.

"Alex," says Aunt Mackie again. "You passed out in the Davises' yard. Mr. Zaccari called the police as soon as it happened. He turned himself in."

I know she's *not* trying to make it sound like Mr. Zaccari didn't just murder my brother.

"Are you serious?" I ask. "You're *defending* him?"

She's still staring off into space. I can't take this silence, so I keep going.

"Mr. Zaccari is a murderer!" I scream. "His prejudiced ass got into that truck, his prejudiced ass followed us for three blocks, and his prejudiced ass ran over Isaiah!"

"Alex," she snaps. At first I think she's going to launch into something that would be the straw that'll break my back.

Something like *You two were never supposed to be at that concert!*

288

What did I tell you about being in the wrong place at the wrong time?

If y'all had just listened . . .

She has every right.

But she just looks at me. She looks into my eyes, and the hardness in her face melts away. She purses her lips, her face contorts into a grimace, and she pulls me against her in the tightest hug she's ever given me. I rest my hands against the soft black silk of her robe.

"Alex, my baby," she says. She plants a firm kiss on my temple and rocks gently side to side as if I really am a baby again, and I wonder if she's thinking back to that day she held me in the hospital, the day she must've looked over at me as she signed the document saying she'd be our caretaker, *if*.

"Didn't he recognize us?" I ask, although I don't know who I'm asking. It's a rhetorical question, really. No, he didn't recognize us. He recognized our hoodies. He recognized two boys sprinting through a neighborhood that had just been hit with a robbery earlier the same day. "Didn't he look close first? Didn't he think for a second that it might be us?"

"Baby," she says, kissing my head again and letting out a deep sigh. "Sometimes these things just happen."

"I'm sick of these things 'just happening.' I'm sick of people assuming things before they know the whole picture."

She pauses at that before responding.

"People make assumptions, Alex. That's what humans do. They shouldn't. But they do."

I've seen this a million times. It's always the same story. Black kids can't sell water on the sidewalk on a hot day without

289

someone calling the cops. We can't play our music too loud. We can't wear hoodies. We can't be out past a certain time in the wrong neighborhood or the right one.

We can't run.

And Mrs. Zaccari wonders why I'm scared of the cops.

"People like the Zaccaris make *way* too many assumptions," I say. "They assumed Isaiah and I were some thugs from somewhere else, who somehow got into the neighborhood, running from the law."

Mrs. Zaccari's words repeat in my head.

Does keeping convicted felons out of our homes sound unreasonable to you?

She didn't mean convicted felons. She meant people who *look* like convicted felons. People, apparently, like twelve-year-old and sixteen-year-old Black kids. Never mind her own fucking son, who at least *knew* about a plan to open fire on thousands of concertgoers just a mile from her house. I wonder how many lives she could've saved if she'd opened her eyes to the real danger.

"They do," says Aunt Mackie. She lets me go and reaches down for my hands. For a moment I panic, thinking she's going to take hold of them, forgetting that my visions are gone. She rests one hand over mine. I get to go another thirty seconds without being reminded of what the future looks like for me. "They make assumptions when they shouldn't. They may not ever get it."

"We have to *make* them get it," I say, "or this'll keep happening."

All this time, I've been wondering what kind of man I'd be

if *this*, what kind of man I'd be if *that*. What kind of man would I be if I let these two—the Zaccaris—go on living the way they've been? Ignorant of just how much power they have? A call to the cops. A turning of a truck key. A *he looked at me* complaint got Emmett Till killed almost seventy years ago. Have we really made so little progress since then?

"We have to make them get it," I say, the determination in my voice surprising even me.

Aunt Mackie shakes her head.

"That's gon' be hard to do, until they live it."

It crushes me, the knowledge that she's right. But I still feel compelled to try. How do I explain to Mrs. Zaccari that apart from the cops, white women are just as scary to me now? How do I explain that just by existing, I'm guilty until proven innocent? That *Isaiah* was guilty until proven innocent?

Aunt Mackie rubs her hand over mine.

"That's the curse of knowledge," she says. "You can't *make* her understand, baby. You live this every day. *I* live this every day. When I wake up in the morning and walk to the garage and get into my Benz and drive down the street, I know I'm an anomaly. I've been pulled over by officers who had nothing better to do than make sure I didn't steal that car. I've had cops assume I'm a sex worker, a drug dealer, the *wife* of one of those."

I realize my mouth is hanging open.

Aunt Mackie?

Strong, formidable, iron-fortress Aunt Mackie? A drug dealer? The wife of a drug dealer?

"This isn't right," I say. "This has to stop."

But I don't even know where to begin in making it stop. If I

291

can't explain to Mrs. Zaccari what we deal with on a daily basis, just because of our skin color, and I can't physically put her in my shoes, then who's to say this will *ever* stop? How do I put this into terms she can understand? Like, *really* understand?

"Maybe one day it will," says Aunt Mackie. "Maybe. But this is *far* too big a burden for just one brave teenager."

There's silence in the room again, and she pulls me into another warm, much-needed hug. She's right. This is too much. It's *been* too much. For once, I don't feel like I have to hold that burden on my shoulders anymore. I take a deep breath, hold her tight, and run through the steps.

Hold my breath and count to ten.

I don't have time to count to a hundred.

I can't lie in corpse pose.

Priya is supposed to be getting me a glass of water.

I can't open the window. I'm sure they're locked to prevent patients from jumping out.

I can't stare at the ceiling from this angle, but I open my eyes and look across the room at the pile of folded clothes on the chair next to Aunt Mackie's empty one—at my jeans, my socks rolled into a neat little ball next to them, my jacket with the photo inside the pocket, and the bloodred Cobra Katjee sweatshirt folded up on top.

Knowing there's a piece of him that I'll always have with me, breathing in all the weight of giving him his last experience on this planet, and breathing out knowing that I was there for him, that he knew he wasn't alone . . .

It helps. A lot.

14

The Reunion

THE MORE I THINK about how it went down—the drive to the graveyard, the drive home, the pizza bites in my room, and the BeatBall, the concert, and the run for our lives—the more I realize that I wouldn't have done anything differently. I don't think I could have. Looking back, it's so easy to make up a million different scenarios in a million different timelines based on other choices I could've made. I could've gone to Isaiah as soon as I saw the vision of the picture, and we might've had a few hours longer to get to know each other.

The photo is in my pocket.

My fingers find it and take hold of the edge, and no vision begins. But when I pull it out and look at it, the memories do.

Mom. Dad. Isaiah. Me. Mom holding her backpack strap with one hand and glancing over her shoulder, as if the photo caught her off guard. Dad's impromptu photography always annoyed her, but she was always a good sport about it. I'm glad he took it. His crooked smile, with one of his front teeth grayer than the others, indicates he was happy to take it. I look at his favorite black hat with the Chicago Bulls logo on the front, and his dark eyes, full of warmth, staring out at me. I shut my eyes and remember his kiss on my forehead after I went to bed angry that one time, pretending to be asleep. If I could go back, I'd sit up in bed, throw my arms around him, and apologize. I don't even remember what I was mad about, but it wasn't worth missing a moment like that.

But I didn't *really* miss it, did I? He still kissed me. He still told me he loved me. We still woke up the next morning and moved on, and we still got years of moments after that we didn't miss.

I look at Isaiah's face, and at mine.

We're in the background of the photo. Mom has her arm around me, pulling me close, and I'm smiling like I'm smiling now, even through my tears. My mouth hangs open mid-laugh with those hideous braces, and I look like I'm excited about what's going to happen. My eyes are alight with anticipation of our first live game ever. I look at Isaiah's face and smile. I look at his grin, at his sparkling eyes. There's something in the curve of his mouth that indicates this photo caught him by surprise just like Mom. But he looks happy. He looks curious. He looks hopeful.

I'm grateful for so many things about the last two days, but most of all, I'm grateful I got to see that life in his face again.

The breeze picks up and I look at the sky and soak in the warmth of the sun on my face. I breathe in the hot afternoon air and look down at the ground. The rectangular hole at my feet is gaping up at me like it did in my vision, and the big white casket at the bottom, covered in bright red flowers—red, for Izzy Rufus, the Red Dragon.

I dry my eyes with my fingers and look around at the solemn faces watching as the undertakers shovel one scoop of dirt after another into the hole, sprinkling it gently, ceremoniously, as if the sound of the granules against the casket would disturb him. I recognize most of these people. The Davises. The Sandersons. There are two kids from Isaiah's class that I don't know by name, and their parents. And there's Talia, whose makeup keeps running, in her black dress with her hair bumped into waves that touch her shoulders. Aunt Mackie, who keeps dabbing a tissue against her eyes, in a black dress suit.

I can't look at her for too long or I might lose it completely.

We all stand in silence. All the words have been said. The pastor, who I guess knows Aunt Mackie somehow—I've never met him before—gave the service. I didn't hear a word. I can tell you exactly what it smelled like in that chapel. I can tell you exactly what color the carpet was and every inscription on the walls under each donated stained-glass work of art, and every red flower arrangement that lined the front podium. But I don't remember a word.

And then, right across from me, there's Mrs. Zaccari, who can't even look at me. Who has a napkin pressed against her eyes or over her nose, careful not to smudge her makeup. She hasn't spoken to me since the murder—the one everyone insists on calling *the accident*.

It makes my blood race through my veins like an angry river.

And I decide, there and then, that not *all* the words have been said yet.

"Enough," the word pours from me softly as I stare across the circle at her.

Look at me, I think. This woman's husband murdered my brother, and not an apology? Not even an acknowledgment of my presence?

"*Enough*, Karen," I say.

She looks at me now, and everyone else in the circle looks between her and me. No more "Mrs. Zaccari" from me. If she and her murderous husband want to kill my brother in cold blood without a fair trial, which even *adults* are supposed to be afforded, the pleasantries afforded to adults shouldn't be wasted on her.

"Enough," I say again, my eyes trained on her.

Looks of confusion are exchanged. Mrs. Zaccari glances around the circle in surprise, wondering what I could possibly mean. She sniffs and clears her throat and cradles her arms around herself.

"Alex, I—"

"Let me spell it out for you," I say, before she can tell me she *still* doesn't get it. "You're just as guilty as Brian."

Since I'm on a first-name basis with Karen Zaccari, I don't know why I wouldn't be on a first-name basis with her piece-of-shit husband.

"Alex," comes Aunt Mackie's voice. I tear my shoulder away from her hand, keeping my eyes on Karen. Until now, I'd held back my tears, through the sermon, the hauling of the casket, the standing around this circle as Isaiah was buried, but I'm not holding back anymore. My cheeks burn, and I let the tears come.

"Isaiah is dead because of the fear *you* foster," I say, surprised at how strong a dam my voice is, holding back the avalanche of rage that bubbles underneath. "Your petitions, and your 911 calls, and your home security systems and your neighborhood watch patrols are getting people *killed*. People who go

296

to break into houses like that guy yesterday, yeah. And yeah, people who get a little rowdy at concerts. *And*," I continue. I can feel my lip trembling, but I know if I stop now, I might not muster up the courage to keep going. "Kids. Like me. Like Isaiah. You *know* us. We're not criminals. But we look enough like criminals to you, don't we, Mrs. Zaccari? When you imagine someone breaking into your house late at night, you picture *us*. You picture *us*."

I remember Shiv up there onstage. I remember Isaiah up there with him, how happy he looked. How nothing else in the world mattered to him. How just for a moment, he got to be twelve again, without having to live in regret. Without being reminded of the darkness he came from, that he had to live with every single day.

What kid should have to live every day in the shadow of four hundred years of bondage and another hundred of lesser-than-dom? Black kids, apparently. But then, how is a Black kid supposed to be a kid?

Who knows?

Who cares?

Apparently not Mrs. Zaccari.

"But *your* son gets to live. He probably wouldn't get run over in the street for looking like he's robbing a house, but he's sitting behind bars downtown with his dad, probably being questioned about his involvement in a mass shooting! How the *fuck* is that fair?"

"Alex," Aunt Mackie bites.

"I *won't* be quiet!" I'm screaming now. Talia takes a frightened step back from the circle and looks at me like I'm a stranger.

Breathe, Alex.

"I won't," I continue, calm again. "I won't be quiet until people like *you* leave us alone. Brian may have pulled the trigger, Brian may have been behind the wheel. But he needed a scout. Someone to tip him off that something was amiss. Something was cause for alarm. And what was it that got my brother killed? What could've possibly scared you into sending your husband to investigate? A kid. A *kid*. Running past your house through his own neighborhood in the rain, in a hoodie, minding his own business. Just trying to get home. Just trying to get somewhere safe. Somewhere *you* tried to convince us you were making even safer."

Mrs. Zaccari—Karen—whatever I'm calling her now, pulls another napkin from her pocket and dabs at her eyes.

"Alex, you don't think this is hard for me?" she squeaks. "My husband *and* my son were arrested. I lost *both* of them this weekend. And how can you say that? We *love* you. We loved *Isaiah*."

Aunt Mackie rests both her hands on my shoulders and leans down to whisper to me. "Alex, let's wait until we have a lawyer, okay?" she asks from behind me, and somehow, I get the feeling her eyes are trained on Karen, because Karen gasps.

"A lawyer?" she asks, her resolve crumbling before me. "MacKayla, surely that's not necessary. We've both lost children this weekend. Surely it would be better to come together and *heal* from this instead? Do we really have to bring lawyers into this?"

"How *dare* you say that to me?" snaps Aunt Mackie, completely ignoring her own advice to wait until we have a lawyer. I take a step back as she steps past me and points an accusatory finger, right in Karen's face. "We've *both* lost children? Please! *You* lost a child because his own actions landed him in jail, Karen. Isaiah was *taken* from me, by *your* husband!" At the word "husband," her voice cracks, snapping through the air like a whip.

"M-MacKayla," whimpers Karen as two tears fall from her eyes, "I'm . . . I'm sorry." She offers the apology, but Aunt Mackie has already turned to lead these people out of this place. She sniffs and shoves her hands in her pockets and glances over her shoulder at me.

"I'll be in the car, Alex," she huffs.

The families of Isaiah's classmates awkwardly shuffle their children across the grass to follow the herd, and Karen and I are left standing here, facing each other. Her blue eyes are pleading with me.

"Now, Alex," she manages, reaching out to me. I recoil, like she's holding out a red-hot coal for me to take.

"Don't," I say.

"You have to know he didn't mean to—" She stops suddenly. I'm not even sure *she* knows how to finish her sentence.

I'm surprised at how dark my voice sounds when I finally speak.

"Didn't mean to kill him?" I ask. I swallow the lump in my throat and feel a tear roll down from my eye. "Doesn't matter. You're both racists."

She gasps and looks at me like I've just stabbed her in the chest.

"Alex," she whispers, "how can you call us that . . . that *word*? We would *never* . . . I told you, we . . . it was an accident—"

"'Accidental' racism," I say, with air quotes, "still gets us killed.

299

And that's really all I care about."

My dad's words come back. . . .

A man's not a man without his paycheck.

And what I thought when I left Scoop's . . .

But a man who doesn't protect his family is no man either.

And my add-on . . .

But one man can't protect everyone.

And a wave of peace comes over me as I bring it full circle.

And a boy shouldn't have to try.

"Goodbye, Karen," I say. If a real man would stand up for himself and ask for help when he needs it, I know I'm saying the right thing. Or headed the right direction, anyway. The silence physically hurts. My chest is so tight it's hard to breathe. Darkness plays at the corners of my eyes, and I wonder if this is what it feels like to pass out. Am I about to faint? Oh shit.

I don't know what else to do, so I sink to the grass and cross my legs, and wait for her to leave. I shut my eyes and bury my face in my hands and wait. And wait. And wait. I hear footsteps move slowly through the grass and fade away until I can't hear them anymore. I'm working on my breathing. *In. Out. In. Out.* I count to ten. It helps a little. And finally getting all of that off my chest?

It helps a lot.

I feel a hand on my shoulder, and it startles me. I look up, my eyes dry, the sun blinding against them, and make out Aunt Mackie's silhouette.

"You ready now?" she asks.

Ready for what?

To let go?

To say goodbye?

To leave this place?

No. No to all three.

"Can I just have another minute?" I ask. "I'll, uh . . . I'll walk home. Or take the bus or something. I'll be okay. Promise."

I don't think Aunt Mackie would've gone for that on any other day, but today she takes her hand away, and nods, and walks to the car.

"Take all the time you need. Just call me when you're ready," she says, "and I'll come get you."

I nod, but I doubt she sees me, as she's already turned and started walking. Then I hear the footsteps stop behind me.

"I love you, Alex," she says. I look over my shoulder.

"I love you, too, Aunt Mackie."

And then I do what I couldn't do before. I push myself to my feet and run to her, throwing my arms around her waist. She reels back from the impact, but then she holds me tight. She runs her hand along my shoulder and kisses the top of my head.

"Mmm, I love you so *much*," she says, choking back tears. "And I'm so proud of you. And I know Isaiah was too."

She has no idea what that means to me. I squeeze her even tighter and pull away to look up at her.

"I'm proud of you, too," I say determinedly. And I am. This is a lot for anyone to go through. Losing a sister, inheriting her two children, and then losing one of them, too?

She nods and carefully wipes a tear from under her eye, which has been carefully concealed and highlighted and contoured and traced with eyeliner and whatever else.

"Thank you," she says. "Thank you. Call me when you're ready."

301

And she turns to leave. I sit back down in the grass.

Eventually, when my shadow has moved just enough to notice, and my spine feels so stiff that it might break, I muster the strength to stand again.

I look out at the field of plaques in the grass, in the direction of my parents', which are only a hundred feet away or so. He won't be too far from them.

I look down at the photo one last time before holding it out over the hole in the ground, and I take another deep breath. The breeze is an invitation. There's a lift in my chest like what happened when Isaiah and I were singing together in my car the other day, and I chuckle a bit, catching everyone's attention for a moment. I don't care.

"Goodbye, Izzy Rufus," I say.

And I let it go.

When Isaiah's beautiful red flowers are six feet under a mound of earth, and so is the photo, people continue to leave, one by one. I'm sure they're all going back to Aunt Mackie's house to eat something and reflect on Isaiah's twelve short years, but I'm not hungry, and I've no energy left. I'm numb, frozen in time here by his side. The classmates leave. Scoop leaves, but not before clapping me on the back and letting me know I can come back to work for him whenever I like, after I've had time.

Time.

What I wouldn't give to have *time*. I always seem to be running out of it.

Talia turns to leave with her mother. Her gaze lingers on me as they go past. I can feel it, and I shut my eyes against it. I'm not ready. I'm not ready for anything. I just want to sit here for a while and think.

So I do.

I drop to the grass, and I bow my head. I think, finally, after days of misery, I've run out of tears. I fold my arms and prepare to blink away a vision of the navy suit jacket I'm wearing and then realize with relief that those are over. I feel the cold dew soak through my suit pants, which are probably dry-clean only. I don't care about that, either.

I feel a tiny tickle along my left index finger, and I open my eyes and hold up my hand to look at it. I find a little lady-bug crawling there. No spots. All red. And I wonder if this is Isaiah's way of saying goodbye.

I smile and watch the little Red Dragon take flight, straight toward the sun, in the direction of my parents' resting place. Then I notice a man walking toward me. He's wearing a brown suit that looks like it's made out of some kind of tweed. He looks like a detective from an old movie, with a huge gray mustache and thin little glasses that sit right at the tip of his nose. My heart starts pounding, and I don't know why. I have the sudden urge to stand up, so I do, careful not to touch the ground. Something about this man, the way he walks, the way he looks at me, seems familiar. He closes the distance between us, shuffling his feet through the grass gingerly, as if every movement causes him pain. When he's a few feet in front of me, and I think he'll walk right on past, he stops. He slides his hands into his pockets and looks up at me. I'm sure he used to be as tall as me. Maybe taller. The years have taken a toll on his height. He looks me up and down in silence with warm, smiling eyes, and he reaches his shaky, wrinkled hand out for a handshake.

I glance down at it for a second, and when I look back up at him, he moves his hand closer to me and purses his lips. His face, his movements, his eyes, they all say *go on.*

I reach forward and take his hand, and a vision crackles to life in my head. At first, panic strikes me. *Not again,* I think to myself in terror, *after all of that, not again.* But this vision feels different, etched in gold around the edges, and strangely comforting. To my surprise, I see Isaiah, tiny, toddler Isaiah curled up in a man's lap, with his oversize head against the man's chest and his black Power Rangers light-up shoes hanging over the man's knees. I don't recognize the man, but something about him feels familiar. Then he looks up at me, and I notice the salt-and-pepper mustache, the slight downward tilt of the eyes on the outside, the strong, wide nose, and I realize it's the man whose hand I'm shaking. A name comes to me like a whisper, as clearly as if I'd actually heard it.

Harold.

My eyes fly open, and I take a closer look at the old man standing in front of me, still holding my hand.

"G-grandpa?" I ask.

He winks at me, lays his free hand over mine, and shakes it. And then, without a word, he steps past me. I stare after him and blink a few times, wondering if my visions have now gone from movies to hallucinations. My heart is racing. What do I do? I look around the cemetery for another person—*anyone* else. Just someone to verify that I haven't lost my damn mind. But I'm alone. I look back to the man, and he's gone. There's not a single trace of him. His shuffling walk left none of the grass around me trampled.

304

Did I just imagine that shit?

I turn back to the open field, and four men are walking toward me. Slowly. *Unnaturally* slowly. All of them are tall, all lanky. All Black. They're moving in a straight line in my direction, like an army, eyes trained on me. I glance over my shoulder to check for anyone else who might be able to confirm that I'm not losing my freaking mind. But there's no one.

Just me and these four men.

One is dressed like one of those old-timey guys who might've worked on a railroad. He's got a railroad hat on anyway, gaunt face, high cheekbones, eyebrows set in a permanent frown of concentration, fists clenched like he's never *not* worked a day in his life.

Daniel Alby.

The name rings in my ears as clearly as if someone had spoken it to me. I just *know* it suddenly, and I wonder if this is what Isaiah meant when he asked me if the world screamed at me. If this is how Isaiah had to live every day of his life, my heart aches even more for him, for a second, and then it lifts as I remember how free he was on that stage. How fearless.

Buddy Lyons, whispers the next name. The shortest of the four, but still taller than me. Striped baseball uniform. Sweat covers his bald head and forehead. A smile is plastered on his face like he's never not *smiled* a day in his life. He marches across the grass slightly ahead of the others, right in the middle of them, like he can't wait to get to me. The man just after him is named John. Just *John*. No last name. And his pants, which look like linen, are stained and frayed at the bottom, and his forehead is creased even worse than Daniel's, but his eyes are

305

soft, and tired, and his mouth is pursed like he wants to speak but can't. His hand is clasped around that of the next man, who is slightly shorter, but looks just like him.

Patience Truman.

Patience? His name is Patience? I look at the grip around his hand and determine that John must be his father. And given the lack of last name, I wonder if John was . . .

The word rattles around in my head like a marble, hurting more with every letter I sound out.

A *slave.*

I'm staring into the eyes of my great-great-great-great-etc.-someone, who has his hand around his son, Patience, who's literally holding on to *patience* as if his life depended on it.

And I guess it does. Or did. I guess the preservation of our whole genealogy depended on patience.

They're all so close now, staring down at me. There's a power that emanates from each of them, as if they're sure of where they stand. Like they know their place in this world, and they're inviting me in with them. John reaches his arm out to me, and I shut my eyes and feel the warmth of his hand on my shoulder. And a second. And a third. Soon my whole body feels warm, and a swarm of arms encircles me, holding me close. I feel the tears come on suddenly, and I look up through the mass of arms and chests and heads as they all hold me close. Between losing Isaiah and . . . *this*, whatever this is, it's all too much, and I bury my face in my hands and sob. I wonder if Isaiah were around to see this, what he'd say. What he'd do. And then I hear my name.

"Alex," says the voice, strong and familiar. I know it

immediately, and my breath catches in my throat. My eyes fly open and one by one, my ancestors step back, parting the way so I can see across the grass to the other side of the graveyard again. One man is there, walking through the grass, his feet somehow not disturbing a single blade. His sweatshirt is black, with a Chicago Bulls logo on the chest.

"Dad?" I ask, so unsure of myself it comes out in a whisper.

He's carrying a small boy in his arms. A small boy in a red sweatshirt with that Shiv Skeptic bandanna around his forehead and that smile I've missed so much it hurts.

"Isaiah!" I scream, sprinting to them through the grass. I don't care that I'm wearing a suit. I care that they're here. That I get to talk to them again!

Isaiah locks eyes with me and squirms out of Dad's arms and runs to me. I throw my arms around him, squeezing him, lifting him into the air. I hold him so tight, and I don't want to let him go.

Then I notice something else. A dark shadow in front of a tree about fifty feet away from me, standing so still it's lucky I noticed him. He's shirtless, wearing plain brown linen pants. His hair is tied up in locs at the crown of his head, and his arms are crossed over his chest. He looks like an extra from *Black Panther*. He looks familiar too, somehow. He moves, uncrosses his arms, and begins walking toward me, staring me down with the most intense eyes I've ever seen. They're dark and determined, and he walks with purpose. When he's about twenty feet away, I notice he's not wearing shoes or socks. His bare feet are somehow dry, even with all this dew on the grass. He's also about six foot five and ripped like an MMA fighter.

He reminds me a little of Shiv Skeptic, especially in the way he looks at me. Like he knows me. He stops a foot in front of me, looking down at my skinny five-foot-seven frame, and I suddenly feel overwhelmed in his presence. He's *huge*.

I look up at his face, hardened by what appears to be years of worry. So familiar. Where have I seen him? I look at his nose, the way it fans out wide on the sides, and at his high cheekbones underneath his black skin, dark and shiny as a well-loved chestnut. Then I look at his eyes—the way they're turned down at the outer corners, just like Grandpa Harold's, and I realize who I'm looking at. When it sinks in, I feel like I can't breathe. My mouth falls open. He must see the shock in my eyes, because his mouth curves into a smile, and he reaches his huge hands forward to grab one of mine. I've seen this vision before. I see Ursa's face. Her big, round eyes looking over her shoulder at me as I stand as still as possible on that mountain ledge. And beyond her, with nothing but determination in his face, is Takaa, who already knows the terrible fate of his son and his son's wife, who has already seen the slave ships and knows they'll be taken from him, who keeps moving anyway.

I reach out for him.

The world collapses into a vortex around me, and it feels like I'm flying through an endless tunnel of light. The blisteringly hot wind swirls so fiercely I have to shield my eyes. Everything aches. Every inch of me is exhausted, like I just ran a whole marathon. Suddenly everything gets sucked up into darkness like a Shop-Vac, and when I'm brave enough to ease my eyes open, I look down to see my hand is still holding Takaa's. I'm half-surprised I'm still standing after all that. The wind was so strong I thought I'd get blown away. I look up at him for answers. Why is he here with me? *How* is he here with me?

His eyes are smiling as he gives me an answer in a single word.

"Kunze."

Somehow, despite it taking me six months to catch onto basic Spanish, I know this word. Somehow, I've heard it before. I know all its meanings.

He said *freedom*.

He said *permission*.

He said *authority*.

Tears well in my eyes. I get it. I really think I get what he's saying. He said *joy*. I clear my throat and take a deep breath before attempting to reply in my best Akoose.

"Kə̂ŋ," I say.

His eyebrows knit together, and he stands a little taller, lifting his free hand into the air, commanding me to say it again.

"Kə̂ŋ!" I say again, feeling it thunder through me as it leaves my mouth. He nods, and before I can say anything else, he pulls me against him and wraps his huge arms around me. I'm suddenly overwhelmed with gratitude—for who I am. For who my father was. For who his father was. For having known Isaiah as long as I did. Here I am, in the middle of Elginwood Park Cemetery, where my entire immediate family will lie buried forever, in the arms of Takaa himself. Unafraid. I don't know how long I stand there before I hear a familiar voice behind me.

"Alex?"

It startles me, and I turn to see Talia walking toward me

in that new black dress, holding a matching black cardigan in her hands. Her shoulders are hunched up by her ears, and she shivers slightly as the breeze tosses her hair in front of her face. She brushes it away and tucks it behind her ear.

"I just wanted to make sure you were okay."

"Uh, yeah," I say, turning back around to face Takaa. But there's no one there.

I look down at my hand, and I swear I can still feel the warmth of his.

"*Are* you okay?" she asks, stepping in front of me again.

I look at her, at the timidity in her eyes, and the way her mouth hangs open slightly after her question, like she's afraid of the answer. I reach down, hoping to everything I know and love that this still works. I take hold of the fabric of my black Gorillaz shirt that I'm wearing under my black blazer. I pinch the cotton between my fingers, feeling the fibers, vision-free again. I have to smile as I nod in reply.

"Yeah," I say. "Yeah, Talia. I really, *really* am."

"Good," she says, reaching into the front pocket of her dress and pulling out a small, round piece of paper. She holds it out to me. "I, uh . . . I brought this home from the concert for you. I thought you could start your collection over."

I take it in my hands. It's all silver, with raised silver across the whole thing, in the shape of the dragon glyph, those sharp eyes staring up at me, a slight but approving smile in the mouth. I grin down at it and know *exactly* where to put it.

"You sure you're good?" she asks again.

I nod and smile.

One of her eyebrows rises half an inch.

"Really?" she asks.

"Yeah," I say. "Can . . . can I hold you?"

She nods, and I wrap my arms around her waist. Talia squeezes me back, tight, and I take in the scent of her hair, which is different, but somehow familiar to me. It's not her usual strawberry lip gloss scent. It's not her *her* scent.

What is it?

It's sweet. Unmistakable.

I smelled it once getting off the bus downtown as a lady in her forties walked past me to get on. By the time I realized what the smell reminded me of and turned around to look at her, the doors had closed and the bus was taking off down the street. But now, it's standing right in front of me. I pull back from Talia and look into her eyes when I ask, "What scent is that?"

"It's my mom's perfume. She lets me use it for special occasions. Do you like it?"

It's exactly what I needed.

I'm going to buy a whole bottle of it myself and keep it in my closet next to Isaiah's Shiv sweatshirt, Cobra bandanna, and Leviathan wrist cuffs, next to my dad's black sweatshirt and my mom's Chicago Bulls hat.

"Can I get the name?" I ask.

"Sure." She smiles. "It'll have to wait till we get to my place, though. I don't remember what it's called."

I search her eyes for any trace of an ulterior motive. *My place*, she said. She notices me staring strangely.

"You *sure* you're okay?" she asks.

I nod.

"Where to now?" I ask her. She must catch the glint in my

311

eye, because she smiles, and her gaze drifts from my eyes to my mouth and back to my eyes. She kisses me softly, cups my face in her soft hands, and presses her forehead against mine. My heart is thundering against my ribs.

"We could go get something to eat. Or some ice cream," she suggests. "Doesn't *have* to be at your place."

I know what she's getting at, and my voice trembles as I say it, but I know I need to.

"Hey, Tal? I'm uh . . . not ready yet. For sex, I mean."

She pauses for a long while, and I wonder if she's changed her mind, if after all this waiting, she's finally tired of me, if it's too little too late. But then she smiles and says it.

"That's okay."

"Yeah?"

"Yeah," she says with a shrug. "I get it. And I'll wait."

"Thanks. I know it's not like, you know, what a man's 'supposed to be,'" I say with air quotes. "But it's . . . y'know . . . *my* truth, and I have to be honest about it. It's not you. I promise."

She grins a little, and her cheeks get a little pinker.

"I'm just happy you're not keeping me in the dark anymore," she says. "If something bothers you like that, you can tell me. And you can tell me *why*. Okay? No judgment. Just be honest with me."

"Deal."

I still don't know if we'll ever live in a house like the gray one with the yellow door. I still don't know if we'll last as long as I hope we do. I still don't know who will buy Scoop's Ice Cream Parlor in about two years.

15

The Future

MOM USED TO TAKE me and Isaiah to consignment shops all the time, specifically a consignment shop a few miles from our house in East Garfield Park named Griswald's. I'd always assumed Griswald was some guy from the days of King Arthur who opened the store hundreds of years ago, and it had kind of always been there. But now, two weeks after the funeral, I'm sitting in an armchair in Mabelena's as Ena floats from counter to counter behind the registers, and it's all sinking in how *real* it is, owning a place like this. Mabel is somewhere in the back office, probably drawing in the coloring book that Talia's mom gave her. Oh yeah, Maria works here now, appraising new items that come in and ticketing everything. It's under-the-table work, so her disability checks are still coming in strong. Warmth settles into my chest at the reassurance that Talia doesn't have to rely on Aunt Mackie for her next meal any-more, and that Maria doesn't have to keep the burning secret of leaning on my checks when Talia's not looking.

I hear a shuffling sound, and I look up from my seat by the dressing rooms—the seat I always sink into when I show up to pick her up at the end of her shift—just in time to see Talia on a ladder, reaching high above her head to get a box down. I jump up and rush to catch it just in time. The box falls and tumbles into my arms, forcing the air out of my lungs as I go sprawling backward onto the floor.

"Oh God, Alex!" she screams.

"What was that?" cries Maria from somewhere in the back room. She and Ena both come rushing back to the counter as Talia leans down to get this box off me.

"Estamos bien," I say to Maria. I look up at Talia with a grin. "Soy bien."

Once she's taken the box in her arms and set it gingerly on the edge of the glass counter, she leans against it and smirks down at me.

"*Estoy* bien," she says, "'Estoy' is that temporary version of 'is,' remember? 'Soy' is a constant state of being."

I push myself to my feet and take both of her hands in mine—I swear I'll never get tired of holding her. I lean forward and brush my nose against hers and say, "In that case, soy bien."

"That's not how that works," she giggles. I kiss her cheek.

"Don't worry about it. Soy bien." I pull her close against me and rest my chin on her head. "Cuando estoy contigo."

When I'm with you.

And I mean it.

"Hey," I begin, clearing my throat as the full weight of the suggestion I'm about to make sinks in. I can't believe I'm doing this, but it's something I have to do. Something I should've done years ago. "When I say 'when I'm with you,' I really mean it. I mean anywhere. Anywhere, even where you've needed me most.

Where I haven't been."

She's looking at me like I'm not making sense, and I'm not sure I am.

"What I mean is," I continue, "I'm free today if you want to go visit Shaun. You know. Since it would've been his birthday today."

Her eyes light right up, as if all the times I've been too scared to go have been forgiven, and this moment is all that matters.

"I, uh," she begins, her warm hands squeezing mine. "I assumed you would've forgotten."

I shake my head.

I never forgot. It just hurt too much to acknowledge it. Even now, my heart is racing with the idea of sitting in front of his headstone and talking to him. My fingers are going numb, and my chest is so tight it feels impossible to breathe. But I need to do this.

"I never forgot, Talia," I say. "I was just afraid."

Joy in the face of oppression is its own kind of bravery, but so is sitting in front of the thing that scares you, and not running.

So here I go. Before I change my mind.

"Wanna go when you're done with your shift?" I ask.

"Yeah," she says, blinking in surprise. "I just have to get this box of jewelry into the case first."

"Oh, I can help," I offer.

As soon as the words leave my mouth, I feel my phone buzz with a text.

Scoop: Hey Alex, like I said, my offer still stands. I know I was

315

very angry when you left after your last shift, but given everything that's happened, I understand your situation. If you still want to work for me, do you think you could come in today? I really need a closer. And frankly, an opener for tomorrow.

I sigh. I *just* offered to help out around here. There's no way. My heart pounds as I answer.

Me: Sorry, Scoop, but I have plans today. I've also said I can't close one night and open the next day.

No idea what he's going to say. I've never spoken to him like this before, even over text. My hands are shaking, and I don't know why. He already said I was fired last time. Then he told me I could come back. Now he *needs* me back?

He's typing.

Scoop: Sorry, Alex, I know you're going through a lot, but Ashley just called in sick. If you're not busy, I really need you to come in.

"Everything okay?" asks Talia, eyebrows raised in suspicion.

"Yeah," I answer absentmindedly, and then I catch myself. "Um . . . actually . . . Scoop is asking me to come in today."

She sighs, and I remember to continue. "No, no, it's not like that. I'm not going in. I just told you I can help sort through the jewelry box."

She grins proudly and turns to put a small box on a shelf.

Me: I can't. I'm sorry.

Talia thanks me and cuts open the box, and we get to work. I enjoy the feeling of every piece, being able to hold all the gold chains in my fingers, and all the earrings, the cheap plastic, and the sterling silver and the jewels. It's hard to tell the real ones from the unreal, for the most part, but when I pick up a ring that looks strangely familiar to me, the metal heavy and cold in my fingers, and the diamonds glinting like stars even under these fluorescent lights, I realize this one is *definitely* real.

"Hey, uh, this one doesn't have a price tag," I say, holding it up to Talia. She looks at it for a long moment before shrugging.

"Like it?" she asks.

"It's . . . it's beautiful," I say. It's *clearly* worth a lot of money. I slip it onto my left ring finger, and then it all hits me. The vision comes back, not as a vision, thank God, but as a déjà vu kind of lightbulb-clicking-on moment.

This is the ring!

The ring!

The ring that belongs to that guy who's going to buy Scoop's in a couple of years!

It's on *my* finger.

I turn my hand over as I hear Talia holler something to the back of the shop, to which Maria replies in Spanish.

"It's yours," she says, catching me off guard.

"What?" I ask, now back in the moment.

"My mom says Ena says you can have it. All yours. It's one less thing we have to bother with pricing. Besides, you've been through enough lately and you've more than paid us for it already. Have one beautiful thing, Alex."

I grin as Scoop's words come back to me.

When you own the shop, you can make the rules.

And Aunt Mackie's words right on their heels.

Whoever makes the rules controls the narrative.

And why not *me?* I think.

In a few years, I thought I'd be off at college, with Scoop's a distant memory, but why not me? Why can't I be the guy who's going to buy the shop in a couple of years? I'd be out of high school, and I'd have two years of savings behind me if I found a job somewhere else. Who's to say I can't be the guy who shakes Scoop's hand?

I don't know. And in the absence of a vision confirming or denying the question, a small spark erupts into a flame deep within me. Hope.

Scoop: Alex, please don't make me beg here.

With hands a bit shaky, and after a deep breath, I text Scoop back.

Me: Sorry, Mr. de la Cruz. I don't think this is working out. You already told me you didn't want me to come back, and after thinking about it, the feeling is mutual. You'll have to find someone else to come in today. Please consider this my resignation.

I nod to Talia.

"Thanks, Tal," I say.

"Sure," she says with a grin.

My Vans are soaking wet and covered in grass, and my heart is fluttering, but I'm here. I'm finally here, next to Talia, staring down at another grave that should be familiar to me, but ashamedly isn't.

Shaun Gomez, it reads.

It's already getting dark out here. The sky is a brilliant orange-purple swirl, and the breeze is picking up and getting colder. Talia wraps her sweater more tightly around her, leans her head on my shoulder, and loops her arm through mine. I lean over and kiss her hair.

"You're shaking," she whispers. "Are you cold?"

"Nah," I say. "Just, uh . . . this is just really weird."

"What? Seeing his gravestone? I'm used to it."

A lump forms in my throat at that, and I shake my head and sigh.

"I'm sorry, Talia," I say.

A long moment passes between us, and she says nothing, which I'm thankful for, because it gives me time to work up the nerve to say what I say next. It all comes pouring out of me.

"I'm sorry I haven't been there for you. I'm sorry I haven't been *here* when you're here. I'm sorry I've been so confused about what I want and need, and I haven't really talked to you about it. I should've trusted you. And . . ."

I swallow and turn back to Shaun's stone.

Shaun Gomez
Son. Brother. Angel.
September 14, 2003—July 2, 2017

Suddenly my knees feel weak, and I take a deep breath and steady myself against Talia.

"I'm sorry, Shaun," I muster. "I'm sorry I'm so late."

Silence.

Silence that stretches on forever.

I don't know how long I stand there, but it's long enough for Talia to pull me back from my dissociating.

"¿Sabes lo que diría?" she asks. *Do you know what he would say?*

I laugh, because yes, I know.

"Mantenlo positivo, bro," I say.

Keep it positive.

That was Shaun. Always smiling, always keeping things balanced. I hope that wherever he is, and wherever Isaiah is, they're laughing. My cheeks start to burn as I hold back my tears.

"Ahora sé un poco de español," I say. "But I'm still not fluent."

"Él todavía no habla fluido," she tells him with a smile. "Pero es un buen estudiante."

"I am?" I ask.

She nods at me and grins.

"Lo intentas, y eso es todo lo que importa."

You're trying, she said, *and that's all that matters.*

I brush my nose against hers and kiss her gently, and just smile at her.

"What?" she asks. "Why are you looking at me like that?"

I let out a laugh and shake my head, soaking in the same feeling I got when I looked down at her that day at the pool when we both almost drowned. I'm just glad we made it. Through death. Through grief. Through a mass shooting. Through a curse.

"Nothing," I say. But that's not true. I realize that I've fallen into my old habit of saying "nothing" as opposed to trying to parse out exactly what I'm feeling, and I correct myself. Somehow the three words feel so natural, like they've gone unspoken for way too long, and it's about damn time.

"I just . . . ," I begin. "I love you."

She smiles, and her cheeks go slightly pinker, and she tucks her hair behind her ear with one hand and squeezes mine with the other.

"I love you, too."

I look down at the gravestone again, and I hope he's proud of me. Even though we were only months apart, Shaun was always taller, and always more mature. So I guess that's why I feel like I owe him a decent existence. Wherever he is, I want him to be happy he spent the few years he had on this planet being my friend. And the same for Isaiah, that he spent his time on this earth as my brother.

That's really all I want.

I pull away from Talia and bring both my hands up to my chest, forming them into the four letters I couldn't make by myself when he was alive.

S-H-I-V.

"I finally figured it out," I say. "I've finally figured it out."

Not everything, obviously. I'm still a kid. And now I have even less figured out because I can't see the future anymore. But I look down at the new tattoo on my palm. That word, kə̂ŋ. That word has just one meaning: king.

King, for Shiv.

King, for Takaa.

King, for Grandpa Harold.

King, for Daniel Alby.

King, for Buddy Lyons.

King, for John.

King, for Patience Truman.

King, for Dad.

King, for me.

King, for Isaiah.

King, to remind me of the strength and beauty that I come

from. King, to remind me what it means to be brave in spite of everything it means to be me. To give me resolve where there could be regret, and courage where there could be fear. I'm still figuring out what it means to live in the present. But at least now, I can live knowing I gave Isaiah joy he'd never had. I can live knowing I've broken a five-hundred-year-old family curse—the curse of seeing, every day, that which others can't. The curse of facing the illusion of certainty. The thing so many people fail to realize is that to most people like me, Black kids trying to make it to adulthood in peace, it *looks* like the future is spelled out for us. All I have to do is turn on the news. But that word—kɔ̂ŋ—says all I need to know about my past, and my future. I can't change the former, but at least now the latter is whatever the hell I want it to be. No visions. No hints. No looming cloud telling me what I'm destined for. No fear. I decide what I become.

Later that night, I lie on my bed, staring up at the stickers from several concerts Talia and I have been to in the last few weeks. So many colors. My favorite, of course, is the big silver one in the middle, with the dragon eyes staring down at me, watching over me like my ancestors have, like Isaiah is, and I wonder where I'll go next. Who I'll see. What I'll do. Where I'll end up.

I wonder where I'll end up.

What a privilege.

Epilogue

A BLACK BOY STEPS off the bus, headphones in his ears and hands in his pockets. He looks around as he walks through his old neighborhood, feeling the ring around his finger in his pocket. He's confident he'll own a business one day.

The barber shop is on the corner just ahead. The boy walks on.

The light is on. The boy swings the door open.

A handful of Black men with shears in their hands turn to look and smile in recognition.

A man steps out from the back room, drying his hands on a towel. He sees the boy. He stops. He smiles.

"Alex?"

The boy smiles back.

"Hi, Galen."

ACKNOWLEDGMENTS

The Cost of Knowing started off as a story all about Black boy joy.

And then, as I wrote about two carefree Black boys with superpowers, I began to sense that something about writing it felt wrong. It felt like there were so many parts of being a Black *man* specifically that I wasn't acknowledging. So many parts of Alex and Isaiah's world that would be at odds with their carefreeness. So many things telling them to worry, to be anxious, to be afraid. Toxic masculinity. Intergenerational trauma. Pressure to be a "provider." The weight of the past. The heaps of anxiety that can come with the future.

As a Black woman, I set out to write a book that speaks alongside Black men, and not *over* them.

One day, I will write a Black boy joy book. But first, I had to write a Black-boy-joy-*despite* book. That's what this is. It's my love letter to the Black men who had to grow up too early, and for whom the task of being carefree and joyful and Black and male might seem impossible.

Thank you to all the Black men in my life. The ones who are joyful, the ones who are trying to be, and the ones who are busy just making it. Your feelings matter.

Shout out to my incredible therapist for listening on my best and worst days. Writing this book was traumatic for me at times. Since the term "emotional roller coaster" would be an understatement, I'll go with "emotional wood chipper." Every draft etched away a piece of me, leaving my spirit raw and grief-stricken. My therapist listened. Therapy is lit. Don't be afraid or ashamed to get a therapist. I believe most of us could use it.

As always, my agent, Quressa, handled my millions of questions from probably her most anxious client (me) with finesse and wisdom. You're a queen.

My editor, Jen, and all the incredible people at S&S did a phenomenal job helping me transform my scrambled thoughts about ancestors, intergenerational pain, toxic masculinity, and mental health in the Black community into something coherent and beautiful. Thank you to the Education and Library team for getting this book to those who have such an important hand in getting stories into the lives of young ones. And thank you to the cover artists—Laura Eckes and Sarah Creech for the design, and Alvin Epps for the gorgeous artwork.

Thanks to my friend Roseanne Brown for distracting me with memes and obscure yet strangely unsettling questions like "does a straw have one hole or two" in the middle of the night when I wasn't going to be doing my best editing anyway.

Thanks to my friend Amber Inoue for keeping me company on all those mornings in quarantine when I woke up too early for no dang reason.

Thanks to my wildly talented NaNoWriMo friends, several of whom aren't published but should be—Jackie Mak, Alexandra Keister, Christopher Mikkelson, and Elayna Mae Darcy.

Thanks to my beta readers, who always give me their best: Becca Boddy, Jackie Mak, Alexandra Keister, and Monica Gribouski.

Thank you to my writer friends in the gaming industry who have welcomed me with open arms and taken me under their wings as I learn the ropes. It's so cool to be able to contribute to an entertainment medium that had such a strong influence in shaping who I am as a storyteller. Thank you infinitely.

Thank you to my mom and dad, who are just as excited about every book update now as they were when I brought home my first place Young Authors award in the fifth grade. And also for being okay with the fact that that's the only first place *anything* I ever won as a child.

To the love of my life—Steven—who I've watched grow as an incredible man of science and feminism. I'm glad our kids will have you as a shining example of manhood and person-hood. Thank you for taking care of me *and* you. I love you.

And to my son, my darling bun, who's not even out of the oven yet. I hope this world embraces you with compassion and love as I hope it does for all men someday. I love you and your father bigger than the universe.

ABOUT THE AUTHOR

BRITTNEY MORRIS is the author of *SLAY* and *The Cost of Knowing*. She holds a BA in economics from Boston University because back then, she wanted to be a financial analyst. (She's now thankful that didn't happen). She spends her spare time reading, playing indie video games, and enjoying the rain from her house in Philadelphia. She lives with her husband Steven who would rather enjoy the rain from a campsite in the woods because he hasn't played enough horror games. You can find her on Twitter and Instagram @BrittneyMMorris, and online at authorbrittneymorris.com.